T0274151

"With a multi-dimensional quality, Steven James writes with a confident, assured ease. Just good, old-fashioned, gimmick free storytelling that pushes the envelope to the edge and beyond."

—STEVE BERRY, *New York Times* bestselling author of *Red Star Falling*

"James is one of those rare authors that can combine complex and intense tension, while developing characters that will keep readers on the edge of their seats reading all night. When you put together a short list of authors that need to be on everyone's bookshelf, Steven James is one of those authors... Steven James sets the new standard in suspense writing."

—JOHN RAAB, editor of *Suspense Magazine*

"Mesmerizing... I need to read more of Steven James."

—MICHAEL CONNELLY, *New York Times* bestselling author & executive producer of Amazon's *Bosch* television series

"James delivers first-rate characters, dazzling plot twists, and powers it all with non-stop action."

—JOHN TINKER, Emmy Award-winning screenwriter

"Pulse-pounding suspense."

—FICTIONADDICT.COM

"Exhilarating."

—*MYSTERIOUS REVIEWS*

"Thought- provoking and thrilling."

—*NEW YORK JOURNAL OF BOOKS*

"James is a master of suspense."

—ROBERT DUGONI, #1 international bestselling author of *My Sister's Grave*

RIFT

RIFT TRILOGY, BOOK ONE

RIFT

STEVEN JAMES

SKY TURTLE

NOVA

Rift: Rift Trilogy, Book One

Published by Sky Turtle Nova, an imprint of Sky Turtle Press
and a division of Oasis Family Media, LLC.
289 S. Main Pl.
Carol Stream, IL 60188

Book design by Jamie Foley
Cover by George Pratt and Rebecca K. Reynolds

First hardcover edition, October 2024
Printed in the United States of America

ISBN 978-1-963559-00-2 (hardcover)
ISBN 978-1-963559-02-6 (eBook)

Also available as an audiobook from Oasis Audio.

www.skyturtlenova.com
skyturtlepress.com/rift

To Crystal,

whose hope inspires me

Other Novels by Steven James

The Bowers Files
Opening Moves
The Pawn
The Rook
The Knight
The Bishop
The Queen
The King
Checkmate
Every Crooked Path
Every Deadly Kiss
Every Wicked Man

Travis Brock Espionage Thrillers
Broker of Lies
Fatal Domain

The Jevin Banks Experience
Placebo
Singularity

Standalone Sci-Fi
Synapse

Young Adult - Standalone Fantasy
Quest for Celestia

Young Adult - The Blur Trilogy
Blur
Fury
Curse

"We turn our pain into narrative so we can bear it; we turn our ecstasy into narrative so we can prolong it. We tell our stories to live."

—JOHN SHEA, AUTHOR

"The only way to get rid of my fears is to make films about them."

—ALFRED HITCHCOCK, HOLLYWOOD DIRECTOR

PART I

THE THIRD ROOM

1

SOME WORDS HAVE THE POWER

to impale your heart.

And sometimes that's quick and merciful.

But sometimes it's terrible and long and torturous and seems like it will never end.

And I've been on both sides of the impaling.

———

I picture it sometimes. What it would've been like to be there when Dad died. Or, more specifically, to *be him* when he died.

I put myself there in the car. Maybe because I want to understand what he was going through. Maybe because I want to remember him. Maybe because I want things to be different and there's a secret, hidden part of me that believes that if I picture it all clearly enough it'll somehow solve the past, change things, tilt reality in his favor. And maybe then it won't be my fault that he's dead.

Chippewa Lake, Wisconsin.

Saturday night.

March 23rd.

11:32 p.m.

And so.

Here you are.

Driving through the fog.

You're not really paying attention as much to the road as you should because you're scanning the ghostly haze created by the melting ice and snow, searching for headlights gleaming toward you in the night or a car pulled onto the side of the road. Her car. Your sixteen-year-old daughter's.

And then you come to the lake.

And hit the stretch of black ice on the south side of the bridge.

And lose control of the car.

You've been told to turn into a skid, taught your daughter to do the same, but in this car, on this night, doing that solves nothing, and the car whips sideways through the fog toward the shoulder of the road, sending an urgent, terror-laced shiver slicing through you as the car's tires refuse to grip the pavement any longer and continue to glance uselessly against the ice toward the incline that leads down to the lake.

The car spins as you slide.

The night curls around you, a blur of your own headlights smearing across the white fabric of haze, and then you careen over the shoulder and there's a jarring impact as the car crashes into the guardrail, torquing its supports out of the half-frozen ground. As the guardrail gives way, it screeches with resistance, a metallic scream that creases through the night and chases you as you plummet down the ravine toward the lake.

Toward the precariously thin ice.

It's been unseasonably warm the last few weeks.

The lake's ice has been melting, and though the surface is still ice-covered, the ice isn't nearly thick enough to hold the weight of a car crashing into it.

The car flips over once, twice, as it tumbles down the embankment. It all happens slowly, too slowly, as if time has paused and taken a step back to watch it all happen. A wild, terrifying descent into the hungry, gaping night in slow, slow motion.

And then, at impact, time catches up with itself.

The car smashes headfirst into the ice—but at least you're not upside down. At least there's that. Somewhere along the line, the airbag has deployed and is now wilting in front of you.

You're bleary and uncertain. You must have hit your head, or maybe it's just the impact jarring you.

Impact.

Yes.

And now.

The car is beginning to sink.

You struggle with the seatbelt, but can't release it. For some reason it's stuck and stubbornly refuses to unsnap.

You flick on the light, which thankfully still works, and assess things, and that's when you see your leg. It shouldn't look like that. The unnatural angle and the white glistening bone glazed with blood poking through your blue jeans near your left knee. No, no, no. It should not look like that at all.

And when you notice that fractured bone, the gate opens and the pain invades you—like it was welling up, waiting for a way in, and by noticing that broken bone, you've given it all the permission it needs. A piercing bolt of pain shoots through you and you clench your teeth as you futilely try to stuff it back to wherever it came from.

Already, water is finding its way in and around your feet more quickly than you expected. It's joltingly cold and you gasp as it rises toward your knees. You need to get out. Now.

You try the seatbelt again and this time it unclasps and zips back into place, freeing you.

Yes, yes, yes.

You try to twist your leg free from where it's wedged in beneath the car's wrenched console, but it's excruciating as the splintered bone rages against any movement at all, and you have to pause to catch your breath.

You attempt once again to bury the pain.

Still no use.

As the car submerges, the night outside the window turns to a sheet of ice, then shifts to black water around you, deep and forever.

And then, a realization—stark and dark and final: you're not going to get out of this. You're not going to survive. You need to make the call. You need to speak to her, one last time.

And so, you stop trying to extricate your broken leg and instead, you scan the front seat for your cell phone. It was beside you, between the seats, but now it's gone—who knows where?

The water inside the car is rising.

Now up to your waist.

Ice-cold.

Death is coming quickly.

Where's the phone?

It must be here. It is here. Where?

Where!

And then, as you sweep your hand through the water on the seat beside you, your fingers graze against it, knocking it onto the floor, toward the far door. You lean over as far as you can and after several agonizing, failed attempts, you're finally able to snatch it up

Maybe it won't work. Maybe the water has already ruined it.

Quickly, you wipe the screen across your shirt to dry it off and hold it up to your face to unlock it. A moment later it wakes up.

It's not dead!

Water.

All around you.

Praying that it'll still work, you tap at the phone's screen to make the call.

No one picks up. The call goes to voicemail. Your daughter's voice comes on, telling you in that tired, slightly annoyed way of hers to leave your message and that she'll get back to you when she gets around to it, if she feels like it.

The water is at your chest.

"I love you," you say into the phone and can't help but cringe from the pain pulsing up your leg. "I'm sorry. Look on my workbench. Tell your mom I love her too, I..." But then the pain is too much. There's more you want to say, there are whole books of things you're leaving unsaid, volumes of apologies and remember-whens. A tragic library of regrets. And maybe good things too. All those unspoken words streak through your mind searching for a way out.

But they will not find it.

It's too late.

The water is up to your neck.

You try once more to free your leg, but it's useless.

A text. Maybe she'll see a text.

You start typing, but the water's at your chin and, as hard as you struggle to keep your mouth above the water, it's no longer possible.

And so, it never gets sent and you gulp in what air you can, and you hold the phone above you and you thumb type, staring up through the freezing-cold water at the screen to see if the call will go through, but by the time you're able to tap in 911 and hit send, the phone is above the water and you're not.

And you close your eyes and your heart cries out a final, soul-searing prayer that your sixteen-year-old daughter will listen to the message, will hear your words, will know that they're true and that you meant them with all your heart.

Love.

Regret.

A second chance.

But then your prayer is gnawed into nothingness as eternity collapses around you and within you and swallows your final thoughts in one grim, ravenous gulp. And then, the icy water from the lake where you taught your daughter to swim when she was a giggling little girl, now whisper-still and silent in the night, becomes your grave.

While it's true that it might not've gone down *exactly* like that, it's close. I pieced it together from the way his body was found and from the message he left me and from what had happened between us beforehand that sent him out on that final and fateful night searching for me in the fog.

And because of what would have been on his mind. My words. Those deadly, impaling words.

That was at the end of March.

It's October 11th now.

He's been gone nearly seven months, but it seems like a lot longer—yet also, somehow, like it just occurred, like he's both been gone forever and also like I just lost him yesterday.

Yes, it happened. It's true. He's dead.

And it's my fault. He'd be alive today if it wasn't for me saying what I said and leaving the house like I did on that night when we argued about my journal.

2

AFTERWARDS, I SAW A THERAPIST for a while when I was still up in Wisconsin, before things fell apart with Mom and I needed to come down to live at Grams' house here, in Tennessee.

I'm not going to lie: Seeing the counselor didn't help and might've even made things worse. He kept talking about the stages of grief and how it was natural for me to feel the way I was feeling, but he didn't know the whole truth. I didn't tell him everything.

"You can't blame yourself for what happened," he told me during our last session.

"Really? Then who should I blame? You tell me."

"Don't blame anyone, Sahara." He glanced over at the clock staring down at us from the wall. A signal of his attention drifting. Not a good sign, but also not the first time he'd looked over there and I wondered if that was typical for therapists. "It was an accident," he added.

And I wanted to say, "Yeah, one that wouldn't have happened if I hadn't said those things to him and then stormed off like that—and if he hadn't loved me enough to come looking for me," but I held back and said nothing.

The clock ticked away.

We had fifteen minutes left.

He jotted something down in his notebook. "I understand you've shut off your phone?"

That wasn't quite the case but I didn't correct him. "I don't want to listen to his message," I informed him.

I could've deleted Dad's voice message, but that seemed like that would have been too much, like it was going too far—almost like it would've been me symbolically deleting *him*. I still used my phone for texting and surfing and posting and as a calculator and a camera and as pretty much everything except for as a phone. I couldn't bear to do that anymore. People who knew me were getting used to it.

"But," the counselor said, "listening to your dad's voice could be a way of remembering him, right?"

I stared at him. "How would hearing his voice help anything? I don't need that—there are a million other ways to remember him." My words had a bite to them, but I didn't care. "He's dead. Why put myself through that, anyway? Why torture myself?"

"Love isn't torture. It's freedom."

"Yeah, well, being constantly reminded of the death of someone you love *is* torture." I stood to leave. "You know what? I'm done here."

As I was heading for the door, he said to me, "If you close off your heart, it'll make it all that much tougher to heal."

Maybe I don't want to heal! I thought. *Maybe hurting is a way of remembering how much we cared about each other—as messy as it was sometimes, as irritated and frustrated as we were with each other at times—and how he'd be alive if it weren't for me. Maybe holding onto the pain* is *love. Maybe that's freedom, even if it* is *painful—because at least it's real.*

But I kept all that to myself. Instead, I just turned to face him one final time. "I'm not about to play pretend with my feelings."

"Sahara, that's not it at all. That's not what I want. But what I want isn't important. It's what you want that matters."

Yeah, well, what I want is a chance to tell my dad I'm sorry and to hear him tell me that he forgives me. A chance to take back what I said to him the night he died.

"What I want"—at that point I was fighting to keep back the stupid tear that was trying to seep out of my left eye—"is to finally be happy again."

Before he could reply, on a whim, I walked over to him, and

before he could pull away, I snatched the notebook from him to see what he'd been writing down during our session.

A shopping list.

The last thing he'd added was soy milk.

Perfect.

Something that's not even what it claims to be—there is no milk in soy milk. No one is out there milking soybeans or nursing little soy babies with it.

It's just a label that's also a lie, caught up in a subtle disguise.

I flung the notepad against the wall that day, and then I left and never went back.

When tragedy happens, they tell you to pick up the pieces and start again, but sometimes the pieces are too big to pick up. Sometimes there's no picking them up, no starting over again. So what do you do when you can't pick up the pieces of a broken life but also can't seem to move on without them?

That really was the question.

And the longer I ask it, the more lost inside of it I seem to become.

So.

Now.

Here it is, the second week of October, and I'm sitting in English class and it's the last hour on Friday before the weekend and I'm praying that our teacher will call on me soon so I don't have to wait until Monday to read my essay. Having it hanging over my head the whole time would ruin the entire weekend.

It's weird. I don't mind telling stories to my friends—I like it, actually—but reading stuff in front of the class—let's just say that is not my favorite thing in the world to do. Mr. Dreyfus, on the other hand, seems to really be into the whole read-your-work-to-the-class thing as A Positive Learning Experience, which has been hard for me all semester.

Storytelling, sure.

Essay reading, not so much.

When I'm in the middle of telling a story, it's like I'm transported to another world, a land of banshees just outside the window and monsters under the bed and straw spun into gold and true names revealed. It's a place of horror and dismay from being abandoned in the forest, and of cleverness and of breadcrumbs leading you back home. And it's a place of castles rising from the mists and curses that make a difference and true love that wins in the end. It's a land of Once Upon a Time and Happily Ever After and a place where dreams might actually, someday, come true.

Or, at least that's what I used to think: that true love might win and happily ever after might wait for you at the end of the story and dreams might come true. Now, I'm not so sure.

Sometimes the dragon wins.

And sometimes the story you've been hoping will unfold before you just withers away, dying right before you on the vine.

Jason Landers is reading his essay, a little too giddily extolling the virtues of drama club and sharing how amazing it is and all I can think of is how long he's taking and how we're probably going to run out of time and how I'll have to stress about this assignment all weekend.

My essay.

If you can even call it that.

I honestly don't even know what to call it.

I kind of gave in to the poem-loving part of my brain when I was writing it. So maybe it's closer to that than anything else.

I sit here in the back of the room of twenty-four students with my elbow propped on my desk. The left side of my head is shaved and the hair on the right side drapes down past my shoulders. Sort of a light red color.

My mom would say I'm too into death and darkness: dark clothes, eyeliner, fingernail polish, that sort of thing. I think I'm just into truth, and the truth is we're all gonna die. I read once that back in the sixth century, a famous Italian saint named Benedict wrote,

"Keep death always before your eyes." So, yeah, I try to do that, but not lose sight of life as I do.

Which is not easy.

Right now, I have my chin leaning on my hand, as I listen to Jason drone on—or should I say, I *try* to listen, but honestly, most of my attention is channeled down into my nervousness.

Nerves. Nerves. Nerves.

Nervy. Nervy.

Nerves.

And I have no idea what's going to happen when I finally walk up there and read what I've wanted to say but have never had the actual guts to say in front of anyone before.

My non-essay essay.

As honest as I can be.

Maybe *too* honest.

Yeah, almost certainly too honest.

3

SO FAR WITH THE ESSAYS,

everyone has ended up sounding pretty much the same as they talk about their families and the sports and music and movies they're into. The assignment was to write a 500 to 600-word essay on the topic of "Who am I?" but everyone so far has gone in the direction of "What I like!" instead.

And that makes me even more nervous about reading my assignment in front of everyone because I actually *did* ask the question Mr. Dreyfus wanted us to focus on.

Who am I?

Which was probably a mistake.

Why'd you even write it like that, Sahara? When you read it, it's going to turn on you and bite you.

But I did write it that way, saying things I've been feeling, but never expressing, not since Dad died. All the stuff I've been bottling up inside. But ever since I turned seventeen last month, I've been thinking maybe it's time to start owning it: who I am, I mean. Because there's a huge difference between what you do and who you are. And sometimes what you do has almost nothing to do with who you are, deep down inside.

You act. You pretend. You hope no one notices the real you—and yet you also beg the universe that they will, at least the right person will, before it's too late.

———

Times might change, but I don't suppose the things that really matter, the true, down-to-the-heart-level parts of being a teen change all that much, even through the years.

The breakups and heartache, the desperate attempts to fit in and find your place. The silent cries for help and the shattered dreams. The longing and ecstasy and hope and terror. The test stress and the acne and the bullying. You want to escape and you want to belong—both, at the same time. To be known and to hide. How can it be both? But it is.

It's homework and sneaking out at night and parties on the weekends, and it's stolen kisses and first loves and soul-scorching disappointment. It's homecoming and prom and pressure to be who you're not in front of people who don't really care at all who you actually are.

And it's broken hearts and crying into your pillow and staring at the bottle of pills for way too long and wondering, wondering, wondering things you know you shouldn't be considering.

It's laughter and drama and hurt feelings and regret and getting back together. Everything's real and bigger than life because everything *is* real and bigger than life, and it's all happening at light speed all around you and inside of you, and every day can totally take your breath away or crush you into unimaginably tiny, jagged, lonely little pieces.

It's wondering if others are thinking about you when they're really just thinking about themselves. And it's wanting to be invisible and also to be the life of the party—both—and nothing makes sense and then everything does and it's all solved and life is full of possibility and wonder and amazement until it's not once again.

And it's longing. So much longing. For things to be better. For things to be different. And for some moments to remain just the way they are, etched in time, forever. You try to both emerge and disappear. You try to stretch your wings to fly, but the adults who're supposed to be teaching you how to soar keep tugging you back to the nest, yanking you backward and cramming you into the mold of a you that you don't fit in anymore.

The Yesterday You.

Conform, rebel, evolve, or die.

Teenage life.

How is it that the years that're supposed to be so magical and memorable can be filled with so many questions and misery and—

———

"Sahara, are you with us?"

I blink and look up at my English teacher through the long strands of hair draping across the side of my face. Perfect for hiding behind.

Got lost in my thoughts again.

Sigh.

There aren't any single words that mean you have an overactive imagination, but the closest is probably being "polyphiloprogenitive." It's a thing. So that's what I am.

It could be worse, I guess. I mean, if I were the opposite, if my imagination was underact—

"Sahara O'Shaughnessy." Mr. Dreyfus dramatically places one of his hands on his hip and raises a formidable eyebrow. He does that a lot with the ol' eyebrows—raising them as if it gives him more authority, or scrunching them up in disdain. Very active, those eyebrows of his. "I asked you a question," Mr. Busy Brows says.

"Yes," I reply lamely, even though I have no idea what the question was. "I know."

"It's your turn," he informs me. "I'd like to hear your essay—we all would—if it's not too much trouble for you to come up front and read it?"

A few snickers around the room.

Why does he have to be like that?

I'm about to reply with words I will almost certainly regret later when I hear a light cough come from my friend Cadence Simerly who's seated two rows to my right. I glance her way and see her shake her head at me—a warning not to talk back to Dreyfus. Yeah, she knows me all too well.

I hold my tongue and gaze around the room. Pretty much

everyone who doesn't have their head down or their phone out secretly—but not really so secretly at all—is staring at me. The school has a cell phone policy, of course it does, but Dreyfus, in his never-ending quest to be The Cool Teacher that Everyone Likes, doesn't concern himself with it, which actually makes people respect him even less.

Lacey, the girl next to me, squishily chomps on a glob of bubblegum that's way too big for her mouth, for anyone's mouth, really. For some reason I notice that, and I wonder if she has any idea what bubble gum actually contains and if she'd jam so much of it in her mouth if she did.

I doubt it—glycerin, resins, humectants, elastomers, emulsifiers, fillers, waxes, antioxidants, and polyethylene—which is used to make plastic.

Yeah, I seriously doubt that she—

"Well?" Mr. Dreyfus says impatiently.

"Coming," I mutter and I grab my essay, which isn't really an essay, and I head to the front of the room.

Alright.

Time to spread those wings and, hopefully, avoid plummeting catastrophically to the ground.

4

I LOOK AROUND THE CLASSROOM.

The walls are covered with quotes that are meant to inspire us to write. Too many, really. Dreyfus is trying way too hard.

My two favorites are probably from William Butler Yeats: "Do not wait to strike till the iron is hot, but make it hot by striking," and from Oliver Wendall Holmes: "Many people die with their music still in them." It's sad, but true. I agree. Too often people are getting ready to live, and before they know it, time runs out.

But there are tons of others from other authors: Hemingway and Vonnegut and Angelou and Faulkner and Fitzgerald. Interestingly enough, they're all writers. No tellers, like my grandma. No true story*tellers*, no one who writes stories with their mouths and not just with their pens, even though we're in the Appalachian Mountains where storytelling is still a thing. Or at least it's supposed to be.

If you ask Grams, there's a big difference between telling a story and writing one down.

"If you snip off a flower to preserve it, you kill it," she told me once. "It'll dry out and wither—but if you leave it in the wild, well then, it'll keep on flowering every year. Stories are perennials. They'll keep flowering as long as they're told and retold and allowed to grow in the wild. You write a story down and it's stuck there forever, encaged in a bunch of little squiggles on a page. Let it live. Don't write it down."

Mr. Dreyfus still has his eyebrow raised at me. Maybe it's a condition.

He nods for me to get started.

I fumble with the papers as a ruinous swarm of butterflies invades my stomach. I find myself fidgeting for a moment, wondering if I should just scrap what I wrote and make up something different on the spot.

Calm down. It's all good. It's going to be okay.

"Anytime, Miss O'Shaughnessy," Mr. Dreyfus says.

I take a deep breath and, trying my best to hide behind the pages of paper I'm holding, I read my assignment to the class:

> I am your next door neighbor.
> I am the daughter of a man ripped from life way
>   too soon.
> I am the child of a woman who never wanted a kid
>   in the first place.
> There is more to me than meets the eye.
> I'm a junior.
> I sit in the back of the room.
> I keep to myself.
> I'm a girl who's easy to overlook.
> I watch.
> I listen.
> I observe.
> I am depressed.
> I am lonely.
> I am hurting.
> I am ashamed.
> I am amused.
> I am amazed.
> I am human.
> I'm changing—
> —maturing—
> —growing—
> —becoming—
> —I am alive.
> I sold you that wood-fired pizza last weekend.

You've seen me.
You've looked at me—
—looked past me—
—bumped into me at the ball game—
—flipped me off for passing you on the highway.
I walk beside you in the hallway and you don't
      notice me.
I drink.
I smoke.
I eat lots and lots of nachos.
I yearn.
I yawn.
I tremble.
I am afraid.
I am aware.
Part of me is asleep.
Part of me is curious.
Part of me is on fire.
I lie.
I hide.
Can you find me?
Are you looking?
Do you know who I am?
I look just like you.
I am just like you.
I'm lost.
I'm found.
I'm listening.
I'm searching—
—hoping—
—dreaming—
—believing—
—hurrying—
—on my way to somewhere—

—on my way to something,
  but I can't quite remember what it was,
  or why I'm going there at all.
Sometimes I cope pretty well.
Sometimes I just give up.
I burp.
I gargle.
I dance.
I kiss.
I cry.
I sing.
I bleed.
I am in debt.
I am in despair.
I am in awe.
I am in love with the idea of being in love.
I feel trapped in time, and the past won't let me go.
I'm ticklish.
I'm hungry.
I like to go swimming in the moonlight.
I laugh.
I vent.
I forgive—
—but I don't always forget.
I have issues.
I hope.
I dream.
I wonder.
I question.
I am alive.
I painted my toenails black on Monday night.
I got a speeding ticket last month.
I wear Doc Martens.
I eat oatmeal.

I wiggle my toes in the sand.
I have pierced ears—
—a pierced lip—
—a pierced nose—
—a pierced heart.
Sometimes I feel like crying, but mostly I hold back.
I stuff my feelings.
I tell people "I'm fine," even when I'm not.
Sometimes I feel like I'm going to explode.
I am a cold dusk falling.
I am a new day dawning.
I am a sailboat, catching a daring wind toward a
    distant shore.
I am a lost ship, crashing into the rocks and sinking
    in the sea.
Sometimes I am a shattered mirror.
Sometimes I am a dream come true.
Who am I?
What am I doing here?
Is there anyone else like me?
Does anyone else like me?
I am alive—
—for now.
Can you find me?
Are you looking?
Do you know who I am?
I look just like you.
I *am* just like you.
I'm a human being... being human.
As I try to figure out who I am.

My heart is pounding, pounding, pounding in my chest as I
finish up and I feel naked having read all of that, laying the real me
out there all at once, in one fell swoop.

For a long, unnerving moment, I stand there staring down at the page, afraid to look up, afraid to see people's reactions, which I know are coming—the smirks, the sneers, the eye-rolling.

Finally, I do, though.

I peer over the top of the paper and gaze at the faces of the students in my class.

5

THE KIDS WHO ALWAYS LISTEN

are staring dutifully at me, their eyes slightly glazed over, and the kids who don't ever bother to listen are doing what they're experts at: looking like they couldn't care less.

Mostly, though no one seems all that interested.

It's almost time to go home—so that may be part of it. The countdown to the weekend.

Saved by the upcoming, proverbial bell.

Well, I tell myself, *at least you didn't completely crash and burn.*

The only person who looks genuinely interested is Tyler Beck. Which is... well, amazing.

He doesn't really fit into any of the cliques around school—sort of skirting along the fringes of the skaters and the soccer jocks. Just enough rebellion to be unpredictable, but not so much to seem dangerous. He's one of those loners other people secretly wish they were like. Kind of a normal face, but green hazel eyes I can hardly look away from. He has this mop of unruly blond hair that's always got just the right amount of messed-up-ness and the just right amount of effortless coolness.

It's almost too much.

I don't even know what to do when he nods to me.

Caught me staring.

Oops.

I dry swallow and quickly, glance over at Mr. Busy Brows.

He takes a deep breath and when he speaks, his words are

crushing: "That wasn't exactly an essay, Sahara. The assignment was to write an *essay*."

A plummet in my gut.

"Oh. Okay."

"Essays have the elements we've discussed in class: a thesis statement, supporting evidence, a strong conclusion. You remember that, right?"

I can feel my face flushing. "Yes."

"And did you say that you drink and smoke?" he asks me, his voice all judgy and filled with *faux* authority—maybe it was a performance for the class. "You do know that you're underage for both of those activities and that they're both unhealthy, not to mention illegal?"

Seriously? a voice inside of me screams. *That's what you got out of that? Out of everything I said?*

Screaming. Screaming. Screaming, deep inside. So much screaming in my heart. Maybe that's one reason why I wrote out all of those things in the first place—to quiet the screams. At least for a little while.

At least to give it a shot.

"Right," I say to Dreyfus. "Don't drink or smoke. Gotcha."

The bubble that Lacey has blown pops.

The bell rings and I head to my desk as Mr. Dreyfus tries to tell us to read something over the weekend, but I can't make out what it is over the noise of everyone grabbing their things and scraping their chairs backward and I doubt anyone else can hear him either.

At least I didn't throw up from the nerves. At least there's that.

Then Cole, this linebacker everyone likes and who was the reason I added the "I walk beside you in the hallway and you don't notice me," line to my non-essay, leans toward me and says in a sly, low tone, "You said you like to go swimming in the moonlight?"

Oh great, I can see where this is going.

I say nothing, just wait.

"What about skinny dipping?" He grins with teeth that are way too straight and he sniggers. "Ouch. Now that's an image I'm *never* gonna be able to unsee."

Oh. Brilliant.

I flip him the bird.

I wish I didn't care what people like Cole say to me, but still, his words burn.

It might be the first time all year that he's actually spoken to me, not *about* me behind my back, and he has to go and say something like that. It's not that I'm way too fat—or too scrawny. I've put on a little weight since last spring when I lettered in track, but nothing crazy.

My face then? Sometimes at my best, I might *almost* be *on my way* to looking pretty—which is about the most I could ever hope for. So, yeah, maybe that was it—but he can see my face anytime... Well, whatever he meant, it was a biting and cruel thing to say.

As I grab my books, I keep thinking about what I just did: *Why did you even read that in front of everyone? You never should have said all those things.*

They were true, but maybe truth isn't really what I needed to be sharing with the people at my school.

Maybe a lie would be better instead.

6

I HEAD TO THE HALLWAY TO

escape to my locker so I can retrieve my backpack, get out of here, and get to the Unicoi County Public Library where I'm supposed to be working tonight until they close at eight, shelving books and putting up a Halloween bulletin board in the children's area.

My new job as of yesterday.

I quit working at Capote's Wood-Fire Pizza food truck last weekend after our county's annual Apple Festival. Try working for ten hours straight sealed up in a shiny steel food truck.

Welcome to the Pizza Oven.

Climb inside, Hansel, it's safe, trust me.

That job lasted a whole two days.

Honestly, I don't do so well keeping jobs—any jobs. Being polyphiloprogenitive, I daydream too much, which makes it tough to focus sometimes, but this time around I thought that the library might be a better fit than working fast food. Immersing myself in a world of books. Surrounded by walls of tales that have the power to set you free like only a good story is able to do.

I guess time will tell. They needed help, and I needed money, and I like reading. We'll see how this goes.

———

Cadence catches up with me at my locker. Blonde. Popular. Unflappable. She has the face of a fairy tale princess. Everything she does is an exclamation point. She's my best friend for a bunch of reasons. Partly, I like her for her quirky, weird sayings. Partly, because, for some inexplicable reason, she seems to genuinely, actually enjoy being around me.

"I heard what Cole said," she says to me. "Don't pay any attention to him."

"Yeah, I know."

"Seriously, I mean it. Forget what he said, Zod."

The Zod nickname has nothing to do with me being a supervillain or the adversary of Superman. It's from a story I told her last month when she was sleeping over one night. For some reason, we were watching the old, animated *Aladdin* movie and I ended up noting that it was nothing like the original, and when she asked me about it I told her the frame story for *The Arabian Nights*.

According to the legend, a certain king would marry a woman, sleep with her one night, and then kill her in the morning. And this went on day after day. Horrific.

But then one day, he marries this woman named Scheherazade, and she knows he's going to kill her in the morning, so she says, "Can I invite my sister over to say goodbye?"

He agrees to it. So, Scheherazade, she invites her sister over and starts telling her a story. It's really gripping and intriguing and she stops right at the climax. A true cliffhanger. And she knows that the king has been eavesdropping on her the whole time and afterward he can't stand not knowing the ending. So he begs Scheherazade to finish the story.

And she says, "I'll tell you more tomorrow night."

They go back and forth like that for a bit, but she's literally got all the cards because she knows he's planning to kill her anyway, so what does she have to lose?

Well, it works. He doesn't kill her in the morning and the next night she continues her story, and once again, she ends it right at the most exciting part. Another cliffhanger.

Then, just like the previous night, she says, "I'll tell you more tomorrow night."

Well, if you believe the legend, things go on like that with her telling stories for one thousand and one nights and finally the king realizes what an amazing woman she is and he tells her that he doesn't want to kill her after all, that he's fallen in love with her.

A bit slow on the uptake, that king, but at least there's a happy ending.

That's the power of a good story.

Sure, I know there's a lot in the legend about oppression and privilege and injustice—no kidding—but what I like most is that everything eventually turns out well for her—for them both.

Resilience. Creativity. Courage.

Scheherazade literally told stories to save her life. She fought against unimaginable evil and cruelty with nothing but her wits and her imagination and she won and became queen of the land. And she didn't just save herself, she saved the lives of at least one thousand and one other women who would've been slaughtered if not for her story.

Yeah, Scheherazade is my kind of woman.

So, anyway, after I told Cadence the story, she started calling me "Sahara-zade" which got shortened to "Zade" which became "Zod." It's how things go.

"Zod?" She waves her hand in front of my face.

"Sorry," I say. "I got lost there for a sec."

"I was just saying, Cole. Don't let him get to you."

"Sure."

My locker door is open and Cadence takes advantage of the moment to lean in and sneak a quick peek at herself in the mirror inside. She flips her hair elegantly to the side for a more windblown look, which somehow, even though there's no actual wind here in the hallway, works perfectly.

Incredible. How does she do that?

"Cole might look good in a football uniform," Cadence acknowledges with a touch of modest admiration, "but that boy is one oar short of a dinghy."

"Did you just say, 'one oar short of a dinghy'?"

"Sure, you know, like, he's not exactly the sharpest marble in the crayon box. His raft is on the water but it's not quite inflated. Like that."

I stare at her. "How do you even think of these?"

"They just come to me."

I finish collecting my things and swing my locker door shut.

"Oh," she tells me, "and your essay [air quotes]—*was*—[air quotes] legit."

"Since when do you use air quotes?"

"I've just started to [air quotes]—*use*—[air quotes] them."

"Hmm... I don't think you quite understand how they work."

"I think I [air quotes]—*do*—[air quotes]."

Oh, boy.

From anyone else it might be annoying but from her it's endearing.

"I'm saying your poem-thing, or whatever, was cool," she emphasizes. "Was it a poem? I don't know. It didn't rhyme."

"Poems don't have to rhyme," I say. "Anyway, I don't even know what it was. A mistake probably. I don't know what got into me."

"No, it was filthy."

We start down the hallway, everyone parting as she approaches. She has that effect on people. "So, what are you doing tonight?" she asks me.

"Working at the library 'til they close," I tell her. "That new job I just got. I'll probably just head home afterward. Maybe watch a movie. What about you?"

She lets the glimmer of a smile slip through. "I aim to misbehave."

"Finally watched *Serenity*, huh?"

"Had to start with *Firefly*," she tells me. "Thank God for binge-watching."

"You got antsy."

"I was born antsy," she says.

"That is true."

She gets a faraway look in her eyes. "I am a leaf on the wind. Watch how I soar."

"Okay," I say. "You really have been doing your homework. Good for you."

"Anyway, there's a party out at Jameson's Gap. A bonfire. Aiden and I are going. You should come."

Aiden is her flavor-of-the-week boyfriend. A guy should not be that impossibly cute, but he is. It's ridiculous. Cadence has this ability to snag the guys that other girls only dream about dating.

"I don't know," I tell Cadence. We're making our way toward the exit but there's a clog of students at the door, slowing us down. "I should probably stay home. Spend some time with Grams, you know?"

Since leaving Wisconsin, I've been living with my grandma who's seventy-four. We're supposed to be looking out for each other, and we get along well, so it's working out. We have something deep in common, after all: We both loved a man named Tim O'Shaughnessy who drowned in Chippewa Lake last spring.

I lost my dad. Grams lost her son.

Honestly, I sometimes forget that—about her loss. Losing a parent is one thing, but I can't imagine how hard it would be to lose your only child.

Gramps died when I was little and Mom's parents have never been in the picture—I think they live in Phoenix, but I haven't heard from them in years. So, right now, with Mom still in Wisconsin, it's just the two of us down here: Grams and me.

We talk about Dad sometimes but I haven't told her why he was out driving in the fog on that icy road on the night he died. And I never told her what mom said to me the day before I came down to live here in Tennessee. Grams doesn't need to know that.

No one should have to hear those words said about anyone, let alone about them.

Here's what happened.

7

AFTER DAD DIED, MOM WENT

off the rails in this emotional tailspin that just about destroyed her.

She was sleeping all the time and the nights became days and the meds weren't working. We managed to make it through a few weeks, but finally, one afternoon after she'd forgotten to eat for who knows how long, she collapsed on the floor in the kitchen, and that's where I found her after track practice, staring off into space, all mumbly drunk, slumped on the linoleum in a pool of her own urine. I was like, "Mom! Are you okay?" And then she started crying and didn't stop and that was it. I knew it was time—*past time*—to get her help.

A couple of workers from Child Services came to the house. They saw Mom's condition, and her bedroom all in disarray, and nothing in the fridge, and they made the decision. It wasn't hers to make anymore, not at that point. Things were out of her hands.

With no other relatives in the area, I stayed at a friend's place for a couple of weeks while Mom was in a hospital for people who are depressed and aren't getting better. At last, she came home and I thought things would be different, but then she unloaded the Truth Bomb of all time on me.

She started by saying, "I need to be honest with you," which is never a good thing to hear. It means someone's about to tell you something for their benefit, not for yours. "You know how I was in grad school when I got pregnant with you?" she said.

"Yes. American Literature."

"I never finished my degree."

"I know. You told me that before."

"Your father really wanted a baby and..."

"Yeah?"

"I... wasn't ready for one."

I felt a sinking feeling in my stomach. "What are you saying?"

"I made the choice to keep you," she said, like it was some remarkable, noble act.

"To keep me. You mean not to abort me. To kill me. Oh. How brave of you."

A silence that spoke volumes. "I didn't want to lose your father," she said, "I..."

"You never wanted a baby."

"I—"

"So basically: You never wanted *me*."

And she didn't deny it, which told me all I needed to know.

"And now that he's gone," I said, "where does that leave us?"

"I think we could both use some space."

"Seriously?"

"To heal. It's time for me to finish my degree. I've spoken with your grandmother and she's glad to have you..."

She let her voice trail off, left the rest unsaid and the silence exploded around me and inside of me and its echo was so deep and so cold and terrible that I didn't think then, and I still don't today, that it's ever going to go away.

"Because you don't want me around," I said. "And you never did."

"You're going to love Tennessee. And then after I get my degree, after I've—"

"Save it. I don't want to hear it."

How are you even supposed to deal with hearing something like that from your mom?

It did something to me. What's that saying about sticks and stones breaking your bones? Should be: "Sticks and stones may break my bones, but words may slay my heart." Fact. Words spoken and those left unsaid. Because words can rip the world apart. And they can leave open wounds and they can leave a family in tatters.

They can impale you with the truth, or the lies you've been told your whole life. Like every time your mom said she loves you.

So that's when I moved down to live with Grams.

———

"So," Cadence says, drawing my thoughts away from that devastating conversation with Mom and back to the invitation to tonight's party, "check on your Grams and then come. She'll be fine for a few hours."

"I don't know, I'm—"

"Seriously, Zod, you need to get out sometimes. Besides, we need to celebrate."

"Celebrate what?"

We finally get to the door, still caught in the crowd of students shoving past us toward the weekend.

"Um..." She considers my question. "Your new job! Do you have to do story time for the little kids on Saturday morning, by the way? I can only imagine the kind of stories you'd tell them."

"The lady who hired me didn't say anything about story time." I pause. "Let's hope not. I might have a tough time making my stories kid-friendly enough."

Cadence nudges my arm. "*Tyler's* gonna be there tonight."

"Why would that matter?" I say a little too pointedly. "I mean, whether or not he's going to be there?"

We step outside.

The autumn afternoon is cool. Jacket weather. A touch of woodsmoke drifts toward us from a house nearby from someone burning wood to heat their home, which isn't super unusual here, at the base of the mountains.

"I don't know why it would matter." Cadence offers me a tiny grin. "Why would it?"

"Why'd you even bring it up?"

"Oh, come on, Zod. I've seen how you look at him."

"And how's that?" I say, but I can feel my face getting red.

"Mm-hmm. And also, how he looks at you. You can't tell me you haven't noticed?"

"He does? I mean, does he?" I stop walking to look at her face for a deeper clue.

She rolls her eyes. "Seriously?"

I process that for a moment. "Yeah, I guess I could go to the gap after swinging home to make sure Grams is fine."

"Thought so."

"Just to celebrate my new job," I clarify. "Like you said. That's all."

"Uh-huh."

We continue toward the parking lot.

Here at the foothills of the Appalachians it doesn't get as hot as you might imagine for Tennessee—the mountains surrounding us help with that, and today they're mad with colors: red and yellow and orange and a touch of brown that winter will eventually spread out across the hills.

This afternoon, the sky seems to be in love with the mountains, sharp and almost too blue and contrasting starkly with the fall colors spreading across the hills as far back as you can see to where they kiss the horizon.

It's like you're stepping into a postcard. The way things ought to be.

If only things were picture-perfect on the inside and not just on the surface.

When I was a kid, my parents brought me down here to visit Grams quite a bit in the summer times. I don't really remember Gramps too much. He died when I was six, but I do remember he would always do these magic tricks like people do with kids—pulling a coin out from behind my ear, or making one vanish in his hand, that sort of thing.

So, because of those visits, I knew about the spell these mountains can put on you, and now that I'm staying here more than just a few days, I know I'll miss them a ton when I have to leave and go back to Wisconsin—or to wherever comes next. The future's kind of up in the air. Maybe Mom will change her mind and want me back. Maybe she's just going through a phase as she mourns Dad.

Honestly, though, I'm not holding my breath on that.

———

Cadence and I enter the parking lot.

They call this area of eastern Tennessee the Appalachian Highlands, and our school is aptly named Skyland High. We're supposed to be the Skyland Hawks. Because of that, there's an eight-foot-tall metallic statue of a bird out in front of the school, situated prominently between the flagpole and the circular drop-off drive.

Our mascot.

Oh, yay.

But the thing is, whoever designed the statue didn't get the eyes right. Hawks have eyes more on the front of their heads, falcons off to the side. So we actually have a falcon mascot. You'd think someone would have noticed when they built it. Nope. Not at this high school. Not at Skyland High where "Academics Set Us Apart!"

Yes, that is actually our motto.

Sigh.

"I'll see you at Jameson's Gap, then?" Cadence says to me.

"Yeah. I'm guessing nine-ish. As long as I can get permission from Grams."

"Perf." She blows me a kiss. "Love you."

"Love you more."

She sashays toward the Tesla her dad bought her last year for her sixteenth birthday. He works at a nuclear fuel plant nearby—makes good money there doing some sort of research that he's never exactly explained to Cadence, or at least that she's never been quite able to explain to me.

He's always into whatever gadget or phone or car is new or next and he passes most of the stuff on to her and her younger brother Casey, who's a freshman, when the next shiny thing snabs his attention.

But in the case of the Tesla, Cadence got that new.

Me, on the other hand, I climb into the clunky Camry that's two years older than I am and that Grams didn't drive anymore and that was somehow still running and that got gifted to me when I moved down here.

I don't really mind, though. I can't exactly trust it to always get me where I'm going, but so far it hasn't conked out on me yet. At least not for long.

I fire it up and after the engine coughs a couple of times, it reluctantly starts and I chug toward the library, thinking about seeing Tyler at the party and about what Cadence said about how I look at him.

She was not wrong.

I wonder if it's really that obvious to everyone.

But especially to him.

I try not to think about him looking at me.

But I don't try particularly hard.

A few minutes later, I roll into the library parking lot and click off the engine.

The library is a blocky historical building in downtown Erwin that serves as the main library for the whole county—which only has about 17,000 people, not counting the people who live off the grid and don't want to be counted.

This library used to be a train station, the Clinchfield Railroad Depot, built back in 1925. From what I understand, it was converted into a library in the 1990s. It still has a ticket window just behind the circulation desk, which is iconic, distinctive, and, in my humble opinion, kind of cool.

Unicoi County is a rural county that stretches up and over the mountains on each side of Highway 26, which pretty much slices it in half. It's like a giant eggplant with miles and miles of national forest land on each side of the highway. On one side, it meets up with North Carolina just on the east side of the Appalachian Trail that stretches along the ridge overlooking Erwin. More mountains lie on the other side of the highway and Grams and I live back there, tucked away in the hills.

––––––

The demographics here aren't so different than the small town I lived in up in Wisconsin. Around here, you get a mixture of country and mountain people and some richer city folks—lawyers and doctors who work in Johnson City, just ten miles or so down the road, but prefer living out here where there's more seclusion on the edge of the national forest.

Locals call this area of North Indian Creek Valley "The Valley Beautiful." There's even an overlook known as "The Beauty Spot," which is actually a good name for it. It's a huge, wide-open meadow at the top of a mountain with the Appalachian Trail skirting along the edge of it. It's far enough from town that you don't have much light pollution at night, so you can really view the stars and meteor showers, but it's still close enough to town that you can drive up there in less than half an hour.

You can see for forever up there—at The Beauty Spot—and in just about every direction you'll find more mountains stretching out toward the horizon. It's not like the rugged grandeur of the Rockies, which Mom and Dad took me to visit when I was nine, but more like a bunch of ambitious rolling hills that decided one day to emerge from the earth and strive for the sky.

Around here they call them the Blue Ridge Mountains. They're part of the Appalachian range, which some people say are the oldest mountains in the world. But despite the name, these mountains aren't actually blue—obviously. Instead, for most of the year they're covered with a thousand shades of green, and it's just that the further back they fold toward the horizon, the bluer they look because of how haze plays tricks on your eyes.

I've always been into astronomy. It was a hobby I could share with my dad. So, one night, soon after I moved down here in early August, I took the telescope he gave me when I was twelve up to The Beauty Spot to watch the Perseids meteor shower.

Seeing something like that reminds you of just how small you really are. I mean, in the Grand Scheme of things.

If there is a Grand Scheme at all.

———

Now, I put thoughts of Tyler and parties and meteor showers aside.

Rather than dwell on all of that, I grab my backpack and stroll past the two slightly rotting pumpkins standing sentry beside the front steps, awaiting Halloween, and go inside the library for my second night of work at my new job.

Let's see if this job lasts longer than that weekend one at the pizza food truck.

8

AS I WALK IN, THE HEAD
librarian, Ms. Mason, is waiting for me from behind the circulation
desk and greets me with a warm smile. "Hey, Sahara. How was
school?"

Disastrous, I think.

"Oh, good," I say.

She looks like she's in her mid-forties but wears old lady glasses
on a silver chain around her neck. Very iconic librarian—except she
dresses like a hippie. Hard to pin down what vibe she's going for.

"By the way," I say, "it's cool if you want to call me Zod." I'd told
her that already, when she interviewed me, but at the moment I don't
remind her of that fact. "I mean, or Sahara. It's fine either way."

She looks at me curiously, maybe trying to piece together where
the nickname Zod might have come from, but she doesn't ask. "Then
Zod it is." She gives the countertop a decisive knuckle rap. "And you
can call me Amanda."

She offers me a warm smile and I have a feeling she's going to be a
whole lot better to work for than the pizza truck guy.

I'm not sure how long calling her by her first name will last, but I
say, "Yes, ma'am. I mean, yes. Okay, I will, Ms... Amanda."

"Good."

Not all libraries have cats, but this one does. A slim, striped, gray
and white tabby cat named Lore who thinks he owns the place and
loves to lounge around on the counter and, even though I'm not
really a cat person, I give him a little scratch and he arches his back
and purrs comfortably as I do.

Maybe I could be converted to be a cat person after all.
I'm just saying, *maybe.*

———

After showing me how to use the circulation software, Amanda
sends me off to shelve books for a while—but there aren't that many
to put away, so that goes pretty quickly. Then she hands me a box of
thumbtacks and points to a pair of scissors and some colorful card
stock on the counter. "The bulletin board awaits! The Halloween
decorations for the children's area are in the basement. Back corner."
She gestures toward the stairs. "Be careful, though. Some people say
it's haunted down there and the light on the stairs is out. So watch
your step."

I don't know how serious her throwaway comment about the
basement supposedly being haunted was meant to be, but it registers
with me.

Honestly, I don't know if I believe in ghosts, but here in Southern
Appalachia, lots of people do. It's pretty common to believe in the
power of faith and of healing and in the reality of spiritual entities—
angels and demons and what Grams calls "haints." A "haint" is a
"haunt." A ghost.

There's a lot of history here in the region, and where there's a lot
of history somewhere, you can be sure you'll find a lot of tragedy.
And where there's a lot of tragedy, there always seem to be a lot of
ghosts—or at least stories about them.

I'm not sure how many decorations I'll need to be carrying, so I
set the tacks down next to the scissors before heading to the stairs.

From the top step, I can see that the stairwell is draped in thick
cobwebs, and I get the sense that no one has been down there for a
long time.

Instinctively, I click the light switch but nothing happens. Of
course not, Ms. Amanda already told me the light was out.

On the step just below me I see an enormous dead cricket. But
then, as I move my foot slowly toward it, all at once, it flings itself

erratically up against my leg, bounces off me, and leaps down the stairs and out of sight into the darkness, startling me.

I catch my breath.

Okay, not so dead after all.

I'm not even in the potentially haunted basement and already I'm jumpy.

I turn my attention to those guardian spiderwebs. To get to the Halloween decorations I'll need to get past them.

It had to be spiders.

Spiders freak me out, so with a slight feeling of revulsion, I grab a nearby broom and use the handle to sweep back the sticky webs, pressing them aside. As I do, a large brown spider scurries, agitated, down my forearm and I cry out and shake my arm to throw it off, but that only snarls gross webbing all over my hand and my arm, freaking me out even more.

The spider hits the wall, then drops unfazed to the floor and disappears into a small opening beneath one of the steps, which is just fine with me.

Crickets and spiders and possible haints in a dark, creepy basement.

Of course, because why not?

I take a moment to calm myself and smear the gooey webbing off my hand and onto my jeans.

"You okay?" Ms. Mason asks, and I realize she's watching me from the circulation desk, and has probably been watching me the whole time.

"Yeah," I mutter, wiping off my hand. "It's just... I'm not really a huge fan of spiders."

"There might be more of them down there. Just to warn you."

Oh, wonderful.

"Thanks."

"Do you want me to get the decorations?"

"No," I say, a little bit reluctantly. "I'll do it."

I don't mention this, but my non-love of spiders comes from a story I heard one time about a woman who goes camping and then comes home and the next morning she starts noticing this itching feeling on her scalp, and then, pretty soon, tiny crawling sensations all over her head. Turns out a spider had laid its eggs in her hair when she was in the woods and they hatched during the night while she was asleep. And now they're everywhere. Hundreds of baby spiders. All over her face and arms, crawling, scurrying.

Ew.

Okay, enough of that.

All because she went camping, which is why you don't see me heading for the hills on the weekends with a backpack on.

Urban legend or not, it terrified me when I was ten.

And it might or might not still sort of, possibly, do so now.

I take the steps slowly, one at a time, and as I descend, I sweep the broom across the dim space in front of me, doing the best I can to clear the stairwell of webs.

At the bottom of the stairs, I find a basement light switch and flick it on, and see that the basement is one giant room spanning the entire floor plan of the library above me.

Back corner. She said the Halloween decorations are in the back.

Looming wooden shelves packed with books tower over me and dominate the main part of the basement, Ninja-slicing up the light from the naked bulbs scattered across the ceiling that are trying unsuccessfully to fully illuminate the room.

Thick, intimidating shadows lurk in the corners where the light can't seem to reach.

Curious, I take a couple of books off the shelf in front of me and find library card envelope slots in the back of them. Old school all the way. And though they're shelved out of order down here, the books are meticulously typed—or in some cases, hand-stenciled—with Dewey Decimal System numbers on the spines. No barcodes or QR codes.

But I can live with that. It's what I grew up with near Chippewa

Lake during oh-so-many trips to our little town's rather ill-equipped library to visit the 398s—the fairy tales and folklore section, where my imagination has gone to play for as far back as I can remember.

Everyone should pay a visit now and then to the 398s and explore the land of lore and tales of pretend.

———

I page through a couple more books. The empty cards in the back tell me that two of them were never checked out by anyone, not even once.

I stare at the shelves.

Thousands of corpses of thousands of authors' dreams stand before me, gathering dust after being relegated down here to the dim and bookcase-crammed, cricket and spider-infested basement.

A placard leaning against the wall announces that there's an annual Friends of the Library sale coming up on November 2, and I realize that these books are about to be sold off in a few weeks—or at least *hopefully* sold off—probably to raise funds to buy new books for upstairs next year. After all, there are only so many shelves up there. So, it makes sense, but still...

November 2 seems appropriate.

It's the Day of the Dead.

In my polyphiloprogenitive mind, I wonder what these books would be thinking if they had feelings—I can't help myself. Rejected, neglected, or hey, maybe just excited to move on? You have your moment in the sun and then you're vanquished to the basement and then eventually sold off—but maybe then you find a home after the book sale with someone who likes older or less popular books.

They say that the Pixar people came up with their movie ideas for years by asking "What if... had feelings?" Toys. Insects. Cars. Monsters. Even feelings—if feelings had feelings. That seems to maybe be scraping the bottom of the barrel, but, hey, whatever works. They had a good run.

———

I reshelve the books and look around.

A discarded artificial Christmas tree sits propped up against the wall in the corner, a string of limp lights still draped loosely across its plastic branches and partly looped in a haphazard circle near its base. It looks like someone might've started to remove them but then just abandoned the project halfway through.

Halloween, Sahara. Remember, you're here for the decorations.

I drift past the shelves and peer into the shadowy, forgotten corners of the basement where a couple of tottering piles of overstuffed cardboard boxes are stacked nearly to the ceiling. I'm not sure what they hold, probably more books.

On the floor beside them, four faded watercolor paintings lean up against the wall: a rustic cabin, a mountain waterfall, a desert populated with threatening-looking cacti, and a wind-swept shoreline with a solitary lighthouse perched on a rocky cliff, its light stabbing valiantly across the canvas, deep into the night.

It makes me think of my non-essay again: *"I am a sailboat, catching a daring wind toward a distant shore. I am a lost ship, crashing into the rocks and sinking in the sea."*

I'm both, somehow, at the same time: the billowing sail and the sinking ship. Somehow, I feel like I am heading toward the future while also being dragged down by the past.

I wonder if anyone else ever feels this way.

None of the paintings are what I'd call masterpieces, more like ones you might find at a garage sale or in a thrift store. I try to imagine where they might've hung upstairs before being retired down here, but no good spots really come to mind.

––––

Once I'm past the paintings, it only takes me a moment to find the kids' area Halloween decorations—a box of cardboard cutouts of grinning ghosts, plump bats, goofy goblins, and friendly-looking witches on poofy broomsticks.

I pick it up and as I turn, I notice another bookshelf out of the corner of my eye, about fifteen feet off to the left, between me and the tottering tower of boxes.

This shelf is positioned away from the others, pressed up tightly against the wall, which strikes me as a little odd since all of the other ones are lined up in strict, careful rows, almost geometric in their precision.

Huh.

I set down the decorations and make my way to the wall where that lone bookshelf stands waiting.

As I get closer, I see a slim line of darkness edging down one side of the bookcase but not the other, making me think that there's gotta be something besides a wall behind it.

A doorway?

A hidden room?

The gap is maybe half an inch wide and I lean in and try to peer into it, but because of the way the shelf is positioned, I can't really see anything. I figure that the bookshelf must be bolted to the wall, but when I lean against it, there's a little bit of a wobble there. Not enough for it to fall over, but enough to tell me that it hasn't been secured to the basement wall.

This particular bookshelf isn't as huge as the others, and it's more sparsely populated with books. I begin to wonder if I might actually be able to slide it aside to see what's back there behind it.

Just to take a quick look. That's it. That's all.

I grab the side of the bookshelf firmly and have to really wrestle against it to get it to move. At first, I'm afraid it might tip over on me, but the way it's built—wider on the bottom than on the top—I realize that's probably not going to happen.

It's super heavy and it almost seems like it's fighting against my efforts to slide it aside, as if it has a mind of its own, but I tell myself that its apparent reluctance is just because it's old and probably hasn't been moved in years.

So far, despite all of my efforts to slide it aside, it's only allowed me to muscle it a few inches from the wall.

Yeah, you can do this.

I lean into it and, giving it one more go, I push harder, and at last it scrapes another six inches or so across the grainy concrete floor.

And I see that indeed, there is something behind it: a rock-walled corridor just tall enough for me to walk into.

I turn on my phone's light and angle it into the darkness.

9

THE NARROW PASSAGEWAY

stretches out directly before me, maybe thirty feet or so further into the earth with three openings—doorways?—that might lead to more corridors?

Hmm. From here I can't tell.

This passageway must have been here from the original days of the railroad station because it wasn't made with modern concrete or cement blocks. Instead, the walls are stacked with large river rocks with interstitial layers of dry, crumbling earth sandwiched in between them, overlooking the packed dirt floor.

When I peer a little more closely, I can tell that the three openings must be where doors were hung a long time ago. Now only remnants of rotten wood remain where the hinges would have been attached. The doors themselves are gone.

One doorway stands five feet away to my left, the other two lie further down the corridor off to the right.

When I tilt my phone upward, I see a flicker of dark movement at the far edge of the light, a shadow that the light doesn't quite dispel but instead seems to frighten off.

It's almost like it's escaping the light. That's the phrase that comes to mind: a shadow escaping the light—but that doesn't make sense because shadows don't try to escape anything or get frightened off.

Something's back there.

What? A cat? Maybe a possum? A raccoon? A giant rat?

Did Lore somehow get down here from upstairs?

No. In truth, none of that seems right.

I feel my heartbeat quicken.

Maybe if there was a crack in the library's foundation somewhere above me, that could explain how the critter, whatever it is, got down here. I hadn't noticed any cracks up there earlier, but then again, I hadn't been looking.

But you only saw a shadow just now, Sahara, not a rat or a possum.

It was probably just my imagination playing tricks on me. It had to have been that.

When nothing reappears, I decide to go in and check out the hallway and the three rooms, just to have a peek at what they might contain.

I wobble-walk the bookshelf a little further to the side, providing me with just enough space to squeeze through into the corridor.

Maybe.

I try one more time to move it in order to give myself a little more room to get past it, but it must have caught on a groove or bump on the ground because it refuses to budge any further.

Because of the way the bookshelf is positioned, I have to squeeze myself super thin to get through the opening, letting out most of my air to make my torso as narrow as possible—something my dad taught me to do when we used to go caving up in Wisconsin and came to narrow passageways. As he told me the first time he took me to a cave, when I was maybe twelve, "Sometimes there are passages so narrow that you'll need to let out all of your air and then you pull yourself forward and hopefully then you can inhale once again."

"What if you can't inhale again?" I asked uneasily.

"Usually you can."

"But what if you *can't?*"

And he smiled and reminded me of the mythical creatures that lumberjacks back in the old days claimed inhabited the Northwoods, "Then you die and the hodags will find you, burrow into your body cavity, and eat you from the inside out."

"Oh. Lovely."

At the time, all I could picture were the bulldog-sized creatures with razor-sharp teeth, spiky backs, and fearsome claws ready to tear into my flesh and eat me from the inside out.

"But you'll be fine," my dad assured me. "Those are just stories."

"Uh-huh."

Then he winked at me, his way of telling me that everything was going to be alright.

I never did get attacked by a hodag, but his advice about how to wriggle through a tight space is what I'm thinking of now as I exhale my air and slide between the bookshelf and the wall of the stone-formed corridor: both his words of advice and his words of warning about those mythical hodags burrowing into my body cavity and eating me from the inside out.

Which doesn't help my anxiety level one bit.

I squeeze through, make my way into the corridor, and inhale deeply once again.

The air is musty and pockmarked with dust motes that I accidentally kick up as I move onto the dirt floor beyond the bookshelf.

It's a forgotten place back here, or at the very least a place that it seems like someone was trying to forget. But at least there aren't any spiders.

I edge toward the first doorway and find that it leads to a small alcove not much larger than my bedroom closet. I'm not sure why someone went through all the trouble of digging it out and supporting its walls since it doesn't look like it would hold much, and I can't figure out what it might've originally even been used for. A root cellar? The air here is noticeably colder than it was in the main part of the basement, so that would maybe make some sense. But a root cellar beneath a train station? Maybe, but that seems like a bit of a stretch.

A small hole appears to be burrowed into the wall near the corner where a rock the size of a bowling ball has fallen away from its spot near the ground.

Maybe that's where the creature came from.

But no—you didn't see a creature, Sahara, just a shadow.

I tell myself once again that shadows don't move on their own or try to escape the light and, proceeding forward down the hall, I come to the next doorway and find a slightly larger room. This one has wide wooden planks piled up in the back corner next to a couple of old hammers and a mouldering box of nails. I wonder about that for a moment, but then realize that some of the boards are in the shape of a coffin lid.

No. They're not just shaped *like* a coffin lid. That *is* one.

Something's not right down here. Why were they making coffins?

But then another thought: *Maybe they weren't making coffins. Maybe they were taking them apart.*

I'm not sure I should go any further—probably not—but something compels me to look in that third room.

Somewhat uneasily, I head fifteen feet farther down the corridor toward the final doorway on my right.

10

AS I WALK FORWARD, THE LIGHT

from my phone flickers for a moment like it's unsure if it wants to keep shining.

Yeah, that would not be a good thing if it decided to die on me now.

It's not like I'd be lost in a maze or anything, but the shadows... I just don't trust those crouching shadows. Let's just say I wouldn't want them to overtake me before I could get back to the bookshelf. I don't want to be overcome by the darkness, not back here.

I find myself gulping as I make my way down the corridor, aiming the light ahead of me as if it's a weapon, as if a beam of light alone could protect me.

The darkness retreats, back to the far corners of the corridor where it's trapped and eventually seeps into the cracks in the wall and disappears as I direct my phone's flashlight directly at it.

It's hard to shake the feeling that light and darkness are clashing here, like the darkness doesn't want to submit to the light, but wants to fight against it instead. It's weird. It makes no sense, but it sure seems to be the case.

I come to the third doorway and peer into the room.

This is the largest of the three rooms, twice the size of the others—maybe twenty feet by twenty feet. For some reason, I'm uneasy about entering it, and instead, I pass my hand in front of me first and find that it's even colder in there than it is here in the corridor.

From caving, I know that the underground world is typically cooler than the air above ground—unless you're in Wisconsin and you're caving in the winter, when it might be sixty or seventy degrees warmer in the cave than it is outside in the subzero forest or field above you.

In that case, you always bring a change of clothes along into the cave, stashing them near the entrance while you explore. Then, when you're done, you make sure to change out of your damp and muddy caving clothes before you leave the cave. If you don't, when you step out of the entrance, they'll freeze on you pretty much instantly. Makes it rather uncomfortable walking back to the car encased in frozen clothes that crinkle and crack and slice into your skin every time you take a step.

What are you doing here, Sahara? You should go back.

I'm just looking.

Just curious.

I'm not super tall—five-six in my Doc Martens—but still, I have to duck as I pass beneath the doorframe and enter the room.

Immediately, I begin to feel queasy. For some reason, the air seems thicker and tougher to breathe than it did just a moment earlier. It's like I'm not just walking forward, but pressing against something that doesn't want me here, like the air—or something invisible inside of it—is trying to hold me back, to keep me at bay, but then sealing itself up behind me after I take a step.

Slowly, hesitantly, I move forward.

It's not cold enough in here for me to see my breath, but it is cold enough to make me shiver.

And for some reason, it's not just getting tougher to breathe, but also tougher to think.

Everything kind of slows down in my mind.

Slowing.

To a crawl.

I see the image of my dad talking to me in the hallway on the night he died, right before I stormed out the door. But it's not like a memory or a dream, it's more like it's happening again, or maybe I'm experiencing it again, as it happens for the first time. But I'm not myself, instead, it's as if I'm standing next to myself, like I'm watching a movie of what's happening rather than remembering it occurring through my own eyes.

Dad tells me about my journal, and I stare at him in disbelief, and then I utter The Words I Can't Take Back.

I see myself push past him, stomp outside the house, throw the door closed behind me, and head to my car, almost slipping on the ice as I do.

I climb in, fire up the engine, and pull forward, fishtailing out of the driveway.

Then I'm driving into the fog, going way too fast and I smack the steering wheel with the palm of my hand in anger and scream into the night, my heart broken for what I think he's done and also because I already regret what I said to him.

The images float and hover around me.

The foggy night outside.

The headlights trying their best to shine through the haze.

And so much anger inside of me.

A silent scream inside of my heart.

A scream that's going to turn into soul-singeing regret within just a few hours.

Here in the third room, I reach forward and touch the steering wheel and can almost feel it solidifying in the air before me.

What is happening? What is going on?

It's no longer possible to sort out what's really happening around me from what I'm imagining.

I'm in the car.

I'm in the rock-walled room.

I'm driving through the freezing night. I'm standing here surrounded by dusty air.

Part of me knows I shouldn't be doing this, but I take another step.

And feel a chill that doesn't come from the air but from a slithering uneasiness awakening somewhere inside of me.

Stop freaking yourself out. Just go back to the main part of the basement. Get out of this room.

The fog clears, and instead of a hazy night outside the car, I see a land, barren and endless and arid, stretching out all around me, languishing under a threatening sky burdened with slabs of dreary clouds, heavy with winter rain.

What is going on?

I'm in the middle of a desert I've never been to before, but one that doesn't want me to leave it.

It makes me think of Scheherazade and her world of Arabian tales.

Somehow, I know this is a land of grief and heartache, of sun-bleached bones and broken dreams. But then, in a moment, the sand morphs and moistens and becomes an endless sea. No shore in sight. Love adrift. Stark longing with nowhere to go, now shrinking into a lake. Chippewa Lake. Dad in his car. Drowning because he loves me.

I see it.

See him, his mouth open in a burbling underwater scream that's being silenced forever by the dark water.

No!

Then everything seems to spin and tilt, and I don't feel like I'm standing up but lying down on my back. The lake disappears into a snarl of gray smoke that morphs into a pine plank, one and then another, that slide in around me and then seal themselves into place above me.

A coffin.

And I'm sealed inside.

When I lift my hands, I feel the rough wood.

I press on it, but it's solid and unforgiving.

I pound against it, my fists tight and frenzied, but it does no good.

"Hey!" I yell to no one because I'm all alone.

I feel my heartbeat racing, skitter-skipping along on its way to the edge of a cliff, with nothing to stop it.

I hear the sound of heavy clods of dirt landing on the lid of the coffin, and I cry out for help, scream for whoever is burying me to stop, to let me out because I'm not dead. I'm alive, alive, alive!

And then I feel the itching on my scalp.

Oh no.

And then movement, light and feathery, tiny, tiny feet.

They've awakened.

Please no.

The baby spiders.

They're scurrying across my face and my neck and under my shirt, and I'm in that coffin, the lid just above me, the sound of shovelfuls of dirt landing on it, growing more muffled and distant by the second.

I try to scream again, but nothing comes out. However, when I open my mouth, the spiders rush toward it and I close it, but not quickly enough. I taste a mouthful of them, squirming on my tongue, and gag on the wiggling legs and moist, writhing bodies and cough them up and spit them out.

I close my eyes and tell myself that I'm just imagining all of this, tell myself that it's not real, none of this is real, and that it'll all go away as soon as I open my eyes.

Heart beating. Hammering.

And then I do.

I open my eyes.

And I'm not in the coffin any longer.

I'm standing in the room once more.

No fog.

No drowning father.

No coffin and wriggling spiders clogging my throat.

Just a voice, whispery and low from right behind me. *"This is where you belong, Sahara. You don't ever need to leave."*

I whip around.

Nothing. No one there.

Get out of here, now!

I'm trying to sort out what's real and what's not, what's just in my mind and what's actually all around me. I back up to get out of the room, but somehow, I back into the wall instead.

I must have gotten turned around.

I search for the doorway, which should be behind me, and see it across the room from me.

That's impossible! You just came in through there. What's going on?

I must have crossed the room while I was disoriented.

Right now, I just need to get back.

I take a step forward to the other side of the room, toward the hallway.

Get out of here. It's not that far. Just half a dozen steps.

Then a whisper: *"But is that really what you want?"*

I feel a quiver inside of me like something deep and secret and arcane is stirring. An ancient tale awakening, one with yellowing teeth and claws and pulsing blood.

And part of me wants to stay here, to step into that dark shadow shrouding in around me, edging into time. It wants to sit down and lean against the wall and breathe deeply of the oppressive air and do that now and do it forevermore.

Drink in death.

Drink it all in.

Something in the air and something deep beneath it.

Get out, Sahara! You need to get out of here!

I take another step toward the opening at the far end of the room, maybe eight feet away now, but when I do, it seems to back up farther away, the distance stretching out, doubling and doubling again. And I think of a torture rack from the Middle Ages and of the grim snap and strain of joints and muscles being stretched beyond what they can bear. That's what's happening to the space before me, the distance expanding and at the same time straining to contain the tightening sinews of air that lie within it, air that's about to snap.

You're just disoriented. That's all.

I think of Dad trapped in that car under the ice. Trapped and dying in the dark.

And I hear his voice calling for me to join him: "I'm here, Sahara. I'm ready for you. Come to me."

"Dad?"

I pivot around and try to find the source of the voice.

And I see him.

He's standing on the other side of the room and he looks just like I remember him—just as tall as he should be, just as strong, just as scruffy. But his left leg is bent and broken in a way that shouldn't be able to support his weight, and his eyes are different. They're blank and white and don't look like they could see anything, but also seem to be staring directly at me. And he's soaking wet, water dripping off him onto the dirt floor.

"I've been waiting for you," he says. "You can stay here."

No. It can't be true.

"Dad?" As I whisper the word I shudder because I know it can't be him. He's dead. And the dead do not come back.

Unless there is an afterlife.

The Great Unless.

"It's cold down here, Sahara." His voice sounds low and gasping and there's a shivery echo to every word. "So cold."

You're hearing things. You're seeing things. He's dead!

He cocks his head. "Why didn't you answer the phone when I called you that night? Why didn't you pick up the call?"

"I didn't know," I mutter. "I swear. I never would have... I had no idea it was..."

It's not real. This isn't real. It's all in your head. It's all an illusion. A hallucination. He's not here. He's not—

"Sahara, stay with me."

"I can't."

"Join me."

Get out of here!

I turn around to leave.

The doorway itself seems to be shrinking and I have the sense that if I don't move now—move *now!*—the space will become too small for me to fit through and I'll be trapped in here forever.

Desperately, I scramble forward, convinced that I can make it, and feel something clutch my shoulder. A hand. But there is no hand. There can't be. Because I'm alone.

Frantic now, I launch myself toward the doorway and tumble through it and I burst through an invisible membrane of sour air that's stretched in front of the door, sealing off the room. It's almost like I can hear it rip open and then tighten with a damp slithery *cinch* behind me once I tumble through.

I'm on my hands and knees, gasping for breath, straining to get enough air into my burning lungs.

Breathe. Breathe. Breathe.

Just breathe.

I have the feeling that a lot of time has passed—hours even. How long was I in there? Is the library even still open? I look at my phone, check the time, and see that it's just after six. It's as if no time has passed at all.

What is going on with you?

I push myself to my feet and, with a slight hitch of hesitation, turn back to look into that third room.

It appears normal, nothing out of the ordinary. No ghostly murmuring voices. No spiders or coffins or fog-enshrouded nights.

And no Dad standing pale and cold in front of me, a revenant from the land of the dead.

I was just imagining all of that. I had to have been. My overactive imagination stringing together nightmares I've had with stories I've heard and the pain I've been carrying around since Dad's death, my stupid story-obsessed brain mixed them all together and frightened me with what wasn't real. That's what it was. That's what it had to be.

Probably because all those things were in my mind when I was writing my non-essay and then there was that thick mesh of cobwebs in the stairwell and that spider on my arm and being alone in that isolated corridor... all of that caught up with me and led me to hallucinate everything I saw, everything I heard.

I figure that, by now, Ms. Mason has got to be wondering where I am, so as quickly as I can, I wrestle the bookshelf back against the wall, retrieve the box of Halloween decorations, and hurry toward the stairs.

I'm halfway there when I see an old leather-bound book on the ground in front of me.

I have the sense that it wasn't there earlier, but it's possible I was distracted and missed seeing it. Or maybe, it fell while I was in that back corridor.

I pick it up and I'm about to shelve it again, but then I see the title *Haints in the Hollers: Southern Appalachian Ghost Lore.*

Well, that's appropriate.

Way *too* appropriate.

A little unsettled, I find myself opening it up. A 1962 copyright. There are half a dozen dogeared pages about different local folktales and ghost stories, and then I get to the last page and as I flip past it, I come to the back of the book and see the library card slot in the back.

My jaw drops when I see the only name scrawled on it.

Tim O'Shaughnessy.

My dad.

11

I STARE AT THE BOOK.

This makes no sense. Dad grew up around here, sure, of course he did, and he liked to read... but what are the odds that one of the books he checked out twenty-nine years ago would end up here in front of me? That it would fall off the shelf just in time for me to find it?

I'm no expert in math, but it's gotta be pretty much a statistical impossibility.

But then, an inner voice: *Nothing that happens is impossible, Sahara. And nothing that's impossible ever occurs. That's one way to tell what's real and what's not.*

Based on the date when the book was checked out, he would have been sixteen at the time he read it.

How could something like this happen? It's almost like something was trying to get my attention.

Or someone.

Dad?

I feel a chill and take in a nervous gulp of musty basement air.

No. that couldn't be. How would that even work?

I blow the dust off the top of the book.

As I do, it strikes me that the dust is only on the top of the book when I hold it up vertically, not on the front cover, which was facing up when I found it on the floor. That means that it would have been upright on the shelf gathering dust and not there lying flat on the floor of the basement. Which also means it wasn't lying there for very long.

So, it quite possibly did fall while I was in the back room.

Or it was placed there.

But that doesn't make sense. I was the only one in the basement. It *had to* have fallen, and I was so distracted while I was in that back passageway that I just didn't hear it hit the floor.

I wonder why he checked out this particular book and I have the sense that if I read it too, we'll have something in common, a bridge between the present and the past, a connection that might even stretch between life and death.

Maybe it'll provide some answers, some sort of contact with him, even though he's gone.

I think back to the sessions with the counselor and how he'd said that love isn't torture.

But maybe it is. Love hurts because to love someone you have to give away part of yourself and—obviously—you suffer when you lose them. And you do all of this willingly. But love is essential, so maybe it *is* torture—the kind that keeps us alive, gives us a reason for living.

Maybe this book would somehow give me a chance to find out.

———

Upstairs again, I paste a carefree smile on my face as I emerge from the stairwell and see Ms. Mason at the circulation desk.

"All good?" she says.

"Yeah." I hold up the Halloween decorations, but keep the book hidden beneath them. "It took me a minute to find these."

"Okay."

My shoulder's on fire beneath the spot where I felt a hand tugging me backward into the room. Dad's hand? I don't know.

I reach up tenderly and touch the fiery spot, and wince.

Ms. Mason looks at me concernedly. "What is it?"

"Nothing. Just... A sore muscle. I'm fine."

A look of concern. "You sure you're okay?"

"I'm good. Can you excuse me for a sec? I need to use the restroom."

"Sure."

I close the bathroom door behind me and peer into the mirror.

I don't look so good. My eyes are bloodshot and I'm pale and still trembling.

I slide the neckline of my shirt over across my bra strap and see a fierce red bruise in the shape of a hand on my shoulder.

So, there was something in there after all.

Yes.

There was.

Someone really had grabbed me. Someone who didn't want me to leave.

It couldn't have been Dad.

He's dead, and he wouldn't have wanted me to join him. That makes no sense.

It had to have been something else.

There's not really any space in my backpack for the book, so I set it nearby on the counter and then spend some time thumbtacking kid-friendly Halloween cutouts onto the bulletin board, but the whole time I'm thinking about that collection of ghost lore and the secret passageway behind the bookshelf and the shadowy form that seemed to be afraid of the light, and the room that didn't want to let me go, and of what Ms. Amanda had mentioned to me—that the basement was said to be haunted.

Yeah, that's a definite possibility. But whether or not it actually is haunted, there's something not right down there, and maybe that book of ghost lore is a clue to what that something is.

I'm not super crafty, so it takes me a while to snip out the bulletin board letters spelling HAPPY HALLOWEEN! and cut out some orange Jack-o-Lanterns, making them only slightly scary so they don't freak out the kids.

As I'm finishing tacking them up, my stomach grumbles, reminding me that I haven't eaten anything since lunch.

It's nearly seven-thirty, so it makes sense that I'm hungry.

Last night, I'd thrown a couple of granola bars in my car, figuring they'd get me by until I got home, but in the aftermath of visiting the basement, I'd forgotten about them and lost track of the whole eating-to-stay-alive thing while I was busy with the bulletin board.

When I return the thumbtacks and scissors to the circulation desk, Ms. Amanda says, "All finished?"

"Yes."

She walks with me to the children's area, studies the bulletin board, and nods approvingly. "The carved pumpkins are a nice touch."

"Thanks," I say, but the pumpkins aren't really that impressive. She's being kind. They just might be misshapen orange turtles with stem-shaped heads.

"Are you good to read stories tomorrow for our eleven o'clock Story Hour?"

"Um... I might not be the best story reader for little kids. I get nervous reading in front of people."

"Oh, I'm sure you'll be fine. There usually aren't more than eight or ten kids plus their parents. Dr. Seuss is always popular... Although, they do get checked out a lot."

"Right." I'm not really sure I want to shirk my responsibility my first week on the job. "Okay."

She consults her watch, "You know, Zod, no one's here and it's almost time to close up anyway. Why don't you take off? It's a Friday night. Go have some fun."

"Really?"

She smiles. "I know you need your hours. Don't worry. We'll still pay you. Personal time."

"Oh, that'd be great. Thanks."

I wonder if I should ask about the weird rooms in the basement. Even though I'm hesitant to at first, in the end I decide, *what can it hurt*?

"Ms. Amanda, what do you know about the corridor downstairs?"

"What corridor is that?"

"The one behind that bookcase that's pushed up against the far wall, over near the stack of boxes in the back."

She scratches her chin reflectively. "Hmm... I'm not sure. I honestly haven't looked around that basement much since I started here in the spring. I didn't even know there was anything behind any of the bookshelves. I suppose you'd have to ask the previous librarian about any corridors down there. Wait—if it's behind a bookshelf that's against the wall, how do you know it's there?"

"I might have peeked."

"Ah. Well, I'd say that—if a bookcase is shoved up against the wall—it's probably been placed there for a reason. Best to just leave it alone and not worry about it."

"Right." I nod agreeably. "Sure. Of course."

At this point, I figure it's best not to mention the three rooms, or especially what happened to me when I entered that last one. Then I have a thought and add, "Do you know if there are any maps of the library?"

"Maps?"

"Or blueprints? Building plans? Anything like that?"

"Well..." She eyes me curiously. "I can't imagine that there are any still around—considering how old the building is but there's an old box of papers that used to be in a local historical exhibit that's still in a closet in the office. There are some documents in there that tell about the library back when it was still a train station. You knew that right? About it being a train station?"

"Yes. Until the nineties."

A nod. "I think those papers are in the box on the top shelf in the back of the closet. There might be some blueprints in there. Who knows? I don't think any of that stuff has ever been scanned in; so none of it's online anywhere. I'd say that box is the place to start. But let's save that for tomorrow—if there's time and we're not too busy. Then you're welcome to go through it."

"Thanks."

———

As I'm collecting my things, she notices the ghost lore book. "What have you got there?"

"Oh, a book I found downstairs." I hold it up. "I like folklore and ghost stories."

"Was it on the Friends of the Library sales shelf?"

"Yes." Then, even though I definitely do not want to go back in the basement, I feel obligated to take it back down there if she wants me to. "Should I put it back?"

"Oh, no. You can have it if you like it. Keep it. Anytime I find someone who wants one of those old books, I'm happy to see it find a home—the goal is to find a new home for all of them."

"Thank you."

I figure I need some answers before I go telling anyone what's going on, so I don't mention the library card in the back with my dad's name handprinted on it.

And I don't clarify that the book actually seemed to find me, instead of me finding it.

———

Outside, before going to my car, I walk around the building and study the foundation.

As far as I can tell, there aren't any holes large enough to let in whatever shadowy creature it was I saw—or more precisely, *didn't* see—beyond the bookshelf.

But something was down there—or at least its shadow was. But, like I kept reminding myself when I was in the basement, shadows don't cast themselves.

That's what I'm thinking as I drive home with the book about Southern Appalachian ghost lore that somehow ended up on the floor when and where it did, lying on the seat beside me.

———

As I drive along the Nolichucky River toward Grams' house

nestled up in the mountains above the river, I'm still pretty freaked out by what happened in that third room.

There's this lingering uneasiness that I have from being in there and it feels like it's burrowing its way deeper and deeper into my soul. I'm not sure that I'm up for being around a bunch of people at the moment, and I'm tempted to bail on the party, but then I think of my promise to Cadence that I'd be there.

And I think of Tyler being there too.

Okay, maybe don't bail after all.

With the time it'll take me to drive home, grab something to eat, and then make my way up to the Gap, it probably will be close to nine, like I'd mentioned to Cadence earlier. That should work.

So, I have a four-point plan for the night after checking on Grams. (1) Grab some food. (2) Get permission to go to the party (a good chance, but not guaranteed). (3) Head to the bonfire where I can hopefully accidentally-on-purpose run into Tyler: *Huh, hey. I didn't know you were gonna be here. Imagine that. What are the odds?*

And then (4) come back home and page through the book that found me, to try to uncover some answers.

BEFORE

———

I heard there's a saying in Portugal: "What is difficult to bear becomes sweet to remember."

Yeah, right.

It's not sweet to remember lying in bed and waking up to the doorbell ringing at two in the morning and then catching the sound of your mom getting up and traipsing to the front door, and then hearing her cry out—a shrieking, "Nooo!" that goes on too long and ends in a strangled gasp. "Please, no."

It's not sweet to remember a sound that echoes through the house and through the night and through your heart, a sound that might never stop echoing there, ever again. It's not sweet to remember the raw, shrill desperation in her voice. There's nothing sweet about remembering running down the stairs and seeing her crumpled by the front door with two somber cops beside her holding their hats in their hands. No, there's nothing sweet about that, about any of it.

And then the one cop puts her hand on Mom's shoulder and in that instant I know; I know without them saying anything.

It's Dad.

He's not home, but he should be.

He's not home and he never will be.

I know it. The deep-down kind of knowing. The knowing that's beyond words.

I find myself rubbing the ring I'm wearing on my right hand, the one that Dad gave me when last fall when I turned sixteen. Sapphire. My birthstone. It's not magical or anything, but it is precious to me.

There's another saying: "What doesn't kill you makes you stronger," but that's not true either. What doesn't kill you makes you weaker. Losing someone you love doesn't give you strength, it saps your strength and has the ability to tear your best intentions to shreds.

Or "Time heals all wounds." That's another good one. I read in a book one time, this guy says, "Time doesn't heal all wounds. Sometimes it throws salt in them and laughs at you as it walks away." That seems more on the right track.

Or maybe, "Time plus tragedy equals comedy."

No. That's another cunning little lie.

I don't think there's enough time in the whole universe to make the loss of my dad comedic in any way. No. Not ever.

How could so many things that people take at face value be so backwards?

So, yeah, that night happened. That ache. And that pain is still gnawing away at me every time I think of it, seven months later.

That night, Dad called me when he knew he wasn't going to make it. He called my number instead of an ambulance.

"I love you." His voice was strangled and weak. He was dying. "I'm sorry. Look on my workbench," he said, but the words are barely loud enough to hear. Because it was almost too late. "Tell your mom I love her too, I..." And his words trailed off into a silence that troubled me as much as the words did.

But when the call first came through, I was still pissed at him so when his name came up on my phone, I didn't pick up. I didn't answer. I let it go to voicemail.

Later, when I finally did listen to it, I heard splashing water after his words, then a final sickening gasp, and then only a cold dark silence.

Yeah, he called me first instead of 911, maybe because he knew it was too late, that the paramedics wouldn't have been able to get there in time and all he wanted to do was make things right with me before he died, and I didn't even let him do that. He finally dialed 911 in the end, and the call went through, but later the dispatcher said that all she heard was silence and couldn't backtrace the call.

Remembering that night brings an ache that rips me apart in a deep, secret way every time I think of it, so I try not to think of it. Of him. Yeah, it's an ache, but it's also a longing to make things different, and a knowledge that that's not going to happen. Not now. Not ever.

PART II

BE BOLD, BE BOLD

12

THE DRIVE UP TO GRAMS'S HOUSE

is steep and windy, like some sort of trail left behind by a giant snake slithering up the mountainside.

Lots of people in this area of Tennessee call their grandma "Meemaw" or "Mamaw," and their grandpa "Pappy" or "Papaw," but when I was born, Grams decided she wanted to be called Grams. When I was little, I had trouble with my "r"s and called her "Gwams" for years, but she never complained and eventually I got it right and it's been Grams ever since.

———

After making my way up our long dirt driveway, I park just in front of the carport, figuring that I'll be leaving in a little while again, anyway.

I stuff the ghost lore book into my backpack and take it with me.

On the porch, I pass the eggshell-white rocking chair where Grams loves to sit and can usually be found during the day. It's her favorite place to tell stories or *spin a yarn*, as she likes to say.

She doesn't look at storytelling as merely entertainment, but as something deeper: as a way to connect with people, and also to your kin who've gone before you and have passed their stories on to you. It's your job to keep those stories alive.

She told me that there's a Native American belief that all the stories that exist are already out there and that sometimes one of them will find you and it's your responsibility to share it with the world. And she takes that job seriously.

That, and also telling each story with a unique flair. As she likes to say, "When you tell a story, you bring yourself to it and leave some of yourself behind in everyone who hears it."

The house has been in the family forever and used to be a one-room cabin back in the 1880s. New generations eventually added onto it, even adding a second floor, until now there are three bedrooms, a small dining room and kitchen, two baths, and a living room, but you can tell where the old ends and the new begins. The old stories giving way to the emerging ones.

———

"Hey, Grams," I call as I step into the living room and let the screen door swing shut of its own willpower and then kick the actual door closed behind me.

"Sahara." Her delicate voice floats toward me from the kitchen.

To join her, I walk past the well-worn couch that her cat used to scratch at all the time before she ran away, and then edge around the faded gray recliner that faces the window. At last, I find Grams drinking some sweet tea at the table.

"How are you doing, dear?" Her words are graced with a touch of southern dialect—not like a deep Georgia drawl, but an East Tennessee accent. More Country than Southern Belle.

It's a little surprising that Dad grew up here but didn't pick up the accent so much and ended up sounding like he was from Wisconsin instead.

"I'm fine." I pat her shoulder gently, lovingly. "You?"

"Better'n I deserve. And that new job a' yours?"

Hmm... Funny you should mention that.

I debate how much to get into everything that went down at the library and decide now isn't probably the best time. "It was good. I had to be crafty."

"How is that?"

"I made some big orange bulletin board pumpkins."

"That's nice."

"That all sort of looked like squashed turtles."

"I'm sure they weren't that bad."

You didn't see them, I think.

Grams is in her mid-seventies, but has had some health scares over the last ten years—heart issues mostly—so she looks frailer and older than she is. As she says, she's not as spry as she used to be. However, she's still very independent, alert, and as big-hearted as I remember her being when I was a kid and we'd visit her and Gramps in the summers.

I wish I remembered more about him. I have images of him laughing and chasing me around the yard and reading picture books to me—that and his magic tricks and this invisible cloud of Old Spice that followed him around everywhere are about all I can recall.

Grams has wispy-white, mist-like hair, gentle eyes, and a face that still holds the grace of the head-turning beauty she had in her pageant days when she was a teenager and almost made it to Miss Tennessee USA.

"I made some pulled pork earlier." She points to the fridge. "I wasn't sure when you'd be home. I can heat it up for you. Let me get you a plate."

She slides her chair backward, but I guide my hand against it. "No, don't worry about it. I got it. Thanks."

I'm normally not too into eating meat, but she does make a mean pulled pork sandwich with her homemade BBQ sauce that she could probably package and sell. That and her bacon usually bring out my inner carnivore.

Grams uses the herbal version of Dr. Enuf in her BBQ sauce. It's a soft drink that's bottled in Johnson City, just down the road. Better than 7-UP or Sprite, in my humble opinion.

And you always gotta go with the herbal flavor rather than the original. Way better.

She mixes it in to make the sauce. It's wild. Delicious, but who would've guessed it?

I drop two halves of a bun into the toaster and nuke the pulled pork in the microwave.

We talk for a few minutes about our days and then the toaster tosses the halves into the air. I snatch them before they can fall, and the microwave dings, telling me the meat is ready.

I pile some pulled pork on the bottom half of the bun and then dollop some slaw on top of it like I learned to do when I moved here to Tennessee. Finally, I slather a little too much of Grams' barbeque sauce on the slaw and nestle the top of the bun over it.

A masterpiece.

With this sandwich and a little sweet tea I'll be in heaven. I grab the tea and an apple from the fruit bowl, and then find a seat at the table across from Grams. After saying grace, I dive in and she respects me enough not to ask me a bunch of questions while I eat my late dinner.

Eventually, as I'm finishing up some of her cherry cobbler for dessert, she excuses herself to the other room to read while I head upstairs to my room with my backpack and the ghost lore book to get changed for the party I still don't have permission to go to.

13

IN MY BEDROOM, I TOSS THE

backpack onto the giant pink beanbag chair that Cadence bought for me for my birthday last month which I thought I'd hate but actually love to lounge in when I read.

It's twice the size of a normal beanbag and tries really hard to swallow you up when you flump into it, but it's never quite managed to get me. Not yet. I'm careful with my flumping.

My room is a micro-me: a bookcase with the shelves slumping under the weight of my packed-in collection of fantasy novels and collections of folklore, an unmade bed, walls covered with posters of the dark wave, synth-pop, and steampunk bands I'm into but that pretty much no one in my class has heard of: Ego Likeness, Necessary Response, The Eden House, The Crüxshadows, and Abney Park. My telescope from Dad faces the window that looks out over the mountains.

I have a pet cactus on my desk—something even I can't kill.

The guy who sold it to me told me it thrives on negligence, which ends up being a good thing for both me and the cactus, whom I've affectionately named Prickles McStabby.

My idea journal sits right next to him. Maybe the most precious thing I own.

On the dresser, I store a couple of cool-looking geodes and a piece of driftwood that looks like a wooden snake frozen in mid-slither that I found on the shore of Chippewa Lake up in Wisconsin when I used to go hiking with Mom and Dad, before she started to drink too much and he started to work too much. Back before the Great Unraveling in their marriage and then, between all three of us.

I might or might not have too many stuffed animals for a room this size, if you count one given to me every birthday for my whole life from my mom. She didn't always make the best decisions as far as Momming me, but she did get that much right. Most of them are in a mesh pet net that hangs above the beanbag.

Mainly, my room is illuminated by the nightstand's light and the white Christmas tree lights that Cadence helped me string up around the room. Sort of subdued, just a touch of the dark, the way I like it.

I was never amazing at track, but half a dozen ribbons hang next to my way-too-cluttered dresser topped with pictures, hair stuff, a bunch of necklaces—neckli? I don't know—and a two-sided circular tilty mirror thingy. One side magnifies you super huge and the other just shows the normal you, instead of accentuating all your flaws.

Clothes are spewing out of my dresser drawers as if my shirts and socks and bras were trying to escape and the drawer slammed itself shut just at the right moment to trap them in the in-between, half jammed in the darkness and half free in the light.

I'm sure there's some sort of metaphor there for my life, but maybe that's just my storytelling brain working overtime.

Probably the coolest thing about my room is the stars.

I have this constellation machine that projects stars onto the ceiling and I can set it to my latitude and longitude and it'll project what's really outside in the sky, in real time. Or I can set it to another time and place in the future or in the past and, even though it's not perfect or a hundred percent accurate, it'll show the sky as best as astronomers can calculate by extrapolating forward or backward in time based on what they know about how stars move and where they are now or might appear in the future.

Sometimes I set the machine for the latitude and longitude of Chippewa Lake, Wisconsin, on the night that my dad died as a way of remembering him. Some people visit graveyards to remember their loved ones. I visit the stars.

———

Cadence said there'd be a bonfire tonight at the party, so I find some older clothes that I won't mind getting dirty or smoky, and shuffle through my dresser to find a sweater that'll keep out the October night air. I settle on a charcoal gray one and, at the last minute, opt for a long silk scarf that I swoop somewhat dramatically around my neck.

My dad bought the scarf for me on one of his business trips to India, but I wear it more Western, wrapped around my neck, than like an Indian girl might, with it draped around the front of her neck and hanging down on both sides in the back.

I glance into the tilty mirror.

Not a bad look.

I slide on my glasses and debate whether to wear them or stick with my contacts. I like wearing contacts that can change my eye color. I'm not sold on the idea that I was just supposed to have brown eyes all the time, so I sometimes mix things up and choose to have blue or green ones, like I did today, just to see if anyone notices. Sort of a test, I guess, to see how closely people are observing me. Almost no one ever does point it out, though—except for Cadence. She's onto me just about every time.

Oh, and Grams notices too.

I've become somewhat of an expert on eye color, the subtleties of the shades, the shy little differences between them, both in my eyes and in others'.

Campfire smoke and contacts might not be the best combination, though, so I opt for glasses instead and head down the hall to the bathroom to take out my contacts.

———

In the bathroom, after taking them out, I splash water onto my hand and use it to tame a springy tuft of hair that never wants to stay down.

They say that women wear makeup to look younger and girls wear makeup to look older. But there must be an age in the middle there, somewhere, when you just want to look like who you are. Who you *truly* are. That's what I'm interested in. That's what I shoot for as I touch up my mascara.

I usually opt for black fingernail polish to match the dark eye shadow I like to wear. Maybe a little too much of it sometimes, but it feels honest, at least, to the sadness there, buried underneath my skin.

"What's with the Batman mascara?" Cadence asked me once.

"Batman mascara? Really?"

"I'm just saying."

Batman: someone living two lives. Someone who has a secret self that he's hiding from the world. So, is it Batman who dresses up as Bruce Wayne, or Bruce Wayne who dresses up as Batman?

That's the real question.

Who am I deep inside? Which is the real me? The one people see, or the other one that lives there, deep inside?

I wish I knew.

One more glance in the mirror and I head for the stairs.

Now for the potentially tricky part: getting permission to go to the party.

14

I FIND GRAMS IN THE LIVING

room reading her old, well-worn King James Bible. The type is so small that I wonder how, with her eyesight, she's able to decipher the words, but then I remember that she's read it so many times—once a year since she got saved when she was twenty—that I don't know if she even needs to see all those words anymore to know what she's reading about.

Taking a deep breath, I dive right in and explain that there's a bonfire that my friend invited me to. I make it sound like no big deal, but I don't usually go out at this time of night so I'm not exactly sure how she'll respond.

The word "party" might have too many negative connotations, so I leave that out. I end by saying, "I promise not to stay out too late."

She processes that for a moment. "Will there be drinkin' there?"

Probably, I think.

"Maybe," I admit. "I don't really know for sure either way."

"Dearie, I was seventeen once too, you know."

"Okay, there'll probably be drinking," I tell her, "but if there is, I promise I won't have any."

"Where is this bonfire? Whose house is it at?"

Here's where things might get a little dicey.

"Actually it's at Jameson's Gap," I say.

"Out by Devil's Falls?"

"Yes."

There used to be a lot of logging in the area. Not so much anymore, since so much of the land in the area is now protected. Back in the day, though, it was logged and lots of those old homesteads have become part of the national forests today: the Cherokee National Forest here in Tennessee, the Pisgah over the border in North Carolina, and on down further southwest you have the Smokies, which straddle both states. But even though the land isn't logged anymore, lots of overgrown logging roads are still there, meandering through the vast, sprawling forests.

With those roads leading back into the hills from Jameson's Gap, if the cops ever showed up—and from what I've heard, they pretty much never do—there are plenty of escape routes to drive off into without getting caught.

Grams considers what I've said and I try to read her expression, but can't quite guess what she's thinking.

"You be careful," she tells me at last. "And don't you be going near those falls, not at night."

"Yes, ma'am."

"Be back before midnight so your old Grams doesn't have to worry about you none."

"I will. Thanks, Grams."

As I'm heading for the door, I debate once more if I should tell her about the library book or about the back room in the basement, then it strikes me that she has lived here in this area nearly all of her life, so if anyone would know about weird stuff happening at the library, it would be her.

So, ask her, otherwise you'll be wondering about it all night.

I face her again.

How to phrase this?

"Grams, Ms. Mason, the librarian, told me that some people think the library is haunted."

"Lots of those old buildings downtown are." She pauses for a moment, then says, "It was the basement, wasn't it? That's where she said the haints were?"

"How did you know that?"

"Back before my time, the Clinchfield Railroad had routes all through here from Ohio down to South Carolina, down through the mountains. If they had any coffins onboard the trains and they needed to spend the night here, they'd unload them coffins and store 'em in the basement of the train depot—"

"Which is now the library."

"Yes. Down in the cellar. From what I hear tell, there was a big room somewhere in the back that they left empty for that. Called it the coffin room."

Yeah, I'm pretty sure I know the place.

"Why would they do that?" I ask. "Put the coffins there?"

"It was cooler down there. It'd help with preservin' the bodies before transportin' 'em through the mountains."

"Oh. Right." I stare at her slightly suspiciously. "And you didn't think to mention any of this when I went to work at the library?"

"I thought to mention it. I just didn't mention it. There's a difference between forgettin' to say something and choosin' not to say it. I didn't want some old stories gettin' in the way of you takin' that new job."

I thought of the hidden corridor behind the bookshelf and the third room in that rock-walled passageway and the living, breathing nightmares I'd experienced there: Deserts turning into endless seas and seas into Chippewa Lake. Coffins filled with spiders. My dad the night he died—all those images seeming so real.

That had to have been the coffin room.

Haunted?

Yeah, or something close to it.

Grams probes me with her eyes. "Why are you asking about all this anyhow?"

I simply tell her that I want to avoid going anywhere that's haunted—which is true.

Then, she says, "You best be gettin' a move on so's you're not out too late. You have fun then, and you be safe."

"Yes, ma'am."

We say our love-yous and I head outside, hop into the car, pull out of the driveway, and head up into the mountains toward Jameson's Gap, thinking of the coffin room and what might have happened there that made it haunted.

It could be that just storing dead bodies there like that, hoping they'd rot a little more slowly, might've done it, but would that be enough?

I reach up and touch my shoulder.

Yeah.

Still tender.

So, something's still down there.

Something.

Or someone.

And all at once, that brings to mind stories Grams used to tell me about thin places.

15

ACCORDING TO CELTIC FOLKLORE, heaven and earth—or maybe a better way to put it is the physical world that we can see and the spiritual world that we can't— are only separated by three feet, but there are places where it's even less than that, where there's only a thin membrane separating them.

As Grams explained it to me: "Think of a veil that separates worlds—ours and the world of lore, of story, of the eternal. It's not so much a place where you see or hear something holy or memorable, but that you *feel* it—a connection to something bigger than you, a place where you might feel in awe or comforted, yet also unsettled."

Once, she told me that when she was twenty-five she visited the Isle of Iona and there, on that rocky island off the western coast of Scotland, surrounded by the northern Atlantic with the free-spirited wind whipping through her hair, she sensed that she was in a thin place, a place where it was so stunningly beautiful and stark and real and wild that it left an impression of something eternal and unnerving that overwhelmed her.

When she told me about that, I thought of the Sunday School stories I'd heard about Moses and the Burning Bush. I don't know if that was a thin place, but it was a thin moment at least.

From what I understand, cultures all over the world have identified places like this—although they might call them different things: Thin Places, Portals, the Narrows.

Just wishful thinking?

Just local lore?

Maybe.

But maybe not.

Grams pointed out that if you go walking throughout the British Isles, sometimes you'll find old signs that tell you that you're in a thin place. "But mostly you don't need to be told," she clarified. "Instead, you know. You're struck with the significance of where you are, and also with the insignificance of who you are."

So, here's what I start to wonder as I drive through the night: If thin places can exist between earth and heaven, could they also exist between earth and darker realms as well? Maybe between our world and the place down below?

A thin place to hell?

But then, why would I have had a vision of my dad there?

I gulp and try not to even think about what that might mean.

———

I wind up through the Cherokee National Forest to the ridgeline where the Appalachian Trail, known around here simply as the AT, crosses the road, its distinctive white blaze visible on trees on both sides of the road.

There are a lot of places around here in the mountains where you wouldn't want to go uninvited, especially at night. Some of the people who live up here don't like being surprised or disturbed by someone they don't know showing up on their land unannounced. You'll find "Don't Tread on Me" flags on people's porches next to their American flags, and people around here mean it: Don't tread on them. Don't tread on their land.

It's best to take those warnings to heart.

So, if you drive up there onto someone's land without them knowing that you're coming, you're as likely as not to find that person greeting you on their porch with a shotgun, asking you in no uncertain terms to get off their land.

Before I moved down here, I thought that was just a hillbilly stereotype, but since I've started living with Grams, I've realized that stereotypes don't pop up out of nothing. In this case, they came from something very specific: people who are proud of their heritage, who believe in protecting their loved ones and their land, and are willing to do that by using whatever means necessary with rights guaranteed by the Second Amendment.

Tonight, though, thankfully, all I have to do is drive past some of those old homesteads on the way to Jameson's Gap, a junction where a couple of old forest service roads converge.

I'll be fine as long as I don't get too turned around, because some of the roads do lead way back into the hills and hollers and to those "Don't Tread on Me" homes.

———

Pulling onto the old dirt road that leads to Jameson's Gap, I try to convince myself that what happened in the library basement wasn't that big of a deal. Yes, I got disoriented and confused earlier. That's a fact. But maybe it was just from not having enough oxygen or ventilation that far back in the corridor.

And I found a book. Okay, so what? My dad checked it out when he was a kid and now I found it. He was a voracious reader and must have checked out dozens or even hundreds of those old library books over the years when he was growing up. And now, when I was poking around down by a bunch of them, I found one with his name in it. Big deal. Coincidences happen, there's no argument about that.

And all those images in the third room? Well, that was just my imagination running wild, as I wondered about earlier. Ms. Amanda told me that some people thought the basement was haunted. So, that idea was planted in my brain. I just smushed together images from everything else that was on my mind: the spiderwebs from the stairwell, the images of the ocean and the desert from those paintings in the basement, and my memories of losing my dad.

So that's what I tell myself.

And by the time I get to the turnoff to the gap, I've almost convinced myself that, as strange as it all might've seemed at the time, what happened to me in that third room wasn't anything significant or all that inexplicable after all.

Yeah, I've almost convinced myself.

Almost.

———

There are a dozen or so cars parked along the side of the dirt road, and I pull up behind the last one and kill the engine, which sputters off into a greasy, creaky silence.

From here, it's about a hundred yards down the trail to the place where everyone will be hanging out. I've only ever been out here in the daytime: once with Cadence and once by myself to hike to the falls that are about a quarter mile further down the path, deeper in the gorge.

I climb out of the car and find that the chilly autumn night is filled with the scent of damp leaves, telling me that it maybe rained up here earlier in the day. Also, there's some smoke languishing round me from the fire, even this far away, but that would actually make sense if they're burning wet wood.

Although the underbrush isn't as thick as it was when I was here last, for the most part, leaves are still draped overhead and are blocking out the feeble moonlight that's trying to peek through. So, even though I'm pretty sure I know the way to the clearing, I still need to use my phone's flashlight to direct me as I start walking toward it along the trail.

16

TO KEEP OUT THE COLD, I WRAP

my scarf around my neck, hoping I look stylish and not stupid.

Even though I'm looking forward to seeing Cadence, I'm mostly hoping that Tyler will be here and that we'll stumble into some sort of serendipitous moment together. It seems to me that serendipity—making happy chance discoveries—has a lot more opportunity to happen when you lean into it and look for it to occur.

———

As I approach the party, the bonfire becomes visible through the trees, flickering and gleaming in the night.

Music throbs through the air—a boppy pop song that I vaguely recognize from hearing it around school, but I have no idea what band sings it or the name of the song. It's not really my thing—not to mention that it seems out of place out here in the forest near the falls. It's almost like a type of pollution—just like throwing a plastic bag into a river. Something artificial that doesn't belong here.

Noise pollution?

Yeah, it's a thing.

When I'm about fifty feet away from the blaze, I make out maybe twenty-five or thirty people gathered around it, and I realize that either there was a bunch of carpooling going on or some people must have driven up from the other direction and maybe parked further down the road or across from another trailhead, maybe on the other side of the falls.

A few of the girls who are wearing glow-in-the-dark bracelets are dancing, moving in sync with the throbbing beat of the music, but mostly people are standing around idly.

No one really pays much attention to me when I enter the clearing. A couple of people glance my way, but then go back right away to drinking whatever it is they're drinking or, in some cases, to making out.

Someone has arranged a bunch of logs around the fire in a random circle, giving people a place to sit, although most everyone is standing at the moment.

I scan the faces of the crowd, searching for people I know, but realize pretty quickly that I hardly recognize anyone.

There are a few kids from my class, a couple of seniors I've seen around school, and two sophomore girls who are dating guys in my class, but for the most part, everyone looks older. College-age. And I realize this party isn't necessarily for people from Skyland High, at least not its current students. It makes me a little uncomfortable, and I find myself wishing Cadence had mentioned that earlier when she invited me.

That's when I catch sight of Cole, the guy from Dreyfus's class who made the comment about not wanting to picture me skinny dipping after I read my non-essay.

Of course he has to be here.

Great.

Then, a familiar voice from behind me: "Zod!"

I turn, and Cadence floats up to me, throws an arm around my shoulder—thankfully it's not the ghost-grabbed, sore one—and gives me a friendly kiss on the cheek. Her boyfriend Aiden wanders toward us behind her like a good little doggie on a leash.

It's true, he is easy on the eyes, but other than that, I think she can do better. Her phrase from this afternoon about someone being one oar short of a dinghy comes to mind as he joins us.

"Love the scarf!" Cadence gushes as she flips my scarf down and then back up around my neck again, taken with the feel of the silk.

"Thanks," I say. "Hey, I need to tell you about something that happened to me while I was at the library."

"Hold that thought." She looks down at my empty hands, then calls out to no one in particular, "Somebody get this girl a drink!"

"No, I'm good," I tell her, but Aiden has already hustled off to do her bidding.

"Okay," she says to me once we're alone. "What is it? Did you see Tyler yet?"

"Is he here?" I look around, all nervous and hopeful.

"If he's not," she says a bit slyly, "he will be. I promise."

"Wait... Did you do the double-invite-y thing to get both of us here? Is that what we're talking about here?"

"I might've done the double-invite-y thing."

"Cadence!"

"What? Can you blame me if I want my friends to be happy?" A smile in the firelight. Then: "So what is it you were gonna tell me?"

"I know this sounds weird, but when I was in the basement of the library I found a hidden corridor behind a bookshelf and I saw something in a back room—oh, and there was a coffin lid."

"What are you saying? A coffin lid?"

"I know it sounds crazy."

She processes that. "So, what'd you see in the back room? What was it?"

For an instant I'm tempted to say, "It's not what I saw but what saw me," but I realize how ridiculous that would sound and I swallow the words before replying. I could tell her about the images of the stuff from the night of Dad's accident or the barren wasteland, or the coffin that sealed me in with all of those horrible spiders—all of that and the ghostly voice of my dad—but I'm honestly not even sure where to start.

"The room was empty," I say at last. "But it seems like it gave me nightmares while I was awake." Then I add, "I saw my dad. I heard him speak to me."

"What? But that's..."

"I know. Impossible. Because he's dead."

A pause. "What did he say?"

Aiden returns with an unopened can of beer for me, which I decline. "Naw," I say. "Thanks, anyway."

"Give me a sec, babe," Cadence says, and he hesitates for only a moment before wandering off toward the fire.

Once he's gone, I say, "Dad told me he wanted me to join him. That he was ready for me."

"That's messed up."

"I also found a book that he checked out of the library twenty-nine years ago."

"How do you know?"

"The library card in the back."

She considers that. "What's it about?"

"Ghosts in this area."

"You know I don't believe in ghosts."

We've been through this before.

"I know," I tell her. "I'm not saying that I do... I'm just saying something's off there and I need to figure out what's going on."

I'm scanning the crowd while trying to not look like I'm scanning the crowd and Cadence reads my mind. "I haven't seen him yet either," she says. "But he should be coming if he's not already here somewhere. Go on. Look for him. He's not gonna find himself."

"What does that even mean?"

"It means you need to go on a Tyler hunt before some [air quotes]—*other*—[air quotes] girl finds him."

"Right."

———

The bonfire isn't massive but it is large enough to give light to most of the meadow.

Mr. Dreyfus had told me that I was underage to drink and smoke, and he wasn't wrong. Plus, I promised Grams I wouldn't drink, so I wander over to get something that isn't a beer or whiskey from a bottle on the stump, and find that there's a cooler with ice and bottles of root beer.

That'll work.

I snag one, unscrew the cap, and then toss it back into the cooler so it can join all of its other little bottle cap buddies.

While I'm making my way back to the fire, someone turns down the music, and a few of the girls who were dancing *Boo*, but then someone has opened a bag of marshmallows and is holding up a couple of boxes of graham crackers. The guy next to him waves a bunch of roasting sticks and a box of Goo Goo Clusters and the girls stop complaining about the music.

Goo Goo Clusters are an East Tennessee thing. I'd never heard of anyone using one to make s'mores with before, but, with its chocolaty, marshmallowy goodness, it seems like a very delicious idea.

Over the next few minutes, the mood shifts from party mode to campfire mode. More sedate. More reflective. Everyone sort of lounging around the fire, roasting marshmallows and making Goo Goo Cluster s'mores or just staring into the flames in a quiet, fire-induced trance—the effect that fires have probably always had on our species ever since we first discovered how to rub two sticks together to create heat and light and medium-rare mammoth burgers.

And to provide a place for stories to be told, and to live and breed and then live on.

I look around the clearing and finally locate Tyler. He's standing on the edge of the night, leaning back against a snarly old oak tree. I can't tell if he's watching me until he smiles and lifts his bottle of root beer in my direction. I quickly look away, embarrassed that he caught me staring at him for the second time today.

Or maybe he was staring at you?

As I'm trying to figure out how to nonchalantly end up on his side of the fire, a guy I don't recognize says, "Anyone know a good story?"

A little hand goes up inside of me, but I stay quiet.

During the pause that follows his question, Cadence eyes me, but I shake my head.

After a moment, Cole blurts out, "Yeah, I know a story." And he goes on to tell a story that I'm pretty sure everyone can tell is going to have a jump scare at the end, but that they listen to intently anyway.

It's about a guy finding a cabin in the woods and he sees this old woman from behind. She's sitting on a chair in the living room facing the fireplace, her frail hands gripping the arms of her chair, her white scraggly hair hanging down across her shoulders. The man asks her if he can borrow her phone and she slowly turns toward him—Cole really milks this part—and then she opens her blood-red lips and—*AAH!*

Cole leaps toward the girl closest to him, who I think is his girlfriend, and screams at her as he grabs her shoulders and she screams and a bunch of people get startled and jump backward, a couple of them coming alarmingly close to the fire, and then everyone laughs and lets out a collective sigh of relief.

The story's not bad, but it's not great.

His timing was on and it tells me that this is not the first time he's told that story.

The guy who'd handed out the marshmallows lays another log on the fire. "Anyone else know a story? A scary one?"

There's sort of this quiet that settles over everyone and then Cadence, who's sitting next to me, says, "Zod does."

I gulp and whisper to her, "Cadence, don't. I—"

"Who's Zod?" the guy asks.

"The new girl," Cole says. "The skinny dipper."

"What?" someone says.

I ignore his explanation and lean close to Cadence. "What are you doing? I—"

"You got this," she tells me.

I look over at Tyler, who's watching me expectantly.

"So." Cole turns to me and everyone shifts their attention in my direction. "You know a scary story?"

"I do."

He lets his gaze drift to my feet. Then he scoffs a bit and points at my boots. "Why do you always wear boots, by the way?"

"How do you know she *always* wears boots?" one of his buddies says tauntingly. "You been checking her out?"

His friends laugh a little at that, and I'm not sure how to take their laughter.

"Because of the Slasher," I say to Cole before he can answer the rather leading question about checking me out.

"What are you talking about?" he says. "What slasher?"

"He waits under cars at night with a straight razor and when you get close enough to the door to get in, he reaches out and slits your Achilles tendons. *Zip. Zip.* And you fall to the ground, helpless. Maybe he allows you to live, maimed. Maybe not. They say he comes up here to the gap, that he's been seen here more than once. I go with boots rather than take a chance." I glance at Cole's sneakers. "Based on those shoes, I think you better check under your car before you get too close to it. Just to make sure. I'm just saying."

He gulps. It's almost imperceptible, but it's there. He does.

A few people laugh.

I smile to myself and think of my girl, Scheherazade. The Slasher is just a story. Or is it? But it's worth seeing the look in his eyes as he tries to figure that out for himself. I have the feeling that someone is going to be peeking beneath his car later tonight before walking up to the door.

However, he quickly grins and recovers. "I like you, Boots. The Slasher. That's a good one. So, you said you know a scary story? Is that it, then? The Slasher?"

"No."

"Alright," he says. "Well, let's hear it."

And I decide to go for it. This is what I'm good at—at least that's what people tell me.

I mentally sort through the stories that Grams has told me over the years and try to come up with one that's scary enough—or at least unsettling enough—for this campfire.

For as long as I can remember, she's told me a mixture of Southern Appalachian folklore and fairy tales and traditional stories from the British Isles.

Sometimes they're true, mostly they're made-up. Old Celtic stories passed down from one generation to the next from when our ancestors came over from Ireland and settled in these mountains back in the day. She tells those with an interweaving of Jack tales and Tennessee ghost stories. They all sort of mix together, and I like it that way. She says stories shouldn't have borders any more than love or hope or truth does, and I like that hers aren't artificially hemmed in.

She always seems to have the right story to tell at the right time. Actually, at any time. I don't know how she does it. I don't know how many stories she actually knows—I doubt if she does either. Dozens of hours' worth of tales. Maybe even hundreds.

I don't remember all of them, of course, but I remember a lot of them.

And right now...

Yes.

I recall one that might be a little long, but it's a good one to tell.

It's an old English folktale, but I decide to tell it my own way because, according to Grams, that's what storytellers are supposed to do—put some of themselves into their stories, so that when they tell them, it's partly words from the past and partly who the teller is right now, flowing out through the story.

Because, she says, otherwise, you're just like a machine, simply repeating what was said to you. Anyone can do that, but she tells me it's not fair to the story to simply repeat it. As she puts it, "An old country preacher told me once't that takin' someone else's sermon and usin' it yourself is like eating someone else's food and then throwin' it up on your congregation. It's the same with stories."

Well, I thought at the time, *that's descriptive.*

Right now I'm not in the mood for puking up someone else's

version of a story, so I decide to change it around and let it happen today and not hundreds of years ago.

Mr. Fox, it's called.

Shadows quiver and dance across people's faces and through the woods surrounding us, shifting and morphing whenever someone near the fire moves or when the wind meandering between the trees decides to toy with the flames.

As I stand there, the only sounds come from the crackling snap of burning wood and the distant murmur of a car on the highway. Someone has tossed some cedar branches onto the fire and the sweet scent of cedar traces through the smoke and encircles me.

Everyone is either peering into the fire or looking at me.

I've told stories to my friends my whole life, so I'm cool with that scenario, but I haven't really told one like this in front of a group of people that I don't know.

Until now.

I gaze out at their faces and take inspiration from the millions of campfires around the world and the thousands upon thousands of years of other storytellers before me—the sisterhood of Scheherazade—and I tell the story of Mr. Fox.

17

THERE WAS THIS GIRL NAMED

Mary, and she was really cute and very clever, and she met this guy that she liked. He never told her his first name. He just called himself Mr. Fox, and he would only visit her at her house. He never invited her over to his place.

So, one weekend, Mary, she said, "Maybe we could meet at your house for once."

And he was like, "Oh, Mary, now's not the time. I'll be gone tonight anyway. Soon enough I'll have you over."

But she was more than a little curious, so that day, when he left her place, she decided to follow him and find out where he lived.

She drove behind him but kept at a distance, thinking that he would maybe swing by his house before leaving for the night, to go wherever it was he was planning to go.

He drove out to a cornfield scattered with dead stalks, and there was a house at the far end of it and she parked along the edge of the road and waited. She was trying to decide if she should drive all the way to the house, or wait for him to leave and then have a look around. And she decided to wait.

It wasn't long before he left again, and she gave it a few more minutes, and then, just in case he would come back—because she didn't want him to see her car—she left it there and walked along the edge of the cornfield until she came to his house.

She wasn't sure exactly what she was looking for, but when she got to the front porch, there was a sign over the door, and it said, "Be bold, be bold."

Weird, right? Well, Mary realized that she wasn't going to be satisfied until she had a look inside Mr. Fox's house. She doubted the door would be unlocked and she was trying to figure out what to do if it was, but she tried it anyway, and to her surprise, it was not locked after all.

She pressed it open slowly and walked inside.

Off to the right, there was a kitchen. Everything looked in order. Clean. Neat. Dishes all put away. A table sat in the center of the room with a coffee mug and a small plate with a few crumbs left on it. That was all.

The living room lay to the left. A couple of chairs. A floor lamp in the corner. Long drapes, pulled across the windows to keep out the late afternoon sunlight.

The house was obviously expensive, but there was nothing unusual, or that shouldn't have been there.

A set of stairs rose before her to the second floor.

You shouldn't be here, she thought. *You shouldn't be doing this.*

But she was thinking about the sign outside the front door and how weird it was, and she decided she needed answers and went ahead anyway. It was almost like she couldn't help it. Like something was drawing her forward.

Mary went up the staircase slowly. At the top of the stairs, she looked down the hall and could see a couple of doors. That was fine. No big deal. But what drew her attention was a sign over the top of the door at the end of the hall. This one read, "Be bold, be bold, but not too bold." And she knew something was definitely not right.

Be bold, be bold, but not too bold? What is that supposed to mean?

She decided that she needed to know, that she wouldn't feel right seeing him again without knowing the truth, so she decided to check it out.

She walked down the hallway and opened the door.

Inside, it was clear that she was in his bedroom.

It was pretty plain, though. There was a lamp to the left of the bed, a pile of books on the end table beside it. She knew he was smart, that he was well-read, so when she saw the titles of the old classics there beside his bed she wasn't surprised. There was also a dresser and a wardrobe, so that was a little odd, that he wouldn't keep his clothes in a closet.

Then she turned her eyes toward the door in the corner. She figured it was the closet door, but with the dresser and the wardrobe here by the bed, she wasn't positive.

There was a third sign above that door. This one said, "Be bold, be bold, but not too bold, lest your heart's blood run cold."

This time a chill caught hold of her, riding down the back of her neck all the way to the small of her back.

Be bold, be bold, but not too bold, lest your heart's blood run cold. You should leave, leave now.

But she didn't.

She was curious in that terrified way like when you know you shouldn't go another step further, but then there's your curiosity in there too, drawing you forward and you can't help it. You give in.

Mary crossed the bedroom and tried the doorknob.

Unlocked.

She opens the door.

It's dark so she feels around for a light switch, but doesn't find one. Finally, she locates a string hanging down. She pulls it and a single lightbulb illuminates the closet.

She looks down, and there's a vat filled with a dark liquid. She dips her finger into it and lifts it up. Blood. And then she sees it: behind the vat is a pile of hair and bones and teeth and skin.

Mary cries out, tries to wipe the blood off her finger onto her dress, and runs back through the bedroom, back down the hall, back down the stairs, but as she gets to the front door and looks outside, she can see a car pulling into the long driveway. Mr. Fox's car. And she knows that if she leaves at that moment, he'll see her. So she does the only thing she can think to do: She slips behind one of the drapes and tries to make sure her feet aren't visible, but the drapes aren't quite long enough.

When she looks back behind her, through the window, she sees Mr. Fox get out of the car, walk around to the trunk, open it, and pick up a young woman about her age. She might have been drugged or asleep because she doesn't fight, doesn't kick or call out or anything as he picks her up. All limp, but he's strong and it looks like it's no effort at all for him to lift her.

He carries her to the front door, leans his back against it to open it, and then brings her inside. Mary can barely see what's happening through a slit in the drapes and the next thing she knows, the woman is on the floor and Mr. Fox has grabbed her hair and he's starting to drag her up the stairs.

But she's awake now and opens her eyes and screams, but he smacks her head down brutally against the stairs until she's quiet again.

As he continues up the stairs, Mary peeks out from behind the curtain, trying to figure out what to do, how to help that woman. But she's terrified. Obviously. Then the woman looks her way and their eyes lock on each other, and the woman opens her mouth like she's about to say something, but it never comes out.

And then, Mr. Fox is at the top of the stairs.

And then, he's dragging her down the hallway

And then, Mary hears the bedroom door open and then close once again.

She doesn't know what to do.

She knows she could call 911, but this is in the middle of the country and she figures there's no way the cops would get there in time. She also knows she needs to get out of there. She needs to run, but she also can't just leave the woman behind, so at last she runs to the kitchen and grabs a big gleaming knife from the knife block and then runs up the stairs and down the hallway.

Be bold, be bold, but not too bold, lest your heart's blood run cold.

And all she can think of is stopping Mr. Fox.

She gets to the bedroom door.

With a trembling hand, she tries to open it like before, but this time it's locked from the inside. And Mary hears a scream that's suddenly cut short. A final kind of scream.

Then she hears gurgling sounds, and she knows that whatever's happening in that bedroom, she was too late.

So she hurries down the stairs again, rushes out the door, runs along the edge of the cornfield to her car, and then speeds all the way home.

But she was so scared she didn't realize that she still had that knife with her.

Well, the next day, Mr. Fox shows up at her house and he asks her how she's been and she says, "Mr. Fox, I haven't been well, for last night I had a dream and the dream terrified me so that I could hardly sleep another wink. You've studied dreams, right? Psychology?"

"Some."

"So, if I told you my dream, you could tell me what it means?"

"Perhaps. I can try at least."

So, Mary pours him a glass of lemonade and sits across the table from him. She has her own lemonade too.

"Thank you, Mary."

"Of course."

She drinks a sip of lemonade and he does too.

"Tell me your dream," he says.

"In my dream, Mr. Fox, I dreamt that I came upon a house beside a cornfield. Right at the edge of it. And the strange thing, Mr. Fox, is that I saw a sign above the house's front door. And the sign said, 'Be bold, be bold.' It was so peculiar. I've never seen a sign like that above a door. I couldn't imagine what it might mean."

A look of surprise and a flicker of concern cross his face. "And was that the end of your dream, Mary?"

"No, Mr. Fox. I tried the door and it opened. It opened wide. And inside the house, I saw a kitchen off to the right and a living room to the left with long drapes hanging down almost to the floor. And there was a staircase between the two rooms. So, I went up the stairs."

"In the dream."

"Yes. And at the end of the hall was another sign, Mr. Fox. And this one said, 'Be bold, be bold, but not too bold.' And I wondered what all of it meant—'Be bold, be bold, but not too bold.' What could that mean?"

His eyes narrow a little bit. "Go on, Mary."

"So, I went down the hallway and I opened that door and walked inside. It was a bedroom. Books beside a lamp. A neatly made bed. And another door—a closet. And another sign."

"And what did it say? This third sign?"

"It said, 'Be bold, be bold, but not too bold, lest your heart's blood run cold.' Do you understand what that might've meant, Mr. Fox? 'Be bold, be bold, but not too bold, lest your heart's blood run cold'?"

"I'm not sure." He's staring at her all cold-like, giving her the dead eye, his jaw set. "Tell me what happened next, Mary. Did you leave?"

"No. I went to the door and pressed it open, Mr. Fox. I found the light and I looked inside. There was a vat, Mr. Fox, and it was filled with blood. And I found piles of bones and skin and teeth and hair. I ran, Mr. Fox."

"I would expect so," he says.

"Yes, yes, I ran. I ran back through the hallway, down the stairs, and I was about to leave when a car pulled up, Mr. Fox, and it was your car."

"In your dream."

"Yes. And so, I slipped behind one of the drapes and waited, and I saw someone get out of the car. It was you! I saw you, Mr. Fox. I saw you go around to the back of the car, and lift out a young woman, and carry her to the front door of the house. You brought her inside. You began to drag her up the stairs. And I leaned out and saw her open her eyes. She cried out and you—in my dream—you, smacked her head down against the stairs until she was quiet. And then you kept going up the stairs. You took her down the hallway to the bedroom and I knew I needed to leave, but I also knew I couldn't leave her there. Not like that. Not with you."

"That was quite a dream."

"Yes."

"And what happened then?" He tightens his grip on the half-empty glass of lemonade. "Did you leave the house then?"

"No, Mr. Fox. I went to the kitchen, and I grabbed a knife, and I ran up the stairs and went to the bedroom door, but it was locked—locked from the other side. And then there was a scream, a terrible blood-curdling scream. And then wet gurgling sounds. And then nothing. And I knew it was too late. What do you think it means, Mr. Fox? My dream?"

And with that, all of a sudden, Mr. Fox shoves himself back from the table and leaps to his feet and lunges toward her, but as he does, he wavers for a moment. And he looks a little dizzy. And then he stares down at the lemonade glass he'd been drinking out of and then up at Mary.

Only then does he see the smear of blood on her dress from where she'd wiped her finger the day before. She'd worn the same dress.

He takes another step and falters and he has to put his hand on the table to steady himself, but it isn't enough. He tries to mutter something, but he collapses heavily to the floor.

Mary walks over to the counter and picks up the knife that she took from his kitchen the day before and she bends over him.

"What did you think?" she says. "That I would've let you leave here today? Don't worry, Mr. Fox, the poison won't kill you. It'll just keep you quiet, keep you from moving. You won't be able to hurt anyone anymore. Oh, but you'll feel everything. The poison won't kill you. This knife of yours will."

He tries to speak, to get up, to strike out at her, but he's helpless there on the floor.

Mary looks calmly into his eyes and says, "This is for that woman yesterday and for all those who came before her. I'm going to take my time. I want you to remember them all, each and every one. Be bold, be bold, Mr. Fox, but not too bold, lest your heart's blood run cold."

And then, she starts by placing the tip of the blade against his lips, the lips that she used to tenderly kiss, and she hums quietly to herself as she carefully removes them and begins her work.

18

THE FIRE SHIMMERS BEFORE ME.

After my story, for a long, uncertain moment, no one says anything. The only sounds are the snap and hiss of the flames devouring the cedar branches, and then, from somewhere up the mountain, the lonely hoot of an owl.

From past experience, I know that, for the most part, the more crackling a campfire is, the less smoke there'll be. So during the story, I'd put some smaller sticks on it to make sure there was enough light for everyone to see my face, my expressions, and to keep the smoke from getting in their eyes and becoming a distraction.

As a result, the blaze is still nearly as bright as it was when I started the story.

I look around, past the flames, at everyone's face. I guess I hadn't even realized it, but I'd sort of lost myself in the story and it takes me a moment to regroup and realize that I'm not in the story world anymore, but that I'm here at the fire, here in the real world.

No Mr. Fox.

No Mary.

No lonely cornfield or thick drapes or poisoned lemonade.

But some of the images are still hanging around, lingering in my mind. They just won't let me go: the vat of blood, the bones and teeth and skin, the blade pressed up against Mr. Fox's mutilated face. And Mary, slicing.

Slicing.

Ribbons of moist flesh coiled on the linoleum, the involuntary twitch of thready, exposed tendons and—

"So, Zod," a girl I don't know says, interrupting my macabre thoughts. "Is that true?" She's on the other side of the bonfire and is staring over it, directly at me.

"It's true enough." I take a drink of my root beer.

"What do you mean 'true enough'?"

"Stories aren't always so much about what happened once as they are about what happens all the time," I tell her, quoting Grams. "And this one is too: Betrayal. Murder. Serial killers. The world is filled with Mr. Foxes—always has been."

"And Marys?" she says.

Maybe there aren't quite enough of them, I think. *Maybe there should be more.*

"Yeah," I say. "And Marys."

"Did you make it up?" a scrawny guy beside her asks.

Before I can reply, Tyler speaks up. "Doesn't matter. It was a good story." He flags me a couple of fingers in a sort of salute. "Respect."

I don't feel like I need him coming to my defense, but on the other hand, it's nice knowing he's willing to step in, that he's on my side.

"It's an old story," I say. "I didn't make it up. It's been around a while. Maybe something exactly like it happened a long time ago. I don't know. Stories like that don't come out of nowhere."

I don't tell them how old the story actually is, or that it's so old that even when Shakespeare had Benedick quote from it in *Much Ado About Nothing*, he said the line was from "the old tale."

So Mr. Fox was already an old story when *Shakespeare* heard it.

Good stories have a long shelf life.

"Your story was cool," a guy says from the darkness, obscured by the shadows on the other side of the campfire. "But what I wanna know is, was Mary a psychopath too? Or did she go crazy after she saw what Mr. Fox did in the house? Did that drive her over the edge?"

"Tragic stuff happening to you doesn't change who you are." It's Tyler again. "It just *reveals* who you are underneath. The real you."

"But people do change, though, right?" the guy counters. "I mean are you saying people don't go crazy—that the crazy was always there, inside of them?"

Tyler steps closer to the fire so that now he's visible across from me. "That question makes me think of a story," he says. "It's not as good as hers, but it's about this nursing student and she was a bit odd. Something's off about her. So, all the rest of the people in her class make fun of her and call her names and pretty much make her life miserable. One day, they decide to play a trick on her. They figure it'll just be a harmless practical joke.

"So they saw off the arm of one of the cadavers in the research department and take it to her room while she's in class. They tie it to the string in her closet that she has to pull in order to turn on the light. Then they wait. They figure she'll go to the closet, reach for the string, and grab the arm instead and be freaked out. It was just supposed to be a joke. That's all.

"They thought that she would show up in class the next day, and they'd be able to laugh at her, but she didn't come. In fact, three days pass and she doesn't show up anywhere. They get worried, so they go to check on her.

"They knock on her dorm room door. No one answers, but they realize that it's unlocked, so they go in and notice that the closet door is slightly ajar, so they open it the rest of the way and find her sitting in there, right where she'd been for three days, staring crazily off into space, gnawing on that cadaver's arm."

Tyler finishes his story and things are quiet and tense for a moment until some guy grabs the forearm of the girl next to him and pretends to chew on it and she punches him and pulls away and it breaks the mood and a bunch of people laugh.

But the guy with all the questions says, "Yeah, so the moral of the last two stories is to stay away from unlocked closets with those stringy light switch thingys..." He waits. I'm not sure if he's expecting people to laugh, or what, but when they don't, he goes on, "But did the arm make her crazy or draw out the crazy that was already in her?"

I feel like it might be my turn to speak up for Tyler. "Sometimes there are cracks inside of us," I say. "And the pain that's in there seeps out. But that doesn't mean we can't get more cracks. So, it's both: We're changed by the terrors we see around us, but we're also revealed by them and people see the terrors within us."

As I say that, I realize that I don't really want to be having this discussion. Truthfully, I'm still in a distant place after telling my story, still processing the emotions within it. I can't help it. Stories affect me, even ones that I tell myself, and there's a lot to deal with in the story of Mr. Fox.

———

As a couple of people begin to debate how crazy someone already is or could become, and whether their shoes or boots are thick enough to stop the Slasher, I slip away, finish off my root beer, and walk over to the bags of marshmallows and boxes of Goo Goo Clusters that are waiting on a nearby tree stump. I contemplate making a s'more, but then decide against it and just go for a plain, raw, naked Goo Goo Cluster instead.

And as I'm chomping into it, Tyler walks my way.

Of course it's right as I take a bite.

Of course it is.

"Hey," he says.

"Hey," I say with a gulp, swallowing down a ridiculously yummy mouthful of chocolate, peanuts, and marshmallow nougat.

"I liked your story."

I wipe a hand across my mouth to take care of any chocolate hanging around on my lips. "I liked yours too."

"You ever hear that one before?" he asks. "About the nursing student?"

I don't want to hurt his feelings so I say, "No." Then I go on, "It was creepy." And then I add, "It's interesting that you don't think people change."

"I guess I just feel like whoever you are—the real you—that's deeper. You said that the pain and terror inside of us sometimes get revealed, sometimes seeps out."

"Yes."

"What about other stuff?"

"Like what?"

"I don't know." He shrugs. "Joy. Beauty. Compassion. Courage. Can those come out of the cracks too?"

I'm not sure what to say to that. "Um... Yeah. That stuff too," I mutter at last.

He eyes me as if he's trying to decide how much he should believe me or if maybe I just felt obligated to say that. "When you were telling that story about Mr. Fox," he says, "you were different."

"Different? How?"

"I mean, it was like a part of you I've never seen before came alive."

"Maybe there's more to me than meets the eye," I say, repeating the words from the non-essay that I read in Dreyfus's class earlier in the afternoon.

"I'm starting to see that," Tyler says in way that borders on being flirty, but I try not to get my hopes up. "Listen, you wanna do something memorable?"

With you? I think. *Absolutely!*

"What's that?" I say to him.

"Walk to the waterfall. You ever see it in the moonlight?"

"No. You?"

"No. But I hear it's amazing, and there's a first time for everything."

Yes. Like getting asked to go on a moonlit walk with the guy you've been crushing on all year. Definitely a first time for that.

Tyler holds up his hands, palms up. "What do you say? It's not far. Just like a five-minute walk."

I think of what I'd promised Grams earlier—that I wouldn't go to the falls.

"Um..."

Tyler takes out his phone, clicks on the flashlight app, and then indicates the trail.

I can hardly believe that he's even talking to me, let alone asking me to go on a walk with him to see Devil's Falls in the moonlight.

I don't want to read too much into it, but I also don't want to read nothing into it.

However, as much as I want to go, I'm nervous because if Grams asks me if I went to the falls there's going to be some lying going on: (1) Either I tell her the truth and turn my promise from earlier that I wouldn't go there into a lie, or (2) I lie on the spot and tell her that I didn't go there at all.

A lie either way.

But I try to put all of that out of my mind.

She might not ask you. It probably won't even come up.

To be alone with Tyler is what I've been hoping for all evening— actually ever since Cadence first invited me to the bonfire, but now that it's happening I'm more nervous than I thought I'd be.

"Yeah," I tell him. "I'd like that. A walk sounds nice."

And, with his phone's light illuminating the path, we start up the trail toward Devil's Falls.

And I find myself walking with Tyler—*Tyler Beck!*—through the woods.

And toward the lie.

19

"SO," TYLER SAYS, "WHY DO THEY call you Zod?"

"Long story," I tell him. "Really—a very long story."

"I'm game."

"No, I mean it would literally take me a thousand and one nights to tell you the whole thing."

Yeah, it's a bit of a test—me throwing it out there to see if he knows the story.

"Ah." He holds a branch up and gestures for me to pass beneath it. "*The Arabian Nights.*"

"You know the book?" I say, glad to be impressed.

"I'm aware of a few of the stories in it. But the nickname...?"

"My real name is Sahara—I mean, you know that, right? Of course, you do. I'm in your class. I mean..."

"Right."

Stop being so flustered!

Sigh.

"Well," I say, "Sahara sounds a little like the name of the girl in the story who tells all the tales—"

"Oh, yeah. Scheherazade. Sure... I see. I get it, now. Sahara-Zod. Is that it?"

"Nice." Now I'm even more impressed. "I have the sense that most people haven't heard of her—or at least don't know much about her."

"I like to read... And since you're good at telling stories like Scheherazade did... Zod. Works for me."

"And what do you want me to call you—Tyler?"

"I'll tell you what, why don't you call me by a story name too."

Before he can tell me which one, I say, "Ah, let me guess... Rumpelstiltskin?"

He smiles. "You do know your fairy tales."

"It's my only superpower."

"Well, if I call you Zod, then you can call me Jack."

His phone's light flickers briefly, then recovers and brightens once again.

"You're not saying, like *the* Jack?" I say. "Like the 'Jack and the Beanstalk' Jack?"

"Yep. It was one of my favorite stories when I was a kid."

I step over a log. "Why's that? What did you like about it?"

"Well, Jack goes out with the best of intentions: to sell the cow and help provide for his mom."

"So, he has a good heart," I say, but that's not exactly what I'm thinking.

"It seems foolish for him to sell the cow for a handful of supposedly magic beans—he's pretty naive, I'll give you that. But, anyway, he's brave enough and adventurous enough to climb the beanstalk all the way up into the clouds and bold enough to steal the hen from the giant."

"The one that lays the golden eggs."

"Right." The trail widens, which allows us to walk side by side. "And he gets away," Tyler says. "He's clever enough to get out of there and start down the beanstalk and then strong enough to chop it down when the giant comes after him, climbing down from the sky."

"Okay," I say. "So far, he's got a good heart, he's a little naïve, but he's also brave and adventurous and bold and clever and strong."

"There you have it. True hero material. What's not to like?"

I'm quiet. A little too quiet.

"What?" he says. "I'm sensing some hesitation on your part."

"I'm not sure," I say, "I mean... If it's your favorite story I don't want to say anything bad about it."

"I'm a big boy. I can handle it. What were you going to say?"

"According to Grams—my grandma—Jack and the Beanstalk was originally told as a story of what to avoid rather than how to act."

A pause. "What do you mean?"

"Jack was foolish—lucky, sure—but not too bright to trade the cow for the beans. Then, he trespassed on the giant's property, stole from him—taking the only means that we know of for the giant to survive. Then he turns the giant's wife against him and when the giant comes after his rightful property and his only source of income to try to retrieve it, Jack murders him instead of returning the hen to him and apologizing."

"So you're saying Jack's a foolish, selfish, cowardly, conniving, cold-hearted killer?"

"Well..."

"And he never changes his ways..." Tyler is clearly thinking aloud. "But eventually lives happily ever after with the golden eggs he stole from the giant that he murdered. So, the moral of the story really is that crime does pay."

"I mean... Maybe."

I'm honestly not sure how he'll respond to that, and I immediately regret bringing all this up.

"Hmm..." Tyler says at last. "Jack appears at first glance to be the hero, but when you look more closely at the story, you see that he's really... a complex guy."

That's one way to put it, I think. *Or, that he's actually the villain of the story.*

"Yes," I say. "He's complex."

"Complex I can live with. I suppose you could say there's more to ol' Jack than meets the eye. Just like you."

"So that makes two of us."

"I guess so."

"Okay," I say. "I'll call you Jack. A boy with a good heart, who's a little naive but also brave and adventurous and bold and clever and strong."

"I like the sounds of that."

We walk for a few minutes. I'm still feeling bad about dumping on his favorite story, so I decide to change the subject and lighten the mood by admitting to a crime of my own. "I have a secret," I say, "that I've never told anyone about."

"What's that?"

"Sometimes I live dangerously."

"Danger can be fun. What do you mean, exactly?"

"I rip the tags off of my mattresses and Teddy Bears."

"Funny, I didn't peg you as a Teddy Bear girl."

"What I'm saying is, you look at those tags and it says it's a federal offense to rip them off. It says you're not supposed to remove them under—"

"Penalty of law," he says.

"So, you've read them too."

"I can neither confirm nor deny that I have ever had a Teddy Bear," he tells me. "Or a mattress. Or read those tags."

"Right," I say.

"And you rip them off?"

"I do."

He shakes his head. "You hardened criminal, you."

"What can I say? I'm complex too."

"Imagine going to prison for that," he says. "The other prisoners ask you what you're in for and you point to the mattress and say, 'This,' and you walk over there and slowly tear the tag off it. And everyone gasps and backs away from you slowly."

"I like the way you put that," I tell him. "The inmate me appreciates that."

"You're welcome."

Things are quiet then, but it doesn't feel awkward, but rather natural, like the silences feel when you're with a friend and no one seems to feel pressured to say something. Finally, he says, "I heard you're from Wisconsin."

"Yes."

"You don't sound like it."

"We lived a lot of places when I was a kid," I tell him. "Moved around a lot. I don't really sound like I'm from anywhere."

"Or maybe, like you're from everywhere."

"Maybe."

By now, I've sort of lost track of the distance we've gone. Time seems to be passing at a different rate here while I'm walking alone with Jack, but it certainly seems like more than five minutes have passed.

"You sure this is the way to the falls?" I ask him.

"Pretty sure."

I try to read his inflection to decide if there's assurance coming through or a touch of uncertainty.

But right when I'm starting to think we might be on the wrong trail, I hear the sound of the falls up ahead of us in the night.

20

WE MEET UP WITH THE RIVER

and follow it upstream as the sound of the water coursing over Devil's Falls gets louder.

Finally, the trail ends at the base of the falls. There's a faint scrabbly path that leads up to the top of it, but it's steep and rocky and I wouldn't want to walk it in the dark.

Besides, I promised Grams I wouldn't.

As long as I don't go near the top of the falls I should be okay with just telling her that I went on a walk with a friend out at the gap. It's not dangerous here at the bottom—just at the top where people have fallen off.

Or jumped.

Depends on what you believe about the stories of this place.

They say that if you walk out there on the river rocks and stand on the boulder in the middle of the river at the top of the falls that you'll hear the devil whisper to you to jump—which is how it got its name, "Devil's Falls."

And some people do jump, thinking that there'll be enough water at the bottom for them to land safely. But there never is. It's an eighty-foot drop and there's a cruel nest of boulders down there. And from what I've heard, at least five people have tried to make it and none of them survived.

Maybe the stories are just a warning about the dangers of listening to the devil whisper to you and then doing what he says.

But maybe there's more to it than that.

Here, at the waterfall, the forest opens up, giving the moonlight space to filter in and glitter off the water pouring over the top of the falls eight stories above us.

At this point, the river isn't very wide—maybe thirty feet or so—and at this time of year it's more of a stream than a river, but still, there's enough water flowing over the waterfall to be dramatic and awe-inspiring in the moonlight.

Jack turns off his light and we take some time to let our eyes become accustomed to the night.

The moonlight pulses and gleams off the flowing water and the river almost seems like a living thing, with its threads of glistening light easing over the rocks and plummeting toward the bottom of the falls.

It takes my breath away.

We stand there for a few minutes and I think of thin places again. I wonder if this would count as one, here on this mountain at the base of these falls.

I feel like I should say something, but I don't want to end up blabbing something stupid and ruining the moment.

But after a while, when Jack doesn't say anything either, I start to get nervous and I point to the swath of sky that's visible above us through the trees. "Do you know much about the stars?"

"Not a ton," he says. "Just that there are trillions of them. Too many to ever count. And some are twice the size of our sun."

"Way more than twice the size," I tell him. "In fact, you could fit seventeen thousand of our suns in some of those stars."

"How do you know that?"

I shrug. "Astronomy. It's my thing. I like stories, right? So when I was little, my dad would tell me the stories of the constellations. When you think about it, ever since humans have been around, we've been staring up at the night sky trying to find our place in the universe. What are the stars? How far away are they? How many are there?"

"And, 'Are we alone?'"

"Yes," I say.

"Do you think we are?" he asks me. "Alone, I mean? Or is there intelligent life out there somewhere?"

"I don't know. You?"

"I think there are lots of other worlds, each one with its own set of stories waiting to be told." Then he says, "Earlier you told me a secret. Here's one of mine: Sometimes I feel like our school and the night sky have something in common."

"What do you mean?"

"The stars. They're millions of miles apart, right? Hundreds of millions of miles, even?"

"Even further than that," I say, trying not to sound like a know-it-all. "There's a star that was discovered back in 2022 that's so far away that it took almost thirteen billion years for its light to reach Earth. And light travels at nearly three hundred thousand meters per second. Or, if you're not too into the metric system, you could think of it as being so fast that it could wrap around the earth seven times in less than a second."

"And it took nearly thirteen billion years to get here?"

"That's what the scientists are saying."

"I don't even know how to imagine that."

"Neither do I... So what were you saying about the night sky and our school?" I ask him. "What do they have to do with each other?"

He gestures toward the sky. "From here, the stars look so close to each other, right? But in reality, they might be billions of light years apart. Yet from our point of view, it doesn't look that way at all. They look like they're almost touching. Some even are."

"But what does that have in common with school?"

"If someone looked at us in class or in the hallway or sitting on the bleachers during a game, they might say, 'Oh, yeah. Those kids are pretty close together.' But they have no idea about the miles that separate us—the distances between us that are almost unfathomable. It's easy to feel lonely in a crowd of people. Everyone else can seem millions or even billions of miles away."

I look at him, his face illuminated by the moonlight.

"Did you just think of that?" I ask. "Because I totally get what you're saying."

"I've thought about it before." He's staring at the sky and appears deep in thought. Then he looks my way. "I've just never told anyone about it before."

Our eyes meet.

"I'm honored," I tell him.

He says nothing.

And neither do I, at first, but then I say what I'm thinking: "I don't feel billions of miles away from you."

"I don't feel that way either."

The moment seems so right, so perfect, like nothing could ever ruin it.

I catch myself still staring into his eyes. It's too dark to see their color exactly, but I can imagine it and I begin losing myself—

"What is it?" He rubs his jaw self-consciously. "Do I have something on my face?"

I tear my gaze away. "No, no. Nothing like that. Um..."

Save this, save this, save this!

"Do you know what an asterism is?" I ask him, fumbling to recover, to draw his attention back to the stars.

"Hmm. I don't think so."

"Well, there are constellations up there in the night sky, right? There are usually eighty-eight of them that are listed officially, although there've been a lot more than that that've been lost to history. Anyway, there's no rule about making up a constellation. Anyone can do it. And when you do it today, it's called an 'asterism.'"

"We should make up an asterism. Maybe someday it'll be famous."

Or maybe, it'll just be ours forever, I think.

Oh, man.

"That would be nice," I say softly.

He gestures toward the waterfall. "If we're going to really be able to see the stars, though, we need to head up to the top of the falls. I think the woods open up a lot more up there. It's not far."

"Yeah, the thing is, I promised Grams—my grandma, she's the one I live with—that I wouldn't go to the falls."

"And yet, here you are."

"Well... Yes."

"Huh..." He considers that. "So if she asks you what you did tonight, you can just tell her that you went stargazing out near Jameson's Gap. It'd be true. Right?"

I guess. "So far, so good."

"We don't have to go up there, though," he says, backpedaling to take the pressure off. "If you don't want to. I wouldn't want you to get in trouble. We can head back to the bonfire instead. That's totally cool."

I bite my lip. "No. We should go up there."

"You sure? Because—"

"I'm sure. Let's make up an asterism."

"Okay." He turns his phone's light back on. "I'll go first, that way I can help lift you up if you need it."

"Okay," I say.

And with the phone in one hand, he grabs a root with the other and starts up the incline toward the top of Devil's Falls.

21

AS WE CLIMB, HE SAYS, "TELL
me about your scarf. It's pretty. Is there a story behind it?"

"Thanks," I say. "Nothing epic or anything. My dad got it for me on one of his business trips to India."

The sound of the falls is louder than it was below, but it's not so loud that we can't hear each other. I can only imagine how deafening it would be, however, in the summer when the water courses over the edge in full force.

"Oh, yeah?" Jack says. "What does he do? Your dad, I mean."

"Computer tech stuff. I mean, he used to. He's... He died last spring."

"Oh. I'm so sorry."

"It's okay."

Then he's silent and so am I and we continue our climb through the night.

Thinking of my dad's death brings my experience in the coffin room back to mind and I'm struck again by his words to me: that he was waiting for me, that he wanted me to join him.

No, it wasn't him. It was someone else.

Something else.

My shoulder is still on fire from when that unseen hand grabbed me with what seemed like a searing grip, almost like a brand, so I'm hesitant to move too quickly or lift my left arm too high. I mask all of that hesitancy under the guise of just trying to be careful on the steep incline.

It takes some scrambling to make it up the vague path toward the top of the waterfall. It's less of a marked trail and more of a narrow channel of boulders and roots that you can grab ahold of and then use to pull yourself up or step onto in order to climb a little higher.

Jack goes ahead of me, then shines his light back down on the exposed rocks and thick roots twining across the trail and offers his hand when necessary to help hoist me up.

Doing this, we slowly ascend to the top of the falls and when we get there, I find that he was right—the forest does open up above us. And even though there's a moon tonight, it's only a crescent moon and I can still see the stars pretty well.

With his light off again, I let my eyes trace the imaginary lines that connect the stars into constellations, tracking them across the vast expanse of the night sky, finding and identifying the patterns I know and recalling the stories that go with them.

Sometimes I think that maybe the constellations are evidence of our need for meaning. There's no reason to think that this star or that star have anything to do with each other—as Jack pointed out earlier, unfathomable distances stretch between them. The constellations only have meaning because we have a certain perspective, here on this insignificant planet in this meandering little arm of the Milky Way, and we have the need for belonging, so we find constellations and find ourselves in the stories that go with them.

Once our eyes are more accustomed to the moonlight, Jack asks me, "What kind of asterism should we make up?"

"Let's do something with you, with your hero."

"You want to find Jack in the stars?"

"Let's find a beanstalk and a giant."

He steps close enough for me to smell the clean scent of his body wash or cologne, I can't tell which. I hadn't noticed it earlier, but it's oceany and breezy and makes me think of seas and dreams and tales of far-off lands.

I am a sailboat, catching a daring wind toward a distant shore.
I am a lost ship, crashing into the rocks and sinking in the sea.

So, at this moment, am I catching a daring wind or crashing into the rocks?

I feel like the wind is definitely in my sails here, talking with Jack.

But where will it take me?

Where will this night lead?

That's really the question that matters.

Our galactic search for asterisms takes a little time and a lot of leaning in close and pointing up at the sky and reorienting each other to the stars that we're trying to get the other person to look at, and I get the sense that if we were in a movie, this would be the scene where he puts his arm around me and I turn and we stare deeply into each other's eyes and lean close and...

Just as my imagination is about to run away with the moment, Jack says, "There. That star just to the left of the three in a row."

"Orion's Belt."

"Yes. That's the middle of the beanstalk." He places his hand on my sore shoulder and I wince. As soon as I do, he immediately draws his hand back.

"What is it?' he says concernedly. "Are you okay?"

He hadn't touched me very firmly, but as luck would have it, he ended up putting pressure on the exact same spot that was still tender from earlier, when something—whatever it was—grabbed me in the coffin room.

"Yeah," I mutter. "It's just... My shoulder is hurting a little. I must have strained it or something."

"Maybe from the climb?"

"That probably didn't help."

"I'm sorry. I didn't mean to hurt you."

"It's all good," I assure him with a somewhat forced smile. "No worries."

He backs up and we finish tracing the stars of our asterism beanstalk. It's a little too tricky to find a giant in the sky, but we do find a huge, slightly squashed, angular golden egg and call it close enough.

When we're done, Jack says, "I have something I need to tell you."

My heart quivers for a moment. "What's that?"

"It's an admission, really."

"An admission?"

"I'm afraid that you're going to forget me."

His words surprise me. "I don't think that's something you need to worry about," I tell him honestly. "Besides, why would I forget you?"

"I just mean that, in time, you'll meet so many other guys that, eventually, I'll slowly fade from your memory until, one day when you're old—say thirty."

"Oh, yeah, that's really old."

"Right. Well, you'll be trying to remember your high school days and you'll maybe recall being at a bonfire, sure, but you'll forget who you went on the walk with to look at the falls."

I doubt that.

"We'll have our asterisms," I tell him. "I won't forget you. Trust me. Every time I look up at the night sky I'll remember you bravely climbing that beanstalk."

"And then slaying the innocent giant," he says, "who was just trying to recover his property."

"You're a complex hero."

"Yes, but I still think you might forget me," he says. "Unless I do something memorable. Something you'll never forget, that you *can't* forget."

I say nothing, but my heart is racing.

"Like what?" I say.

"Like this."

He turns toward the riverbank, leaps forward, and lands on a flat rock about four feet away in the water. Then, stone by stone, he makes his way toward the boulder at the center of the river.

Though we've pocketed our phones, my eyes are used to the dark by now and I can see him outlined in the gentle moonlight.

"What are you doing?" I call to him over the sound of the falling water.

"Something memorable!" he shouts back over his shoulder.

He finds the boulder overlooking the top of the falls.

Rushing water circles, curls, courses past it—past him—and then plummets over the edge, dropping eighty feet to the deadly cluster of jagged rocks waiting at the bottom.

It looks like the river is about a foot deep here, so the force of the river wouldn't be too intense, but it might be enough to sweep him over if he steps off the boulder. I can't be sure either way.

"Come back," I say. "I'll remember you. I promise!"

He holds his arms out to the sides like they're wings.

"I'm listening!" he says. It almost sounds like he's talking to someone other than me.

"For what?"

"For the devil to whisper to me!"

"Stop it. Come here."

But he doesn't come back.

Then I hear another voice, someone coming our way up the trail, calling out. I can't tell who it is at first, but it almost sounds like Cadence. A flashlight of some type points the way for whoever is ascending the path, but honestly, most of my attention is directed at Jack.

He leans his head back and stares up at the sky, arms outstretched like he's about to do a swan dive off the boulder.

"That's enough!" I yell. "Come back to shore!"

He shifts his weight. I can't tell if he's positioning himself to jump or to return to the shore, but either way, that's when his foot slips and he crashes heavily backward into the river.

If this were summer, I imagine he would've been swept immediately past the boulder and over the falls by the force of the water, but instead, he's able to jam his left foot against it, the water splashing past him as he props himself up until he's seated in the river. Then, he grabs a handhold on the boulder to keep from being dragged to the side and over the edge.

It looks like he's steady for the moment, but I also get the sense that, on his own, he's not going to be able to get to his feet again.

I turn and see Cadence and Aiden making their way up the incline. Aiden is wearing a caving headlamp and its light illuminates the trail for them.

At first, I wonder if we could reach a long branch to Jack, but I doubt we could find one long enough quickly enough, so I realize that's not an option.

No. To help him, I'm going to have to go out there.

"Hang on!" I yell.

Aiden gets to the top of the trail and gasps when he sees Jack.

"Hold my hand," I tell him urgently as I step toward the bank.

It takes him a moment to comprehend what's happening, then Cadence grabs his left hand and I take his right one. She holds onto a thick branch hanging from a tree beside the water, and I edge out, one rock at a time into the river, with Aiden right behind me, supporting me.

But when I reach for Jack's free hand, I find that I'm not quite close enough to get there. I can't help him from here, and I won't be able to reach him unless I let go of Aiden's hand.

"Aiden, you need to let go," I say to him.

He hesitates. "What? No. I—"

"Hurry!"

"Careful," he tells me.

"I'm good."

He lets go, and now I'm on my own and I'm wobbly as I step forward unsteadily to one more rock that seems to be covered with moss or something because it's super slippery and my foot careens off it and plunges into the river. Somehow, I'm able to shift my weight at the last second enough to avoid going down.

I'm about to try to find another rock to stand on, but then I figure that one foot's already wet. Why not both? It's better than slipping again.

Somewhat tentatively, I place my other foot into the rushing water and move it to the side until I secure my footing. I ease forward and when I reach out, I'm finally able to grab Jack's wrist, and he grabs mine.

I'm a bit off-balance, however, and I'm praying that he doesn't pull me down next to him because I have the feeling that then we'll both end up going over.

But instead, he carefully pushes himself up, and with me gripping his wrist, he manages to get to his feet without yanking me down into the water beside him. Now we're both standing there next to the boulder.

And that's when I hear the devil whisper to me to jump.

22

"YOU CAN MAKE IT PAST THE
rocks down there," a voice in my head assures me. *"You'll be alright. Just climb up onto the boulder. It's that easy. Freedom is that close. Just up and over."*

It's almost like when I was in the coffin room and I heard my dad's voice, but this isn't my dad at all. Something's telling me to get onto the boulder and then leap off it into the heart of the falls.

"Do it, Sahara. Do it with Jack. Hold his hand and go together."

But a more sensible voice inside of me screams, *Don't listen! Don't get any closer to the edge!*

However, I do shuffle closer. I can't seem to help myself—just to see if I can catch sight of the bottom of the falls from here. Just a little closer in order to—

"All you need to do is step onto that boulder and—"

"Zod, no!" It's Cadence, and her words shock me back to the present.

Jack is still holding my wrist, and then, in the moonlight, he nods to me and says, "Let's get to shore, Zod."

"But—"

"Trust me."

I do, I trust him, but part of me also trusts that voice that's trying to convince me to climb up and then leap over the edge.

My footing is uncertain, so to steady myself, I take Jack's other hand as well, forming a kind of circle, and we side-step our way to shore where Aiden and Cadence help us onto dry land.

Once I'm there, I finally get my senses back.

I feel like punching Jack. "That was a stupid thing to do!" I yell. "Going out there like that—what were you even thinking?"

"I wasn't thinking. I just—"

"No, you sure weren't," I say, interrupting him. "I can't believe you did that. You could have fallen. You could have gotten us both killed!"

"You heard it, didn't you, Zod?" His voice is soft and filled with concern. "You heard it too."

"Heard what?"

"The devil's voice."

I shake my head in exasperation. "Let's get back to the fire."

He's soaking wet and his shirt and jacket cling to him, revealing his somewhat wiry, yet athletic frame.

Tearing my eyes from him, I pull out my phone and turn on the light to see where I'm going as I make my way down the trail. It's sketchy and I actually have to turn around and back down. I end up holding my phone between my teeth so I can use both hands to scramble down, backing my way to the bottom of the incline. I'm just glad no one got hurt up there.

But the devil did speak to you.

No, I tell myself. *It wasn't the devil. It was just my imagination.*

We're all quiet as we descend to the base of the falls, and after we've regrouped, Aiden and Jack go on ahead, which is just fine by me because it gives me a chance to talk with Cadence.

"What happened with you two?" she asks. "I was looking all over for you earlier before I realized you two had sautéed off into the woods together."

"*Sautéing* would be cooking with gusto. I think you mean we *sauntered.*"

"Picky, picky—but I like that: cooking with gusto. I'm going to do that the next time I make an omelet."

I tell her everything—about our walk to the falls and the dreamy feeling of being alone with Tyler, about us telling each other secrets, and about calling him Jack and making up the asterisms, and about him saying he was afraid I would forget him.

"Yeah," she says, "I'm not thinking [air quotes]—*that's*—[air quotes] gonna be a problem."

"Me either," I reply, ignoring her unfortunate use of air quotes. "He went right out there into the river. I thought he was going to jump."

"I thought you were too."

I'm quiet.

"Listen," Cadence says. "He was just being a guy. It's a scientifically, psychologically proven fact: a change comes over a guy when he sees a girl that he likes."

"Oh, yeah? And what's that?"

"He begins to act stupid."

She does have a point.

"Well," I say, "if that's evidence that Jack likes me, then he must *really* like me."

"Yeah," she says after a moment. "He must."

———

As we get closer to the bonfire, I can hear people chanting, "Big-ger-fire! Big-ger-fire!" and when we reach the meadow, I see that a couple of the guys and one of the girls are lined up on one side of the bonfire, facing the blaze, maybe thirty feet away from it.

The guy in the front of the line is stretching out like he's about to run a race and at first I'm confused, but then I put two and two together and anticipate what's about to go down.

It's definitely a horror show waiting to happen. Drunk college students trying to jump over a bonfire in the middle of the night? No, nothing could ever go wrong with that.

For some reason, the guy who's getting ready to run isn't wearing a shirt.

I point to him and ask Cadence, "Who is that?"

"Ryan something or other," she tells me.

Aiden, who has joined us by then, adds, "Ryan Halbertson.

Graduated last year. His biggest accomplishment in life was learning to smoke two cigarettes at the same time, one from each nostril."

"Oh," I say. "Wow. What a legacy."

"I saw him do it."

"I believe you. And is he really going to try to jump over the fire?"

"If I know him, he is," Aiden replies.

The chanting for more pyromania continues until two people grab some branches and toss them onto the bonfire. Now the fire's pretty legit: the stack of wood is at least three feet high, with the flames slithering up another three or four feet into the night. There's no way to avoid flying through those flames if you're going to leap over the fire.

I figure it's like when you pass your finger through a candle flame and you don't get burned. It's all about the amount of time you're in the flame: Hold your hand steady there and you'll be in trouble, but go quickly enough and you'll be fine. Same here. The fire needs a chance to find you.

So, maybe this guy would be able to fly through those flames quickly enough so that the campfire wouldn't have a chance to burn him, but I'm not really sure either way.

Ryan raises his hands in victory as if he's already made the jump, and then, to the cheers of the crowd, he sprints forward and launches himself over the fire, clearing it by a rather shocking amount, flying effortlessly through the flames.

When he lands, he stumbles and scrambles to get his footing, but after a tense moment, he manages to avoid ending up either sprawled on the ground or tottering back into the fire, which seemed pretty likely a second earlier.

More cheers.

And he's not shrieking in pain or covered with burns.

That jump was not nothing. Mr. Nostril Smoker really had some hang time. Maybe he's a hurdler or a long jumper. When I point that out, Cadence says, "Long jumpers always amaze me. I mean, the way

I see it, anytime you're in the air long enough to comb your hair and walk your dog, you know you're good at the long jump."

"You are not wrong," I say. I'm looking around for Jack, but don't see him and I hope I wasn't too harsh on him earlier when I got mad at him for going out into the river. I might very well have ruined my one chance to get something real started with him.

"Who's next?" Ryan calls.

Cole steps forward. "I'll go." Then he flags a hand toward me. "Be bold, be bold, right, Boots?"

Oh. Wonderful.

He finds his way to the front of the line and makes a big deal out of encouraging the people to chant again, "Big-ger-fire! Big-ger-fire!"

Ryan listens and loads on some more sticks.

A bunch of people have their phones out and are filming everything, even though posting anything with their friends drinking out here would probably be a mistake since I'm guessing that at least half the people are underage. But that doesn't stop them.

The guy next to me has a can of beer in each hand. One is still unopened. He lifts the other one in a pre-celebration of Cole's jump.

Cole tosses his jacket to the side so that now he just has on a polo shirt and jeans. He takes a deep breath and then bolts toward the bonfire, but before he reaches it, when he's maybe ten feet away, he trips on a rock or a root or something.

However, instead of falling down, he fights to regain his footing and ends up half-stumbling, half-sprinting toward the blazing bonfire, his momentum carrying him unforgivingly forward.

I snatch the unopened can of beer from the guy next to me, and rush toward Cole, shaking the can as I do.

23

COLE SEEMS TO FALL IN

slow motion.

As he lunge-tumbles toward the fire, he instinctively throws his hands out in front of him to take the brunt of his fall, inadvertently aiming them right at the blaze, but it's too late to stop now and he crashes with a terrifying cry, face-first directly into the heart of the bonfire.

And then time catches up with itself and there's an explosion.

Of sparks.

Bursting.

Into the night.

Burning sticks fling themselves at the crowd, everyone jumps back, and a few girls start screaming as Cole tries unsuccessfully to disentangle himself from the flaming branches and rolls to the side to get free. His left arm took the brunt of the fall, but his face doesn't look so good either. Scalding white ash clings to his cheeks and his arms and he shrieks in pain, batting frantically at his face.

He shoves himself to his feet and I run to him, shake the can violently one last time, aim it at his face, and then pop the tab and direct the spraying beer at him.

He coughs and sputters and there's beer and sizzling ash and sparks and smoke everywhere. I can't tell how severe the burns are going to be, but I smell burning flesh.

Once the beer has stopped spraying, I pour the rest of it over his arms and his hands to put out the smoldering cinders that are still singeing him.

The next thing I know, Jack is beside me, whipping off his soaking wet coat and wrapping it gently around Cole's left arm to soothe the burns and put out any lingering cinders clinging to him.

I have the sense that Cole might pull away, but he doesn't. And although the damp makeshift bandage might be helping some, I have the sense that he's definitely going to need some attention at the ER.

People are scattering. Then someone is dumping the cooler full of ice onto the fire and thick smoke surrounds us as one of Cole's friends hustles him toward their car to get him to the hospital.

Once everything has settled down, I look around and realize that most everyone is already on their way to their cars, little lights from their phones marking the way, bobbing along the path through the forest, back to the trailhead.

In the end, after a few breathless moments, it's just Cadence, Aiden, Jack, and me.

"Well," Aiden says, "I guess the party's over."

"I hope Cole's okay," I say. "His face did not look good."

"He'll be alright," Jack assures me. "That was quick thinking with the beer."

I shrug it off. "Anyone would've done it."

"But no one else *did* do it. Just you. You probably saved him from having scars all over his face and arms."

Cadence brushes her hand tenderly across my sleeve. "You got beer all over you, girl."

"Grams is going to love this," I mutter. "I'll probably get grounded until I'm thirty."

"How'd you know the beer wouldn't ignite, wouldn't burn him worse?" Aiden asks. "I always thought alcohol was flammable."

"It is," I say. "But there's not enough of it in beer to ignite. You'd need a way higher proof. At least, I don't know, maybe sixty-proof? Maybe more? The whiskey that some of the people here were drinking would've been enough. That wouldn't have been pretty if I'd have sprayed that on him instead."

Aiden looks at me curiously. "How do you even know all that?"

"I read," I say, echoing what Jack told me earlier when he was explaining how he knew about Scheherazade.

———

On the walk back to the cars, he ends up next to me. "Listen," he says, "I'm sorry about earlier at the river, there at the top of the falls. I shouldn't have gone out there like that."

I say nothing to him.

"Are you still mad at me?"

"I might be," I say stiffly. "I was scared you were going to get hurt."

"It was a dumb thing to do."

"Uh-huh. Keep going..."

"I'm sorry." And then, "Will you forgive me?"

I barely hold back a sigh. "Grams would say you were acting crazier than an idiot."

"I like that," he tells me. "I guess I was." Then he adds, "It won't happen again. Promise."

I consider that, but I'm doubting that we would ever be back at the falls again together, anyway. Still, it's the sentiment that counts.

"Okay," I say. "Apology accepted."

He stops walking and extends his hand. "Still friends?"

I pause as well and shake his hand. "Still friends."

He doesn't let go of my hand right away.

And I don't let go of his.

Not a bad deal.

"I enjoyed seeing you here tonight," he says.

"Me too."

He's still holding my hand. Who knew a handshake could last this long?

"Right," he says, "Well, I was wondering...."

"Yes?"

He finally lets go. "I mean, maybe we could hang out again sometime? Maybe tomorrow night—if you're not doing anything? Maybe we could find an asterism for you this time?"

"Um..."

"You're probably doing something. You're doing something, aren't you?"

I give him a side-eye. "Is this you asking me out, Jack?"

"I should start over, shouldn't I?"

"Depends on if you want me to say yes or not."

He clears his throat dramatically. "Zod, would you be so inclined as to spend time with me tomorrow evening?"

"I *would* be so inclined," I tell him. "Thank you for asking so nicely."

I debate whether or not to bring something up with him, and finally decide that I should just go ahead and ask him what's been on my mind. "Earlier," I say, "when we were up there at the falls, you asked me if I heard the devil whisper to me when I was in the river."

"Yes."

"I never answered you."

A pause. "I remember."

"I did hear something. I don't know what it was, but I'm just glad we both made it off that waterfall. If you hadn't... Well, I'm just thankful I listened to your voice instead."

"Me too."

"So..." I say. "You heard it too?"

"I did." A nod. "And I never want to hear it again." He pauses and it seems like he's going to add more, but he doesn't. Instead, he says, "Can I have your number?" Then he adds quickly, "I mean, just to be in touch about tomorrow night."

"I'll give you my number, but don't call me."

"Why's that?" There's a look of curiosity on his face, or maybe it's confusion. "You have a jealous boyfriend?" I can't tell if he's being serious or not.

"No. No boyfriend. It's because I won't pick up. I don't answer my phone. Just texts. Text me. I'll get the message. And don't leave me a voice message either. I never check them."

"A quirk." He nods. "That's cool. I like that."

I don't explain to him the origin of the quirk. Now's not the time.

I could just tell him my number, but instead, I ask him for his phone, and then I add my number and my name, Zod, to his contacts.

When I hand it back, he says, "You're full of surprises, Sahara O'Shaughnessy, you and all of your mattress tag villainy."

"And Teddy Bears."

"That's right."

"I'm complex," I say.

"Yes, you are."

"Text me."

"I will."

And then he smiles at me in the moonlight before sidling off into the night.

And I float back to my car.

24

WHEN I GET BEHIND THE wheel, the engine refuses to turn over and the car won't start, which is the first time this has happened, but considering the car's age and, well, let's just say slightly less than stellar condition, it isn't the biggest surprise in the world. Cadence is rolling past me in her Tesla when I flash my headlights at her to get her attention.

It works, she slows down, backs up to me, and rolls down the passenger-side window. "What's up?"

"My car won't start."

"Climb in. I gotcha covered."

I get out and pat my car's hood affectionately. "What should I do with ol' Alfie?"

"Since when is your car named Alfie?"

"Just now. I'm in a naming mood."

"Ah. Well, we'll pick him up tomorrow or jump him or whatever. My dad can get you a tow if you need one: He's friends with this guy who's a mechanic. For now, just leave Alfie here. He's not in anyone's way, and I don't like the idea of hanging around here waiting for a tow truck at this time of night. It's pretty late. Besides, we're in the middle of nowhere. It would take forever."

She's right. We are in the middle of nowhere, and it is pretty late—almost eleven-thirty, and I promised Grams I'd be home by midnight. It's about a twenty-five-minute drive to the house from here, so even though it looks like I'll be cutting it close, I should still be in the clear.

I open the door and join Cadence in her car. "Where's Aiden?" I ask her.

"He drove separately."

As she accelerates quietly through the night, I smile. "Tyler asked me for my number. He wants to hang out tomorrow night, to go stargazing with me again."

"That's what I'm talking about." She smacks her steering wheel in celebration. "Now we're gargling with our mouths open!"

"Wait... What? That doesn't even make sense, Cadence. How could anyone ever gargle with their mouth closed?"

"I'm just saying... How about, 'Now, we're vacuuming with the nozzle attached' Or 'Now, we're swimming with our floaties on.' That any better?"

"Um... okay," I say. "We'll go with the floaties one because I like to swim better than I like to vacuum."

"Me too. Oh, and by the way, I wanted to ask you earlier, you're okay, right? I mean, you didn't get burned at all?"

"I'm good."

A nod. "Cool... Hey, listen, totally different topic: Earlier, when you first got to the bonfire, you were telling me about a coffin room and your dad appearing to you. We never really finished that conversation. What was that all about?"

I explain in detail what happened in the library basement, tell her what Grams said about bodies being stored down there when the trains would come through, and then summarize my thoughts about thin places.

She takes it all in. "So, you think that's what's down there? A thin place to... what? Hell?"

"I don't know," I admit. "But it sure seems like a portal to somewhere."

"And something came through it from the other side and grabbed you."

"Yes. Something did."

After a pause, she says, "You never told me exactly what happened in Wisconsin, why you ended up here in Tennessee. Just that your dad died. Is it okay to ask about it? I don't want to pry."

"Yeah, no, it's fine." The words are out of my mouth before I realize I've said them. But, the more I think about it, the more I realize that it might be good to tell her, to tell someone, what happened—or at least to share part of it. "All last winter Mom and Dad were going through a rough time. We all were, I guess. They were trying to keep it from me, but I could tell, you know?"

"Sure. Were they gonna get a divorce?"

"I'm not sure. I think they were trying to do all they could to avoid that, to patch things up. I got the impression that even with all the arguments, all the tension—all that—there was love there somewhere, under the pain, trying to find its way up to the surface again. I think sometimes people can love each other a ton and still have a tough time being together or making things work."

"Yeah," Cadence says. "I get that."

"Anyway, after the funeral, Mom couldn't stop being sad—all-the-time sad—depressed, right?"

"Sure."

"She wasn't getting any better. She stopped getting out of bed in the mornings, and I had to get myself up and going and then to school, which wasn't easy because I'm not exactly what you'd call an early riser."

"Unless we're talking about early afternoon."

"Ha. Well... You're not wrong," I say. "Point is: Sometimes Mom'd still be in bed when I got home after school, after track practice."

"Is that it, then? She was too depressed to take care of you, so you came down here to stay with your grandma?"

Okay, here we go.

"Well... That was part of it," I say, "but..."

"But?"

"But she basically told me she didn't want me around. That she wanted to go back to grad school to finish her degree and... that she'd never wanted me in the first place."

"Are you even kidding me?"

"No."

"That's horrible." She cusses my mom out with words I'd thought of myself over the last few months but had never quite uttered. She finishes by saying, "That must have been... I can't even imagine."

"I'm not gonna lie," I tell her. "It just about ruined me. But it also helped me understand why she'd treated me the way she had my whole life. I'd sort of always wondered what it was that I ever did to make her so mad at me."

"But it wasn't anything you did."

"No. It was just me. Just the fact that I was alive."

"Zod, that's terrible."

I try to blow it off as no big deal. "It is what it is."

But, in truth, as I think about it, it's almost like I'm there again, reliving the night when Mom told me how she really felt about me, and it's too much. I feel a tear coming to my eye and I do my best to squeeze it back in, but end up having to wipe the back of my hand across my face.

Cadence pats my knee to console me, and says nothing, which is probably the best choice.

When I'm done, she removes her hand and I look out the windshield and notice movement at the far edge of the headlights. A young woman in a faded yellow dress is walking along the side of the road heading in the same direction that we're going.

"Slow down." I point. "There's someone there."

25

CADENCE IMMEDIATELY SLOWS

the car down.

I don't remember seeing anyone wearing a dress at the party, but as far as I know, there aren't any houses nearby, so this girl had to have been up there. Maybe someone kicked her out of their car, or her car refused to start like mine did. Whatever it was, there was no way we could leave her here, walking down this mountain road by herself in the dark.

Cadence eases the car down to a crawl, and since the girl is on my side of the road, I roll my window down.

She pauses and looks our way when Cadence parks beside her. Before I can even say anything, she says, in a voice that's all soft and fragile, "I need a ride home."

"No problem," Cadence says. "Climb in."

She looks about our age, but her face is so sad and pale that it gives me a chill.

My imagination starts running wild with what might have happened to her, coming up with all sorts of tragic and terrifying scenarios that would have left her out here alone on the road like this.

"Are you alright?" I ask her concernedly. "Did something happen to you?"

"I'm okay."

As she slides into the backseat, I feel the cold air swoop into the car alongside her. She shivers as she closes the door. Maybe it's from the change in temperature from the night air to the warmth of the car, but still, I'm worried about her. I don't have a jacket to offer her or a blanket or anything, but I unwrap my scarf and pass it back to her. "You look cold," I say simply. "Put this on." I hold the scarf out to her until she accepts it.

When she does, her fingers glance across mine and her skin feels like it's way colder than it should be. It's like I'm touching a fake hand made of cool clay instead of the real skin of a living girl. It startles me and I jerk my hand back a little too quickly.

But she doesn't seem to notice that and simply thanks me and wraps the silk scarf snugly around her neck.

Cadence turns up the heat and then says, "Were you at the party?"

"Yes," she says in a near whisper. "The party."

"Did you miss your ride?" I ask her.

She nods. A girl of few words.

As we pull forward, I introduce myself and then Cadence. "What's your name?" I ask.

"Lily," she says.

"Well, it's nice to meet you, Lily."

"You too."

When Cadence asks her where she lives, she says, "It's not far, only a couple of miles. I'll tell you where to turn."

"Perf."

Curious, I flip my visor down to get a better look at her. The dress is delicate and frilly, not something most people would wear to a bonfire. More like something you'd wear to a dance.

I try to place her from school but can't seem to recall seeing her in class or around the halls, and she doesn't look old enough to be in college. A different high school, maybe? But there aren't that many close by, not in this county, and I'm not sure that would make sense if she lives close by, like she said. Maybe a North Carolina high school on the far side of the mountains?

When she sees me looking at her, she smiles. I think that sometimes smiles are the result of happiness, and sometimes they're an attempt to find it. I have the sense that, in this case, it's the second kind of smile.

I flip the visor up so I don't make her uneasy and turn to face her instead.

"So, Lily," I say lightly. "Where do you go to school?"

"I'm homeschooled," she says.

"Oh," I say. "Cool."

"Love the dress," Cadence says to her. "Vintage. Rocking it old school. You make it work."

Lily looks out her window at the black night that we're passing through. "Thank you."

I get the sense that something bad happened to her after all, but I don't want to upset her, so I don't bring it up again, don't force the issue.

We ride for a few minutes in a stalled-out kind of silence and then, at last, Lily says to Cadence, "Turn left up ahead."

Cadence slows and rounds the corner. We're going deeper into the mountains, and I'm not very familiar with these roads. As we wind down through a gorge, I wonder if we'll run into one of the "Don't Tread on Me" homes.

"Is it far?" I ask Lily.

"Not too far."

I see a small graveyard on the right side of the road. It's not that uncommon, really, to find old cemeteries up here in the mountains. People who homesteaded in the area would often have small family or community plots up in the hills.

I haven't spent a lot of time tooling around them, but I did walk through one soon after I moved down here in August and found that many of the gravestones were so worn down by the years that the words that'd been engraved on them weren't even visible anymore, but some of the graves that I could read dated back to the early 1800s.

We're not too far past the cemetery when we come to a long gravel driveway that leads up to what looks like a single-wide trailer, maybe two hundred feet ahead of us. A tilted mailbox that's seen better days stands as a lone sentinel beside the entrance to the driveway.

"You can stop here," Lily says quietly. "I can walk."

"I can take you," Cadence says. "No prob."

"It's okay, Cadence," Lily tells her firmly. "I'll walk. It's not far."

"Oh... Alright." I can tell Cadence is struggling with how much to press Lily because she wants to be helpful, but also wants to let her choose because it really is her decision.

Lily opens her door and quickly gets out of the car. We all say goodbye, and Lily pauses for a moment and then says, "You were both very kind. Thank you."

"Sure," Cadence says.

Then Lily faces me. "It's always about the skin," she says cryptically. "That's what he wants." And then, without another word, she starts down the driveway toward the trailer home.

I'm trying to figure out what on earth that was supposed to mean when Cadence turns to me. "What was that all about?"

"I have no idea."

"That's one odd girl."

"She seemed so sad," I say.

"Yeah," Cadence agrees, "I swear I didn't see her there—at the party, I mean."

"Me either."

"Why do you think she wanted to walk from here?"

"I don't know," I say. "Maybe she just didn't want her parents to see some strange car driving up to the house in the middle of the night."

"Maybe."

We sit there for a moment, letting the car run silently as Lily walks away from us into the night. Finally, Cadence says, "I suppose we can go. I guess she'll be alright."

"Yeah," I say, but I'm distracted.

I'm processing everything, specifically trying to unriddle what skin Lily might have been talking about and who would want it. Skin? Like from the story of Mr. Fox? But if she wasn't at the party, how would she know about it?

As I'm deep in thought, Cadence takes us back onto the road to town, and only after we've driven maybe three or four minutes does it strike me. "My scarf," I say. "I forgot to get it back."

"Oh. I'll turn around. Your dad gave that to you right?"

"Yes, it's well... It's kind of special."

"No worries."

She finds a place to pull off, whips the car around, and we head back to the driveway where we dropped Lily off.

Since we don't know her parents, I'm a little nervous to be driving to their trailer at this time of night.

Cadence must be thinking the same thing because she says, "Okay, here we go," as she passes the tilted mailbox and pulls into the driveway toward the mobile home.

26

A RICKETY SHED CROUCHES beside the trailer. Chickens roam freely inside a fenced-in pen to the left of the home, and an agitated mixed-breed dog emerges from the darkness and bolts toward us, chasing the car and barking ominously.

Everything that's happening with Lily begins to feel vaguely familiar even though I've never seen her before, never been on this driveway, never been to this home.

A sense of disquieting *déjà vu*.

"Something's not right," I say.

"You don't think this is the place?" Cadence asks. "Looks like it's the only home down this driveway. This is where we dropped her off."

But I'm not thinking about the driveway or even the mobile home up ahead. I'm thinking about a story about a hitchhiker, a story I've heard and retold. A story I don't want to be remembering at this moment. There's a ghost in it and a twist at the end and it's not a story I want to be a part of.

The dog won't stop barking, and an outdoor light beside the front door cuts on. We park maybe twenty-five feet from the front of the mobile home.

"I'm not getting out with that dog there," Cadence says.

"No kidding. Listen, I was just thinking—it's okay. I don't need the scarf. We can go home."

"What are you talking about? We're here. We'll get it."

"It's not that big of a—"

The door opens up. A man appears from within the trailer, but since he's backlit by the lights from inside, I can't see his face.

I'm half-expecting him to be holding a shotgun, ready to order us to leave his property, but it doesn't look like he's holding anything. Instead, he calls to the dog, and it quiets down as it trots obediently to his side and takes a seat, facing us.

"Can I help you?" the man calls to us, his voice thick with a mountain accent. "It's late," he adds unnecessarily.

Cadence opens her door and gets out, holding up her hands to show him that she means no harm and isn't a threat.

And, figuring it can't hurt, I do the same, my heart hammering wildly in my chest.

"Come closer so's I can see you," he says.

I'm a little afraid of what he'll do if we don't do as he asks, so I edge closer to the trailer home, and so does Cadence. Now we're both maybe fifteen feet from him and his dog.

The man steps forward then, to where the outside light and the headlights meet and I can see his mop of gray hair. He's gotta be in his sixties. Maybe he's Lily's grandpa.

"Whatch'all doing out here at this time of night?"

Lily hasn't come out yet.

She's not going to, a voice inside of me says.

No, I tell myself. *I'm not in a ghost story, this is real life.*

"We dropped Lily off a couple of minutes ago," Cadence says. "And—"

"What'd you just say? You just dropped who off?"

"Lily, like maybe five or ten minutes ago. She still had my friend's scarf. We forgot to get it back and we just—"

"I think you should go." His words are brusque. Unfriendly.

"If she's here—"

I turn to Cadence. "We need to listen to him. We need to go."

But she ignores me and says to the man, "She said she lives down this driveway. Is there another home further on down?"

There's a long silence. "This girl, was she tall and thin? Blonde hair?"

"Yes. And wearing a yellow dress."

"And she told y'all her name was Lily?"

"That's right," Cadence says. I can hear the confusion along with a sense of growing uneasiness creeping into her voice.

"I don't like these games you're playing with me." The man's tone has become steely and hard and is laced with a threat. The dog must notice the change in tone because it starts growling in a low, menacing manner. "You best be getting on your way," the man tells us.

"We're not lying," I tell him. "I swear to you—everything she just said is true."

"You're talking about my daughter."

"Yes," Cadence says. "If that's Lily. We just want the scarf back, that's all. We're not trying to cause any trouble."

"Listen, we're sorry to bother you," I tell him quickly. I tug Cadence's sleeve and say, "Come on, let's go."

She looks slightly annoyed. "What's going on with you? We're here to—"

"I can't get Lily for you," the man says quietly. "She's not here." He's holding the dog's thick collar in his right hand and I have the feeling that if he lets go, that dog is going to tear forward and attack us. "Not no more."

Cadence looks at him quizzically. "But she was—"

"He can't get her," I tell Cadence urgently, remembering the story, but not wanting to have to explain it to her.

"Why not?" she asks with a touch of fear and concern.

"Lily's in the ground," her father says with grim finality.

"What?" Cadence gasps. "You mean she's—"

"Yes." There's a long silence and when he goes on, his voice is strained with heartbreaking sadness. "Dead and buried. In that graveyard, up yonder. She was hit and kilt by a drunk driver on that road there, twenty years ago." He points past his driveway. "The backside of the graveyard is just over that hill. She's in the southwest corner. Go and look for yourselves if you don't believe me. But it's time for you two to leave."

Then he disappears back into the trailer, leading the dog with him.

"What is this?" Cadence says to me. "I don't understand."

"It's the old story," I say, "playing itself out in real life."

"What old story?"

"About the ghost hitchhiker."

"I don't know that story, but I don't believe in ghosts." We start back to her car. "Lily was here with us," she says firmly. "Do ghosts open up car doors? Do they talk to you? Do they wear scarves?"

I'm not sure what to say. After everything that's been happening to me today, I really have no explanation for our encounter with Lily—except that it reminds me so much of the story.

We climb in.

"Look," Cadence says. "We're going to that graveyard. And you're going to tell me this story. I want to know what we're gonna find up there."

So, as we drive toward the cemetery, I tell her the vanishing hitchhiker story that Grams told me five years ago when we were visiting her in the summer.

27

"ACCORDING TO THE STORY," I SAY,

"there's a girl who's coming home after a party and her boyfriend is mad at her for some reason and he kicks her out of his car. So she's walking along this deserted road at night and she's tragically killed in a hit and run."

"Or by a drunk driver?" Cadence says.

"Yes. Maybe. Well, years later, someone else is driving down the road and he sees her walking there by herself and he picks her up. It's cold that night and she shivers so he gives her his jacket to wear."

I pause. I can hardly believe how closely the events of tonight are mirroring the ones in the story.

I take a deep breath. "He drops her off, just like we did with Lily, but forgets his jacket, just like I forgot my scarf. Well, he drives to the house where she said she lived and her parents tell him that she was dead but that she appeared on that highway sometimes on the anniversary of her death and to go to the graveyard and that he would know her grave when he saw it."

"How would he know?" Cadence asks, but then anticipates the answer: "Because her name was on it?"

"Well, that, and because when the guy goes to the graveyard, he finds his jacket hanging over a gravestone."

"Hers?"

"Yes."

Cadence lets that sink in. "But this girl, tonight, Lily, she can't be dead. It can't be the same girl as that man who said he was her father was talking about."

I don't want to argue, but I also can't deny what seems to be happening here, so I tell Cadence, "Lily's hand was cold when I touched it. You remember how pale she was? How sad she looked?"

"But she said she was at the party."

"Yes, but kids have been partying up there at Jameson's Gap for years. Decades even. It could have been a different party she was talking about."

"I don't know." She shakes her head. "Ghosts? Seriously?"

"I'm just saying."

"The guy at the trailer had to have been messing with us," she says adamantly, but I get the sense that she doesn't quite believe it herself.

"I guess we'll find out soon enough."

————

We drive in silence the rest of the way to the cemetery that we passed earlier—the one the man had pointed to.

"I have a bad feeling about this," I tell Cadence as she parks on the side of the road. There's no shoulder here, so she leaves her four-way flashers on in case another car comes down the narrow mountain road so they won't hit hers, leaving the night outside the car window, pulsing red around us.

On and off.

Red and dark.

"You're saying we're going to find Lily's grave, right?" Cadence says. "And according to your story, we'll find your scarf draped over a gravestone?"

"According to the story, yes."

Red.

And dark.

We're both still sitting in the car.

"At least there isn't any danger, though, right?" Cadence says carefully. "I mean, it's a chilling story, but the ghost girl doesn't attack anyone. No one gets hurt."

She does have a point, and since we're here and we know what's going to happen, I say, "Okay. Let's go get my scarf and get out of here."

She scrounges up a flashlight and we leave the car and head to the cemetery that waits dark and still ahead of us, about fifty feet from the road, red light and dark night alternating behind us as we do.

————

A sturdy, waist-high metal fence surrounds the graveyard. The gate isn't immediately visible, so we help each other over the fence and then, together, we make our way past the angled and worn gravestones that stick out of the ground like rows of ancient chipped-off teeth.

Based on the position of the stars and the orientation of the road, I anticipate the southwest corner will be up ahead to the left. "There." I point. "Just past that old tree."

The wind has picked up and sends a chill through me as it blows across the graves, scratching at the exposed skin on my face and hands and neck.

As we get closer, I see a figure standing beside a gravestone just beyond a rise in the corner of the graveyard past the tree I'd pointed to a moment ago. Even from here, maybe thirty feet away, in the moonlight, I can see that it's someone in a dress, wearing my scarf, facing the other direction.

Someone tall and thin.

Something's not right. This isn't how the story goes.

"Lily?" There's a catch in my throat. "Is that you?"

"See?" Cadence says to me. "She's right there. She has your scarf. She wasn't dead at all."

Then, as she angles her flashlight toward the figure, the person slowly turns to face us, and as she does, I can see that it is Lily, but her dress doesn't look so clean and well-pressed, but is rumpled instead, and stained with dark swaths of blood. Her left arm hangs loosely from the elbow down at a gruesome, twisted angle. Half a dozen jagged shards of glass are sticking out of the side of her face. The one slivered into her right temple looks fatally deep.

Cadence stands beside me, frozen in fear.

Lily's not supposed to be here. We're just supposed to find my scarf on the gravestone. So, since this isn't playing out like the story anymore, I have no idea how she's going to act if we startle or upset her.

"Lily," I say at last, my voice quavering despite my best efforts to appear calm. "We're sorry about what happened to you. We're going to leave you alone. We didn't want to disturb you."

And that's when she speaks. "You were both very kind," she says, repeating what she'd told us earlier, right before she left for the mobile home. But this time, her voice is moist and juicy, as if she has some liquid caught in her mouth or throat. When she finishes, a thin trail of blood burbles out of the side of her mouth and trickles down her chin. "This is yours," she says.

Then she reaches up to her neck and I remember another story.

"The yellow ribbon," I say softly. "Oh, no." I lean over and whisper to Cadence, "Let's go. We need to go. Now."

But she's confused, overwhelmed. "What?"

My words are urgent, rushed. I don't want to say them, but I have to: "It's a different story. A girl always wears a yellow ribbon around her neck. Come *on*."

Cadence hesitates, so I take her hand and we begin to back up. "What are you talking about?" she asks me. "A yellow ribbon? What is all this?"

Lily is slowly unwrapping the scarf. "You were kind..."

More blood oozes from her thin, red lips.

I go on quickly, my voice hushed and with a catch in my throat, summarizing for Cadence the ten-minute story in ten seconds: "This guy she likes, he's always asking her why she never takes off the yellow ribbon, and she always has an excuse and puts off telling him the reason. But then, once they're older and married, he finally convinces her, and she takes it off and—"

"You're not making sense—"

"Her head," I say. "It falls off. It drops to the ground."

Lily is almost done with the scarf. "The skin. Don't let him get the skin... A kiss will break the curse..."

"No, Lily!" I yell. "It's okay!"

But she doesn't stop.

Just one final loop of the scarf.

I tug on Cadence's hand. "Run. Don't look back!"

We turn toward the car, and as we do, a narrow scream slices through the night from where Lily is standing, overtaking the cold wind and echoing all throughout the cemetery.

We're running toward the car, trying to avoid the gravestones and plots, but as the scream fades in the night, Cadence stops, pulling me to a stop as well. "I need to see," she says.

"I don't think that's a good idea."

But in the end, I can't keep my curiosity in check, and so we both turn at the same time to face Lily and Cadence levels her flashlight at the place where Lily had been standing a few moments earlier.

Lily is gone and my scarf is slowly floating to the ground, fluttering lazily in the wind. There's no sign of a head lying anywhere nearby.

"We need to see if it's her grave, there, where she was standing," Cadence says.

"Do we, though?"

"I have to know."

I swallow, admit to myself that I want to see it as well, and at last I agree, and the two of us head toward the gravestone.

We make our way through the rows of weathered grave markers to the scarf.

When Cadence shines her light on the gravestone beside it, we see the dates of Lily's birth and death etched in stone, along with the words "Lily Greer - Beloved Daughter." And sure enough, she died twenty years ago this week.

When I lift my scarf, I catch the scent of perfume, but it's not the kind of perfume I use.

At least there's no blood on it.

At least there's that.

———

Back in the car, neither Cadence nor I know what to say, and so we ride together in silence toward my house.

Finally, when we're only a few minutes out, she says, "I don't understand what happened tonight. I have no way to explain it."

"Neither do I," I say. "Ever since I went into that third room in the basement of the library, weird things have been happening to me."

"But this wasn't just you." Cadence takes the final turn toward Grams' house. "This was both of us. Lily was here in the car. I saw her, talked to her."

"I don't know if it was really her or if she was a ghost or what," I say. "I don't know what she was or what's happening, but I do know that I need some answers."

"How are you going to get those?"

"Hopefully by looking in that book my dad checked out. Maybe talking to Grams—she's lived in this area pretty much her whole life and she knew about the library's coffin room. Maybe she'll know what's going on and what to do. There's also a box of old documents at the library. The librarian, Ms. Mason, said I could look through them tomorrow if it's not too busy."

"Wait." Cadence looks my way. "Did you say the librarian's name is Ms. Mason?"

"Yes. Why?"

"You do know who that is, right? I mean, if it's the same person I'm thinking of?"

"What are you talking about? What person?"

"Cole's mom, Zod."

"What?" I gasp.

"I mean, I'm not a hundred percent sure, but I think that's her. After his parents got divorced last year, I heard she went back to her maiden name and he kept his dad's last name."

"I had no idea."

"Yeah, and you helped stop him from those burns tonight. That's quite a coincidence."

"There are a lot of those happening lately," I say. "Too many." We pull into Grams' driveway and I add, "I have the feeling that they're not coincidences at all."

"What do you think they are?"

"That's what we need to find out."

Cadence pulls to a stop and I look at the clock.

12:22 a.m.

Okay, let's see what happens when I walk in after my curfew, smelling of beer.

28

BEFORE I GET OUT OF THE CAR,

we make arrangements for tomorrow: Since the library opens to the public at ten and I need to be there a little early, Cadence offers to swing by to pick me up at nine-thirty to drive me over there. Then, while I'm at work, she'll check with her dad about towing my car, Alfie.

"You sure that's cool?" I say.

"Couldn't be cooler."

"I really appreciate it, and so does Alfie."

"No prob."

I hand her my car keys, and we say goodbye, but she stops me as I'm climbing out of her car. "Hang on a sec. I think it might be best if we keep what happened tonight with Lily to ourselves. I mean, go on and ask your Grams what you need to, but let's not tell anyone about Lily until we have some answers."

"Deal."

―――――

As I walk up to the porch, I'm nervous that I might wake up Grams, that she'll smell the beer I wasn't drinking but will *think* I was drinking, and then ground me—a term I'd always been uneasy with. When I was little, I was always terrified of getting grounded because in a movie I heard about ground beef and meat grinders, and all I could think of was ending up that way myself.

It sounds silly now, but it wasn't silly at all to me until I was maybe ten and I finally found out what it really means to be grounded. I was quite happy that it had nothing to do with meat grinders, but just meant being stuck at home with a bunch of books to read with no distractions and no one showing up to disturb you. Just a slight little difference there.

As quietly as I can, I open the door and enter the living room. The lights are off, so I'm expecting that maybe Grams is asleep or at least in her bedroom. I don't see any light coming out from under her door either, so that's a good sign.

I carefully close the screen door and then the front door, easing them both silently shut.

Then, I sidle across the room and tiptoe up the stairs, being careful to avoid that one step three from the top that likes to squeak when you put weight on it.

Grams doesn't do well with stairs anymore, so she sleeps on the first floor in a bedroom just off the kitchen, which is good for me because it gives me a lot of privacy up here, having the second floor all to myself.

I pause at the top of the stairs, listening.

Nothing.

Well, at least one thing is tilting in my favor tonight.

In my room, I grab my pajamas and head to the bathroom to get cleaned up and change.

After peeling off my clothes that are still damp with beer, I take a quick shower and rinse them out so they won't reek of booze and campfire smoke in the morning, and then hang them up in the bathroom to dry.

I change into my pjs.

Earlier, I'd planned on spending some time tonight going through the book of ghost stories that Dad checked out when he was sixteen, but at the moment, I realize there's no way I'm up for that tonight, not after everything that's happened today. I'm exhausted and have had enough ghosts and the unexplained for one day. I just need some rest.

I climb into bed, hoping to fall asleep quickly, but I can't get everything off my mind.

Thoughts of my dad and the coffin and the spiders overwhelm me. The sound of the devil's voice whispering to me to jump off Devil's Falls and Lily's final, blood-curdling scream haunt me. All of those things end up climbing over each other and tumbling through my mind and after a little while I doubt that I'll be able to sleep at all.

I try to figure out how to make sense of what's happening. It looks like stories that I've heard and told to my friends are coming to life—but not *quite* in the way I remember them. So, rather than find the scarf on Lily's gravestone, we found her there wearing it. And rather than her head falling off when she removed the scarf, she disappeared altogether.

So, it seems like there are twists in the tales that are unfolding with me and my friends inside of them—which means that no matter how well I know some of my stories, there are still going to be surprises along the way.

When I try to relax and calm my breathing, I find that I'm still rattled from the events with Lily.

The more I think about it, the more I realize I don't want to be rushed or stressed tomorrow morning on only my third day on the job, so I find my phone and text Cadence to see if she can pick me up at nine instead of nine-thirty in order to give me a little extra time to get ready for people coming into the library.

As I consider that, the librarian, Ms. Mason, and Cole—the guy I sprayed with beer—come to mind and I send Cadence another text, this time to see if she's heard any news about how he's doing.

Then, I set my phone beside my bed in case she texts back, and I let out a long sigh that I didn't even realize I'd been holding in.

I can't help wondering what I might've seen if I hadn't turned my back when Lily was unwrapping the scarf from around her neck. I'm just glad that nothing worse happened.

My phone vibrates.

Figuring it's Cadence replying to me, I wake up the screen, but find that the text is actually from an unknown number. I hesitate for a moment, then tap the icon to bring it up.

Four words appear on my screen: "Be bold, be bold."

I feel a deep chill and text back, "Who is this?"

Those three little ghost dots appear, telling me that someone on the other end is typing, but then they disappear and don't come back.

My dad was a computer technician, but unfortunately, he never taught me how to backtrace emails or text messages. I tool around online for a few minutes to see if there's an easy way to locate the identity of someone who has texted you from an unknown number, but I don't find anything very helpful, or at least nothing that works in this case.

Someone is definitely messing with me and it's not funny. I think of the words that Cole said to me when he was about to jump over the campfire—the same phrase as the text—and I figure he's probably the one who sent this, although I can't begin to guess how he could've gotten my number or why he would be texting those words to me.

Then another slightly troubling thought strikes me: I did give my number to Jack and I don't have his number yet in my phone, so it's possible that he's the one who sent this. But why wouldn't he have put his name on the text, and why would he send me such a cryptic and rather unsettling phrase from my story about Mr. Fox?

I text, "Is this Jack?" to the number.

No one replies.

Actually, as I come to think of it, I realize that just about anyone who was at the party and heard the story might have texted me that. But still, it's chilling because I know how the tale of Mr. Fox goes and I know what the girl in the story who reads those words ends up seeing and what happens to her in the end: She snaps and does to him what he had done to all those women.

Bones and teeth and hair and blood and skin upon the floor.

You won't snap. You're not going to go crazy. You just need to get some sleep.

I check the phone a couple more times over the next few minutes, but no more messages come through.

Hoping to find some way to relax, I turn on my constellation machine and set it for tonight's night sky, here at our latitude and longitude in northeast Tennessee.

I want the asterisms that Jack and I made up to be watching over me, but I end up thinking of my dad instead, telling me stories about the constellations when I was a kid.

So, then, with the two of them on my mind—with memories of the past wrestling with dreams of tomorrow—I close my eyes to try to get some sleep.

BEFORE

It was the damaged guardrail and the broken stretch of ice on Chippewa Lake that led the cops to Dad's car. Without those two things, they might never have found him.

He was a good dad.

He didn't do everything right—of course not—but he did the big things right, the ones that matter most. He did the being-there-for-me-when-I-needed-him right, and the buying-me-ice-cream-when-I-had-my-tonsils-taken-out right, and the hugging-me-after-a-breakup right, and he came to my track meets when he could—just enough of them to let me know how much he cared, but not *all* of them so it never got weird.

For the most part, he listened to me and, no matter what else happened between us, I always felt safer with him around. No question about it. He had this love for me that was somehow both tender and fierce at the same time. It's a dad thing. When they get it right, you can tell, and when they get it wrong, well, you can tell that too.

He wasn't perfect, but he was the perfect dad for me.

He would've done anything for me. I knew that, even though he and Mom were having problems, even though he told me something the night he died that wasn't true. I forgive him now. I do. But that night in March, I thought I never would, not after what he said, and what I said to him in return.

If you go by the cops' official report, my dad's death was an accident. But if you calculate things in a different way—in the truest way—I was the one responsible. After all, I was the reason he was on the icy road that night, and I still can't shake the feeling that it was my words right before I left the house that killed him.

PART III

DAZIA AND THE PRINCESS

29

8:14 A.M.

I WAKE UP TO THE WARM GLOW

of sunlight streaming through my window, all optimistic and cheerful, and it almost seems like all the weird stuff that happened yesterday couldn't have been real: the coffin room, Devil's Falls, Lily disappearing in the night. Yesterday feels like a dream—a nightmare?—that I'm finally waking up from. I wonder if a new day is just what I need.

Though normally I'd still be feeling sleep-deprived this ridiculously early in the morning, today I feel remarkably rested.

I check my phone and find no new texts—either from the unknown number or from Cadence updating me about Cole's condition or confirming that she can pick me up at nine.

Just those four words come up on my screen: "Be bold, be bold." At least whoever sent them didn't add the rest of the saying, didn't take things any further.

———

I smell bacon cooking downstairs, so after turning off my constellation machine and getting dressed, I wander down the steps and find Grams busy at the stove with a dozen thick bacon strips sizzling on the griddle. She cracks open an egg and drops the yolk into a cast iron skillet next to the griddle and smiles at me as I enter the kitchen. "Good morning, Sahara."

"Morning, Grams." I'm maybe not looking directly in her eyes because I *was* late getting home last night and I don't really want her to confront me about it, even though I had a good reason to miss my curfew since we were trying to help Lily get home safely.

Also, I don't want to tell her that I went to the place I promised her I wouldn't go: Devil's Falls.

So there's that.

"And did you have a good time last night?" Grams flips a couple of the bacon strips over and adds another egg. There's already a heaping plate of eggs beside the stove and for a moment I wonder if she might be expecting company.

"Yes." I think of my walk with Jack. "It was... memorable."

A pause. "I didn't hear you when you got in." It comes across as an observation, not an accusation.

I try to figure out what to say. "I was a few minutes late—just twenty minutes or so—but first, my car wouldn't start, and then there was this girl walking down the road alone in the dark so Cadence and I drove her home." I leave it at that, deciding not to go into detail about the incidents with the scarf and the graveyard.

Grams doesn't confront me about getting home late, but instead looks out the window at the empty driveway. "I don't see your car. I'm guessin' you never got it runnin'?"

"Yeah, no, we didn't, but Cadence is going to see if her dad can get it either jumped or towed today while I'm at work."

"That's very kind of her."

Grams' words remind me of what Lily said to Cadence and me when she thanked us last night right before she reached up to unwrap my scarf from around her neck.

The scarf that still has the scent of her perfume on it.

I'm a bit worried that Grams will ask me about Devil's Falls and I prepare myself to tell her the truth—even if it gets me into trouble—but she doesn't go there.

Instead, we end up talking for a few minutes about my work at the library and I mention the spiders in the stairwell.

"You never did like them spiders," she notes.

"Nope. Never did."

That leads us to talking about other things we don't like, and she mentions when folks give their pets people names, expiration dates on ketchup, and camouflage flashlights.

"Think about it," she says.

I do. She's right, there is no reason in the world to have a camouflage flashlight. Because, why? It'd just be harder to find in the dark when you need it, and when it's on, no one will be able to see its color anyway.

Then, since I know she's no fan of them, I mention snakes.

"Speaking of snakes," she says, which is her way of transitioning into a story. "When I was a girl we had real trouble with rattlesnakes all 'round the house one year—'specially this one rascally six-footer that kept comin' after our baby chicks."

Surprisingly, this is a story I don't recall ever hearing. "What'd you do?"

"Well, 'bout that time, there was a certain travelin' hypnotist come to town and he went about hypnotizin' people and gettin' 'em to act like chickens on stage. So, that gave my daddy an idea."

"What was that?"

"It took some doing, but he hypnotized that ol' rattlesnake and got him to act like a chicken himself. Then the other rattlers commenced to bitin' him and daddy done got rid of that troublesome snake."

"But if he was close enough to hypnotize the snake," I observe, without trying to be too critical of the story's logic, "wouldn't that make him close enough so that he could've maybe killed it? Like with a garden hoe or something?"

"That woulda defeated the whole purpose."

"Of getting rid of the snake?"

"Of gettin' a *story* about gettin' rid of the snake. Ain't no story worth telling if'n you just hack the snake up dead with a hoe. That's just something that happens; it ain't even worth the breath it takes to tell about it. But if you *hypnotize* a rattlesnake and get it to act like a chicken, well, now, that's a story worth tellin'."

I smile. "I like that, Grams. I'll keep that in mind if I ever meet a troublesome rattlesnake."

"You be sure to."

By then, the bacon and eggs are ready, and we pile them onto our plates, find some seats at the table, say grace, and dig in.

I'm not really into drinking coffee unless I can kill the taste with ridiculous amounts of honey and vanilla creamer, but Grams goes for her coffee black. This morning I opt for orange juice instead.

"You sleep alright, then?" she asks me as she takes a sip from her favorite ceramic coffee mug made by a potter over in Weaverville.

"Yes, ma'am. You?"

She sighs. "My sleep schedule these days is all a'kilter. Got it from my momma. Sometimes she'd wake up so early that it'd be yesterday when she climbed out of bed, and then she'd sleep in until tomorrow and miss livin' today altogether. Once, she missed a whole month that way 'til she could wake her way back up to the right day once again. I remember missin' her plenty that month she was gone."

Once more, I'm amazed at how naturally Grams shifts to and from tale-telling mode. It isn't that she's telling me the truth necessarily, but I don't take it as a lie either. Telling her stories the way she does, it's kind of her way of threading between the truth and not telling the truth, between lying and not lying either.

I figure this is as good a time as any to find out more about some of the things that've been happening to me lately. I drink some OJ and then say, "Grams, when I was a kid you told me about thin places."

"Yes."

"I was wondering, can they happen with bad places as well as good ones?"

"What do you mean?"

"Just that if you can have a thin place to somewhere that's beautiful and awe-inspiring and all of that, can you also have one to the opposite kind of world?"

"You mean tell, can there be a thin place to somewhere evil?"

"Well... Yes."

She takes a bite of eggs smothered with strawberry jam—one of her many culinary peculiarities—before answering, then swallows them and says, "Yes. Most often it's light that tries to shine in from the other world, but sometimes darkness tries to seep on through."

"Are you saying from heaven and hell?"

She shakes her head. "It's not so much that thin places occur between this world and the next, but this world and the one that sits right beside it—the world of tales and imagination, the place of fairies and trolls and dragons and haints. A thin place might just be a doorway separating the way things are from the way they might be, between this world that we do see and the Fairy World that we don't."

"But those are just legends and lore."

She holds up an authoritative finger. "Don't you be too sure about that. There's more to what's real than just the things you can see with your eyes." She looks at me quizzically. "Why all the questions about thin places?"

"Just curious," I say somewhat evasively.

"Uh-huh."

We both eat for a minute.

After a few bites, I say, "Can thin places rip open so that things from the other world enter into ours?"

"It can happen. That's how fairies get through. You can't be too curious about thin places without also being curious about changelings and elementals, because those are the things that might come through with a stain of darkness on 'em."

I'm not sure if she really believes in fairies and changelings and elementals—whatever *they* are. I can't tell for sure.

She's told me about fairies and changelings before, but I can't recall ever hearing about elementals. "Tell me about that," I say. "About those things coming through."

She sets down her fork. "Well, changelings look real, like your own young'un, but the fairies done replaced your baby in the night with one of their own."

I think back to what she's shared with me about them in the past. "And you can tell the difference because the baby maybe starts to suddenly cry all the time or fuss—or stops crying at all."

A nod. "Yes."

"But how do you get your baby back?"

"Well now, that's a question the stories don't have a good answer to. Some people say you need to go back to the Fairy World yourself to save your child, others that you need to make an exchange of yourself... I don't know, but I do know that many years ago, the beliefs about changelings were so strong, that babies were sometimes left out in the woods if the parents were convinced their child had been replaced by one."

The implications of that naturally trouble me. "That's terrible."

"And yet, elementals like it when that happens." Her voice has a cold chill to it. "They're worse than the worst of the fairies."

"What are they?"

"They're like livin' shadows, formless and hungry and bent on causin' nothing but pain and suffering. Some people say they feed on fear and tears and the dread of children."

I let that sink in.

I can't help but think of the shadowy form I saw lurking in the corridor beneath the library, the shadow that seemed to be trying to escape the light, or maybe fight against it. Grams said that thin places don't necessarily lead to heaven or hell, but I have to ask the question that comes to my mind during this talk of elementals. "Are they demons?"

"The Good Book talks about spiritual forces of darkness in the heavenly realms and it mentions rulers and authorities. Some people believe those are elementals. Others say elementals are the souls of the Nephilim from the book of Genesis. I don't know where they come from. I don't know if they're demons or if they rule over the demons, if they were ever alive and can even die, I just know you don't want anything to do with 'em. You ever see a dark, shadowy form in the night that seems to be from another realm, you scamper away from that place just as quick as you can." She pauses and then adds, "You'd tell me if it's more than just curiosity that's behind all these questions, wouldn't you?"

"Sure, of course," I say hastily. I don't want to lie, but I'm also uneasy with the thought of telling her all that's happened to me since yesterday afternoon. The time doesn't feel right for that.

Also, I'm distracted by this discussion of elementals and changelings and I can't help but think of Cadence's one-year-old baby sister. As far as I know, she hasn't been acting strangely, but it's something I begin to wonder if we should maybe keep an eye on.

As I'm thinking about that, Grams says, "There's something I need to tell you."

"Yes?"

"Last night when you were gone, your momma called. She wants to talk to you."

30

"WHAT?" I GASP. "MOM CALLED?"

"Yes. And I don't know all that's goin' on between you two, but I'm not blind. Somethin' is there. Maybe it's your daddy passing away. Whatever it is, it's not helping anything to pretend nothing is wrong."

I don't touch on what's come between Mom and me. "I'm pretty busy today. I'll have to see if I have time to talk to her."

A pause. "Don't shut her out, Child."

Grams doesn't know what Mom said to me. She doesn't know how much she deserves to be shut out—since she shut me out of her heart first, choosing not to love me before I was even born, before I even had a chance.

When I'm slow in responding, Grams says, "Sahara, don't you be lettin' pain become your home. The deeper anger grows roots in your heart, the harder it is to weed it out when the time comes. And that time better come."

I think about that for a moment. "I can maybe do a video chat with her this afternoon. I should be done with work at three."

"Go on, now," she tells me. "Set it up. Let's see it." She waits until I take out my phone.

I send a brief, somewhat curt text to Mom that I'll meet her in a video chat room on Krazle—the only social media app she uses—at three-thirty, which is two-thirty her time.

I see that Cadence has texted me back that she'll be here at nine to pick me up.

We finish eating.

I still have fifteen minutes before Cadence will arrive.

―――――

As Grams and I clean up breakfast and put the leftovers away, she turns on an AM radio station with a radio preacher that she likes to listen to. He's in the middle of a sermon, but it's pretty clear from the start that it's about death and hell and trusting in Jesus to avoid eternal punishment. A true fire and brimstone, Bible Belt, "Ye must be born again!" message.

"Let us turn to Revelation chapter nine and verse six," he says in an earnest, quavering preacher voice. "Here is what the Lord sayeth, 'And in those days shall men seek death, and shall not find it; and shall desire to die, and death shall flee from them'."

Then he goes on to talk about the End Times and the Lake of Fire and the Final Judgment.

But all I can think of is what it would be like to suffer that way, to seek death and not find it; to desire it, only to discover it fleeing from you.

Death is terrifying enough as it is. I can hardly imagine how frightening it would be to suffer so badly and feel so trapped that you *want* to die and yet you see it fleeing from you. I don't know if that's what hell is like, but that sure seems like it would be hellish to me.

My phone chimes with a notification from Cadence that she's here and I realize I was so caught up thinking about the sermon that I didn't even notice her drive up to the house.

"Coming," I text back.

I grab my things and, figuring that I might get a little free time later on to look through the ghost lore book, I jog upstairs to grab it. When I get back to the living room, I hear Cadence knocking on the front door: Six raps in her own special rhythm, always six so we know it's her.

Rat-a-tat-tatty-tat.

I open it up for her and she calls out, "Mornin', Grams!"

Grams loves Cadence and told her early on to just call her Grams, as if she were a part of the family. "Good morning, Cadence," Grams says. "You need any breakfast? There's extra here in the fridge. Come get you some."

"I'm [air quotes]—*good*—[air quotes], thanks."

I tell Grams goodbye and then Cadence and I head to her car.

"There's a lot happening," she says as she opens her door. "Climb in. We need to talk."

31

"FIRST," I SAY, "HOW'S COLE? Have you heard?"

"He's at the hospital."

"Man, I hope he's alright."

"Yeah, me too... So, I—"

"Wait, hang on," I interrupt her. "One more thing." I show her the anonymous "Be bold, be bold," text that I received last night. "Do you have any idea who might've sent that to me?"

"What? Cole, do you think? Based on what he said to you at the campfire?"

"Maybe. I don't know."

She starts the car and as she turns it around to head out of the driveway, I say, "You said there's a lot to talk about?"

"Three things," she tells me. "First, you're all over the Internet."

"What do you mean?"

"Spraying the beer."

"Oh, no." I rub my forehead. "You gotta be kidding me."

"Yeah, pretty much everyone in class posted something about it. You're memeing."

"I'm not sure that's a word."

"It will be from now on," she tells me confidently. "Second, my dad said he's glad to take a look at Alfie and get him towed back to town if we need to. So, don't even worry about that."

"I don't have a lot of money for repairs. Did he say how much it might be?"

"Don't worry about the tow. That's free. We'll see what fixing Alfie might cost, if he needs it. For now, don't stress. Dad said he wants to help out, if he can. That you're like a second daughter to him."

Though she says the words off-handedly, they mean a lot, more than I can say. "Thanks. That's amazing. What's number three?"

"Okay," she says, "I've been thinking a lot about what happened last night."

"Me too," I tell her. "It kept me up late."

"So." She taps the steering wheel knowingly. "The thing is, we didn't actually *see* Lily disappear, did we?"

"Well... our backs were turned at that exact moment, but..."

"Right. What I'm saying is that she was unwrapping the scarf and then we turned around and she screamed and vanished. She could have thrown the scarf into the air and then run off and hid in the night. Maybe behind that tree, or maybe one of those other gravestones."

I consider that. "What about her injuries? You can't tell me that you didn't see the blood on her dress... Her broken arm... Those glass shards jabbing into her face."

Cadence answers quickly, making it clear that she really has been thinking about all this and already has an answer for me. "It was our imagination," she says confidently. "After hearing the guy who claimed to be her dad tell us his daughter was killed by a drunk driver, we saw what we expected to see."

"But what about the gravestone with her name on it? And her dad's story? You're saying it was all an elaborate trick they played on us?"

"I just... I'm trying to make sense of it."

"Sure," I say. "I get that." After a moment, I add. "Based on the date on the gravestone and the guy's story, I think if we search online we can maybe find a picture of the actual girl who died. See if it looks like whoever it was we picked up."

"Good call."

So, while she drives, I search on my phone, and by the time we're halfway to the library, I've found what I was looking for. I show her the screen and she bites her lower lip when she sees the picture of the girl who died on that road twenty years ago at the hands of a drunk driver.

"It's her," she whispers. "It's Lily. So, it's all true."

"Yes," I say. "It looks like it is. Or at least that much of it is."

"So what was all that about the skin?" Cadence asks, a thread of fear in her voice. "When Lily warned us about someone wanting skin?"

"I wish I knew," I say, but then immediately wonder if that's actually true. Maybe, in this instance, ignorance is bliss.

I can't help but think of the story of Mr. Fox and the skin and teeth and hair in his closet. Then, it's almost like both of us think of the same thing at the same time. We look at each other. "Do you think it was her?" I say. "That Lily is the one who sent the text? Is that even possible?"

"I don't know how, but if so, she might reach out to you again."

That was not a very reassuring thought.

"Keep your eye on your texts."

"I will," I tell her a little uneasily.

We're quiet for the rest of the drive until Cadence pulls into the library's parking lot. "So here's the plan," she tells me, switching topics entirely. "I'll swing by around twelve-thirty, bring you some lunch. You get a break, right?"

"I should, yes. But you don't need to."

"It's okay. I'll bring Aiden. We can tell him about what happened last night. Sort all this out. Besides, I want to see the coffin room you told me about yesterday."

"That's probably not a good idea."

"Just see it, not go into it." Then she adds, "Oh, and Jack texted me earlier. I told him that you were working today and he said he'd stop by [air quotes]—*if*—[air quotes] he could. He wanted to hear you read stories to the little kids at eleven."

Oh, that's right. Story Hour.

I wonder if he might be interested in serving as a guest reader, maybe read Jack and the Beanstalk to the kids, but I figure I'll ask him that when I see him.

I get out of the car. "Love you," I tell Cadence.

"Love you more."

———

Ms. Mason is waiting at the circulation desk and hurries to the door when I walk up to it.

She unlocks it for me and welcomes me inside. She looks pretty frazzled and like she didn't get much sleep last night, which I would understand if her son came home burned like that and was still at the hospital.

"Ms. Mason, are you okay?"

"Yes, yes, yes," she says somewhat distractedly. "I understand you helped my son last night? Cole?"

"There was an accident at the fire." I leave it at that. I'm not sure if she knows that he was trying to jump over a rather substantial bonfire and I figure that's best left to him to tell her.

"Thank you," she tells me.

"How is he?"

"He's... He's fine." I hear a mixture of relief and worry in her words. "It doesn't look like there'll be any permanent scarring. Hopefully at least."

"Well, that's good," I say. "I was worried about him."

"If you hadn't helped him I don't know what might've happened." She shakes her head. "I can't even bear to think about it." She studies the time. "Listen, I know this is unusual and it's your first week here at work, but I do need to check on him so I may be in and out today. Will you be able to take care of things here if I need to leave you alone? There really isn't anyone else I can call."

The library is pretty small and I can't imagine their budget would allow for a ton of extra workers, and it probably would've been especially hard to find someone anyway, on such short notice.

"I'll be fine," I assure her. "No worries."

"Okay," she says. "You're... Wait how old are you? You're seventeen, right?"

"Yes."

"Okay. As long as you're older than sixteen, we should be fine—but I don't want to ask you to do it if it's not something you're comfortable with."

"I am."

"Well, I should probably go then. I don't know if you heard, but Cole's still at the hospital. I told him I'd swing by after you got here to see how he's doing."

"Don't worry about the library. I'll take care of things. I promise." Then, I think of how Cole might be a jerk, but that doesn't mean he deserves what happened to him. "Tell him I'm glad he's okay."

"I will. I was going to grab some books to get them ready for you to read at Story Hour at eleven, but I didn't have a chance to do it. There should be a bunch of Dr. Seuss books over on the shelf."

"Oh," I say. "Sure. Okay. It's all good. I'll find something."

"Thanks." Her voice is rushed, and I sense that she's already thinking about being back at the hospital. "Alright." She hands me some keys, shows me which ones open what, then hustles out the door.

I spend some time perusing the books in the children's area looking for something for Story Hour, but I can't really find anything that looks appropriate for kids, or that has enough pictures and is also worth reading.

And then it's ten and I haven't found anything yet.

I glance at the front door. There are three people lined up, waiting outside.

I unlock it and officially begin my third day on the job, telling myself Story Hour will work out, that I'll have a chance in a few minutes to find what I need.

32

DESPITE MY BEST INTENTIONS,
however, things are busy at the circulation desk and I don't get the
opportunity to slip away to find an appropriate book to read after all.

Being the only one working makes it a little tricky as I man the
circulation desk, get people logged into the public-use computers,
and recommend books to parents showing up for Story Hour. I had
no idea Saturday morning would be so hectic.

———

Across from the library, there's a building with a giant mural
of a Bigfoot in The Valley Beautiful. When through-hikers on the
Appalachian Trail come to town, they often swing by to get their
picture taken with it. And now, at quarter to eleven, through the
window, I see two people park bikes beside the mural. I recognize the
bicycles from one of the hostels just off the AT where they loan bikes
to hikers so they can ride down and visit Erwin.

After the two hikers have taken their Bigfoot selfies, they cross the
street and enter the library: a young man and a woman who both look
like they might be in college. As they approach the circulation desk, I
notice that they smell like they've been on the trail for quite some time.

The guy, whose blond dreadlocks hang down past his shoulders,
speaks first before I even get a chance to ask if there's anything I can
do for them. "Is it true, what they say?" He has a gleam in his eye.
"About the Bigfoots?"

Oh, boy, I think. *Here we go.*

"What have you heard?" I ask him.

"That there's a huge cave inside of Big Bald Mountain, and that's where the Bigfoots live and they come out at night, and there are people there on the North Carolina side who have their cantaloupes and melons stolen all the time and that proves there are Bigfoots there because they like melons."

There is so much wrong with your logic there, buddy, you do know that, don't you? I think, but I keep that to myself.

"That wouldn't surprise me," I say, not clarifying if I'm talking about the fact that people tell that story, or that the missing melons proves the presence of Bigfoots in the area. "There are a lot of black bears in these mountains. There was a nation-wide study recently that found that the counties where there are the biggest concentrations of black bears per acre also have the highest number of Bigfoot sightings."

He takes that in with a nod. "Hmm... That's because Bigfoots eat black bears," he concludes, exhibiting that razor-sharp logical thinking of his again.

Yikes.

"Along with their melons?" I say.

"Yes."

Ooookay.

Now it's his partner's turn. "We heard the story of Mary the elephant," she says. "Is that for real?"

I hold back a sigh. I'm not exactly thrilled to retell the story.

Whatever actually happened with Mary the elephant and Red Eldridge in 1916, it was quite dramatic. From what people say, he was riding her in front of the crowd at the circus and she apparently either threw him off from her with her trunk and then smashed his head, or lifted him with her trunk, slammed him into a pole, trampled him and then threw his body repeatedly onto the ground. Either way, it was shocking to the crowd as people watched the death occur right in front of their eyes.

According to the newspaper reports, a man there shot Mary five times to try to kill her, but that didn't do the trick. Towns in the area announced they were going to ban the circus with the killer elephant in it, so the owner of the circus agreed to kill her and, since the bullets hadn't been very effective, they decided to hang her.

Yeah, this happened.

Red died in Kingsport, about thirty-five miles away, but the authorities needed a crane large enough to lift an elephant, and the closest one was here in Erwin, at one of the railroad yards.

So, they brought Mary to town and there, with two thousand people watching, they wrapped a chain around her neck and lifted her on this huge derrick in the railyard, but the first time they tried it, the chain broke and she fell and broke her hip. People were horrified, kids screaming in terror and running away. Your basic, only slightly controlled PETA's-worst-nightmare chaos.

So, they got a new chain and tried again and this time when they hung Mary, she finally died.

You can't make this stuff up.

Even to this day, there are still portraits and paintings all throughout the town of an elephant hanging from a railroad crane. It's crazy.

I summarize the story to the hikers and then add, "But, on a happier note, people around here donate to a bunch of different wildlife funds that help with elephant preservation."

They look at each other, then the woman says to me, "And the Expulsion?" She eyes me critically as if it were my fault. "We heard about that too."

I check the time.

Eight minutes to eleven.

It's an important story. I don't want to rush it, but I also have Story Hour coming up.

In 1918, a Black man named Tom Devert was found beside a fifteen-year-old White girl who was dead. It's not really clear what happened, but a vigilante group of White townspeople assumed he had raped and murdered her and they killed him and there was so much prejudice in the area at the time that, at first, the men were planning to burn down the homes of all the Black people in the county, just burn everyone out. But a guy stepped up at the last minute and convinced them to just expel all the Blacks instead. Still horrible, of course, but not as bad as mass murder.

So, by nightfall, nearly all the Black families had left the county.

You can't really tell the story of Erwin without those two tragic stories: The story of Mary the Elephant in 1916 and the story of the Expulsion of the Blacks in 1918.

The woman hiker shakes her head and scoffs. "It's nuts how, after more than a hundred years, this place is known mostly for its cruelty, racism, and injustice. Your town sucks. That's terrible."

Okay, and now is when I just might get in trouble.

"Maybe it's not all that terrible," I say.

"How's that?"

"Every town everywhere has dark chapters. It's just that here we don't hide them. History teachers always say that the point of studying history is so we don't make the same mistakes as the people made in the past—right? Well, if that's true, then remembering those stories isn't a bad thing, it's a *good* one—the best one, actually, since it helps us learn to never let anything like that happen again."

They look at me stiffly, obviously unconvinced, as if they want me to feel guilty for someone else's actions rather than being inspired to do the right thing because of them instead. And there's about as much logic to that as the guy's Bigfoot conclusions.

I'm about to point this out to them when they decide to take off, shaking their heads as they do.

By that time, it's just three minutes to eleven and I still have no idea what book to read to the kids.

People have gathered in the children's area: eight kids who look like they're maybe from three years old to about nine, plus a bunch of parents. The kids are sitting on the rug and the adults have pulled up chairs facing a rocking chair in the corner that I guess I'm supposed to sit in when I read to them.

Feeling doubly stressed now by having to read in front of people and also not knowing what to read, I grab a pile of children's books.

Yesterday, Ms. Amanda had said that Dr. Seuss was always popular, but someone must have been on a Dr. Seuss kick because most of them are gone, checked out. All except for *The Lorax*,

I'm hurriedly paging through it when I realize it's missing a bunch of pages in the middle.

Perfect.

That's when I look up and see Jack enter the library, glance around for a moment, and then head my way.

Oh, great. He was going to see me crash and burn in front of these people.

It's now eleven and I have chosen exactly zero books.

"Hey," he says.

"Hey."

He eyes the imposing pile of children's books beside me. "How many days long is Story Hour, again?"

"Ha. I'm not sure what to read. You know of any good books for kids? Maybe a version of Jack and Beanstalk that you could read?"

"Nope." He shakes his head. "Not my specialty. So, tell them a story instead. You're a storyteller, anyway, right?"

"Most of the ones I know are too scary for little kids."

"I have faith in you, Sahara-zade."

I'm not sure how to reply to that. I don't know if anyone has ever said that to me before.

Jack smiles at me, pats my shoulder that's not sore, and then finds a seat on the floor with the kids. One of the moms looks at her watch and says, "Is this going to take long? I need to get some things from the store before lunch."

"Oh," I say. "No, it won't take long."

I scribble out a sign saying that I'll be back in a few minutes and prop it up on one of the book holders on the circulation desk.

And then, I decide to do what Jack suggested and tell a story. Why not? He's right. I'm a storyteller, after all. After a quick deliberation, the one I land on is a story I've never actually told anyone before, but one that I made up last winter and have only jotted a bunch of ideas down for in my journal.

The story of Dazia and the Princess.

I take a seat on the rocking chair, clear my throat, and begin.

33

ONCE UPON A TIME, IN A FARAWAY

land near a shimmering, distant sea, there lived an orphan girl named Dazia who longed to be like the princess of the land, for Princess Alamore rode her horse more skillfully, shot the bow and arrow more accurately, and danced more gracefully than anyone else in the kingdom. And, she was also quite beautiful.

In fact, all the other girls wanted to be like Princess Alamore. They wished they could ride like her and shoot like her and dance as she did. And of course, all of them wished they were as beautiful as the princess.

So they watched from a distance and made notes on how she sat upon her horse and held the reins and moved with the horse's movements. And they tried to imitate her, but when they did, they fell off the horse and into the mud. Yuck.

Then they used the same kind of bow and arrow as Princess Alamore. But when they tried to shoot like her, they missed the target and hit someone right back there, in the bottom! Ouch!

And when they danced, they pretended to be Princess Alamore, but stepped on the toes of their partners so much that the young men had to wrap feather pillows around their feet and tie them there with string just so they wouldn't leave the dance floor all black and blue and with bruised toesies.

Because no one wants bruised toesies.

So, one day, Dazia said, "I want to be just like Princess Alamore!" But her friends laughed at her. "You'll never be like the princess," they said. "She's beautiful and graceful and you're ugly and clumsy!"

Their words made Dazia sad but determined. So one day, as Princess Alamore was riding through her orchard, Dazia went out to meet her. She bowed low and said, "Your majesty, I would like to learn to ride like you, but I don't know how and there's no one to teach me."

"Oh, Dazia! You don't know how long I've been waiting for one of the girls in the kingdom to ask me that!"

"You know my name?"

"Of course. I know the names of all the children in the kingdom. Here, climb up and let me teach you what I know."

And so, Princess Alamore taught Dazia how to ride straight and true and balanced upon the horse's back by using her legs and not the reins for balance. And she taught her how to shoot and to look past the arrow to the target and let the bowstring glide off her fingers instead of simply letting go of it. And she showed her how to disappear into the music when she danced, by letting the music disappear into her.

But the more time Dazia spent with the princess, the more the other girls were cruel to her. "You think you're better than everyone else now, just because you're spending all your time with the princess!" they said.

"No, it's not like that," Dazia said to them. "She would spend time with you too, if only you'd let her!"

But the other girls just kept saying mean things as they walked away, leaving Dazia alone.

Later that day, Princess Alamore came up to her. "I'm going to visit my father at the other end of the kingdom," she said. "While I'm gone I want you to remember everything I taught you."

"I will," Dazia told her. "I promise."

Then Princess Alamore left. And for a while Dazia did just as she'd promised: She remembered to ride and shoot and dance just like Princess Alamore. But then, in time, when the princess was slow in returning, Dazia began to go back to her old ways and her old friends once again.

And when she rode, she began to fall off the horses again, down into the mud. Yuck!

And she began to miss the target and hit people once again back there, in the bottom. Ouch!

And she began to step on the toes of her dance partners just like her old friends did while they danced. Out came the string and big, puffy pillows.

Then, one day, a nearby ruler named Lord Oscuro heard that Princess Alamore had left to visit her father, the king. *Aha!* he thought, *this is my chance! I'll ride in with a hundred of my best swordsmen now that she's gone and take over her part of the kingdom!*

So, he gathered one hundred of his strongest swordsmen and one hundred of his fastest steeds and rode straight toward Princess Alamore's region of the kingdom. When Dazia heard he was coming, she wished that Princess Alamore was there, but then realized she could use what the princess had taught her to help rescue the other people in the land.

Dazia told herself that she needed to be brave, just like the princess would have been.

So, Dazia ran out to the field with her bow and arrow as Lord Oscuro approached. And she followed the strides of his horse and let the arrow fly straight and true, not at him, but at the horse's reins. The arrow cut the reins and Lord Oscuro said, "Uh-oh!" and fell off the horse face-first into the mud. Yuck!

He leapt to his feet and drew his sword. "I'll run you through!"

"Oh, no you won't!" said Dazia, gracefully dancing out of the way as Lord Oscuro lunged at her and missed and landed once again in the mud. Some of it even went up his nose. Ew!

Dazia climbed onto his horse.

"You'll never be able to ride that horse!" yelled the muddy Lord Oscuro.

"Oh, yes, I will!" Dazia said, and she remembered all that the princess had taught her about riding without holding onto the reins. She rode to the far side of the kingdom and told Princess Alamore and her father, the king, about Lord Oscuro. The king brought his knights and captured Lord Oscuro and all of his swordsmen and threw them into the darkest part of his dungeon. Then, Princess Alamore went to talk to Dazia.

"While I was gone, did you remember what I told you?"

"At first I did," Dazia said. Then she shook her head sadly. "But then I forgot and went back to doing things the old way. I'm so sorry." Dazia thought for sure the princess would be angry at her and maybe not want to spend any time with her anymore.

But Princess Alamore didn't yell or scold or accuse. "I'm just glad you remembered what you needed when the time came," she said. "And I wanted to tell you, my father has invited you to live with us at the palace. He wants to adopt you, Dazia. He wants you to be his very own daughter."

"But I don't deserve it, I—"

"Of course you don't deserve it," said Princess Alamore rather sternly. "He's a king! No one deserves it. But he's *chosen* you, Dazia. He loves you and I do too and we want you to join our family. Do you understand?"

Dazia nodded.

"Do you accept his invitation?"

There were tears in Dazia's eyes. "Oh, yes! Oh most certainly, yes!"

And so, Dazia became a child of the king. She moved into the palace and spent all of her time with Princess Alamore. And as she did, she became more and more like the princess.

So much so, that when princes would visit from faraway lands, some would ask to dance with Princess Alamore, and some would ask to dance with her sister, Dazia. For they'd become so much alike, that it was hard to tell the two of them apart.

And whenever Dazia got the chance, she would teach other girls all that she had learned from the princess, and those who listened and actually put into practice what Dazia taught, lived happily, and pillowlessly, ever after.

The end.

34

I FINISH THE STORY AND TAKE A

moment to remind myself that I'm not in that faraway kingdom near the sea. I let the images of the scheming Lord Oscuro and the lovely Princess Alamore and the plucky Dazia fade as I try to leave the land of pretend, which seems so at home in that strange, inscrutable world nestled somewhere in between my ears.

"What else happens after that?" one of the girls asks. "Does a dragon come?"

"Actually," I say. "Yes. It does. A big one."

"And unicorns?"

"How did you know?"

Now that I'm in the zone, I start making up more adventures about Dazia riding a unicorn to battle a fearsome dragon with a valiant prince by her side who, at least in my imagination, looks ridiculously like Jack, and how she solves a tricky riddle to find out the true name of a mischievous troll and save the kingdom from an evil and cruel queen who wants to rule all the lands in that realm.

As I tell Dazia's story, Lore, the library cat, finds a place to lounge in the sunshine that's easing through the window to my left and yawns at me, but no one else does. It's been nearly half an hour and no one, not even the youngest kids, appear restless or bored.

When I finish, I ask if there are any other questions.

"So, what was it?" one of the dads asks.

"What was what?" I ask.

"The riddle. The tricky riddle that she solved. What was the riddle?"

Oh. Of course he had to ask me that.

I have no earthly idea.

I scour my brain to come up with a riddle to tell him, but can only think of riddles I've heard before, and nothing original comes to mind now, when I'm suddenly put on the spot.

That's when Jack speaks up. "I remember when you told me this story before, the riddle you said. It was a good one." For a moment it seems like he's setting me up for failure, but he goes on right away, "When you said, 'I think this riddle should be fun: Halfway made is not yet begun. The larger it is, the less there will be. If you know the answer, come talk to me.'"

"Oh," I say, figuring that it's my role at the moment to play along. "Yes. That's right."

I'm desperately trying to solve Jack's riddle and I think I have it, when the curious dad says, "So, what is it? What's the answer?"

"It's—" I begin, and Jack, who must have anticipated that I might not guess it correctly, says, "A hole. If you've made half of one, you haven't yet begun making it because you can't have half a hole. And the larger it is, the less of something you'll have because, well, you've made a hole after all."

Yep. A hole. That's what I was thinking.

The man grunts softly in acknowledgment.

I gaze out at the children and their parents and ask if there are any other questions about the story.

A little towheaded boy, who looks maybe six years old, raises his hand.

"Yes?" I say.

"Did Lord Oscuro really get mud up his nose?"

"He did," I say. "Lots of icky, gooey, oozy, *slimy* mud. Plus all over his face and even in his ears—which I forgot to mention earlier."

The girls wrinkle up their noses. "Ew." But the boy who asked the question smiles like he thinks it's cool.

However, his mother doesn't look too pleased at me for elaborating on the details of the oozy mud, but I flash her an innocent smile and then say to the group, "The library has lots of wonderful fairy tales that you can read to your kids. Check the 398s. There are also books of riddles here as well."

"Huh," the woman mutters quietly to the man sitting next to her—but not so quietly that I can't hear her. "I wish she would've read a book instead. Then we could've checked it out."

I'm trying to figure out if I should apologize when she collects her two children and bustles them off toward the picture books. Within a few minutes, all the other families have meandered away as well to look for books or pet Lore, leaving me alone in the rocking chair beneath the HAPPY HALLOWEEN bulletin board and mutant pumpkins that I put up last night.

Well, not exactly alone, because Jack is still here. "You really are a good storyteller, Zod," he tells me with a nod of approval. "Princess Alamore and Dazia. I like it. Not too scary. Just right for the kiddos. I knew you could do it."

"Thanks. I... I appreciate that. And that was kind of you to come to my rescue with that riddle. Did you make it up?"

He shrugs. "I like riddles. I've made up a bunch of them."

"Really? Tell me another one."

He barely has to think about it before responding. "What no longer exists, and yet you use to plan for a trip to where you will never arrive?"

I chew on it for a moment and then say, "As far as the trip we're planning for to where we'll never arrive, I'd say that's something we all want to face, but no one wants to face it alone. Am I right?"

"Maybe..." A smirk. "So, the answer is...?"

"The past. And the trip is to the future."

"Impressive."

As I let his compliment sink in, I say, "I need to get back to the circulation desk. Walk with me."

As we make our way through the library, Jack says in a library whisper, "Hey, I never thanked you for last night."

"Thanked me?" I keep my voice low as well. "For what?"

"When I was at the top of Devil's Falls," he says, "you came to my rescue."

"I was scared you'd go over. Besides, I couldn't let you listen to the devil telling you to jump."

"I shouldn't have gone out there like that," he acknowledges, then adds, "Honestly, I had something else on my mind."

"Oh, yeah? What's that?"

A pause. And this time his voice is even softer. "Stargazing with someone."

"Really."

"Yeah. Kind of an awesome someone, actually."

My heart flutters a little. "What else is this someone like, besides being kind of awesome?"

"Clever and curious and brave. And good at making up asterisms and fairy tales."

Oh, man.

"This someone sounds fascinating," I say.

"Oh, she is."

We arrive at the circulation desk and I take my place behind it. No one is waiting to check anything out, so I go on and ask him a question that's been on my mind ever since he walked in earlier, but I haven't had the chance to discuss with him. I lean toward him and say quietly, "Jack, did you send me a text last night?"

"A text?" He looks confused. "I've been meaning to, but... Why do you ask?"

"Someone sent me a text that says... well..."

I pull out my phone and show him the "Be bold, be bold," message.

"It's that line from your story about Mr. Fox." His voice is serious and hushed. "So it must have been someone at the party." His eyes narrow a little and I wonder if it's a sign that he's feeling protective of me. "You don't know who sent it?"

I shake my head. "It's from an unknown number and I couldn't figure out how to backtrace it to find out who's behind it."

"Listen, I'm going to give you my number and I want you to let me know if this person texts you again." He pulls out his phone and sends me a skateboarder emoji that I add to my contacts under the name Jack. "Are we still good to hang out tonight?" he asks.

"Yeah... About that... What are you doing today? As in, right now?"

A shrug. "Nothing. Why?"

"I'm here alone. Ms. Mason, the librarian, is at the hospital with Cole. She's his mom."

"Wait—your boss is Cole's mom?"

"Yes. That's why she's not in today. I'm not sure when she'll be back. From what she told me, it's sort of up in the air. Anyway, I was wondering if—and if you can't do it, I totally understand—but I was wondering if you might be able to stay here and give me a hand, and just... if everyone leaves then I wouldn't be in here all alone."

I don't mention the possibility of the library being haunted, which is definitely in the back of my mind.

"Yeah, sure," Jack says. "I can stay. What did you want me to give you a hand with?"

"Actually, if you don't mind doing some research for me, that'd be great."

"Research about what?"

"The room where they kept the dead."

35

HE LOOKS AT ME CURIOUSLY.

"What are you talking about?"

I fill him in about the basement, and the room for the coffins, and what Grams told me about them. I'm not sure how much I should explain about the weird stuff that's been happening to me, and decide that it might be better if I don't go into all of that at the moment so Jack won't think I'm going crazy, so I hold back from mentioning changelings and elementals.

He lets all that I've told him sink in.

"There's a box of old historical papers in the office," I explain. "I was wondering if you could look through them to see if there's anything about the history of the library that might seem... well... off."

"Off? In what way?"

"Anything odd about the basement in particular. Really anything unusual or tragic that might've happened down there—I don't know... A suicide? A murder?"

"Seriously?"

"Seriously seriously."

In the cluttery, jumbly, paper-strewn library office, I direct him to the closet. He's tall enough to reach to the back and retrieve the box of papers off the top shelf without having to stand on a chair.

We set him up at an empty table in the main part of the library and as he pulls up a chair, he eyes the imposing stack of papers, newspaper clippings, and old railroad yard ledgers. "So... Anything odd or off, huh?"

"Yep."

"And you're sure this is okay? To look through this box?"

"Ms. Mason told me I could go through it today if there was time." I pat his arm congenially. "You're just taking my place as the lead goer-througher."

I invite him to join me and Cadence for lunch at twelve-thirty, and when he agrees to stay, I make arrangements with her to bring an extra sub for him. I'm hoping Ms. Mason will be back by then, but if not, I figure we can always postpone lunch until she is.

———

Back at the circulation desk, I help a bunch of parents who've decided to go ahead and check out some fairy tale books and collections of riddles and while I'm helping them, I see that the boy with the mud question has a whole stack of picture books to check out.

Nice. Good job, little man.

Working at the desk, answering people's questions, and shelving books keeps me busy until about twelve-fifteen when Ms. Mason bustles through the front door and apologizes for not being around more during the morning.

"Everything going okay?" she asks.

"Yes." I tell her. "How's Cole?"

"He'll *hopefully* be able to come home this afternoon. Fingers crossed. The doctors said they'll know by about three-thirty or four, so as soon as we close up here I'll be heading over there to pick him up."

"Oh, that's good."

She studies the neatly arranged counter where I've been working hard to keep things organized and under control. "Did you get a break *at all* yet?"

"No, but my friend is bringing some lunch over in a few minutes. Could I take my break then?"

"Of course! Oh, by the way, what books did you end up reading at Story Hour?"

I hesitate for a moment. "I didn't actually read anything. I told them a story I made up instead."

"Oh, really?" She looks at me inquiringly. "What was it about?"

"A resourceful girl who helps save the kingdom from an evil lord who tries to conquer it. She goes on to battle a dragon with a gallant prince and outwit a troll and face off with a cruel queen, but in the end, good triumphs over evil."

"Sounds like quite a story."

I shrug. "I like telling stories. Grams—my grandma—she always told me stories growing up. I guess it stuck. I've been told I have an overactive imagination."

"Sure beats the alternative, doesn't it?"

"Yes." It was something I'd thought myself. "It does."

Her eyes gleam for a moment. "I'm guessing your story's climax required a valiant choice or a selfless act, because 'happily ever after' always comes at a cost," she says knowingly. "Right?"

I'm not sure what to say to that. I've never thought of story climaxes in quite those terms before, but I guess the observation makes sense coming from a librarian. "Yes," I reply at last. "I guess it does."

I could maybe stand to improve the ending if I tell Dazia's story again. Maybe play up the selfless act idea.

"You know," Ms. Mason says. "That's something that's always bothered me about the Sleeping Beauty story: there's no selfless act or valiant choice. After a hundred years, the prince simply arrives, the brambles part before him, and he enters the castle grounds without any obstacles or setbacks. Then, he awakens the princess and they get to be together."

"A kiss will break the curse," I mutter without thinking and then realize that's what Lily told me last night.

"Yes," Ms. Mason says. "But it's all too easy, no courage needed, no virtue necessary, no sacrifice, and no cost."

"The way my Grams tells Sleeping Beauty, it's a bit more gruesome."

"How's that?"

"Over the years, dozens of princes try to hack their way through the hedge, but it surrounds them, impales them, and holds their bones captive as a warning to others to stay away. But then, eventually, there's a prince strong enough and brave enough to slash his way through the thicket and get to her."

"And his scars bear witness to his commitment," she says thoughtfully. "So, there is a cost, and there is a sacrifice."

"Yes. I guess there is."

"I like that version better than the original."

"And there's even another version of it that she's shared with me," I tell her, "where the prince faces a choice—if he kisses the princess, he'll take her place, freeing her from the curse, but falling under a curse himself: a century of sleep for a girl he hasn't even met."

"A truly selfless act."

"Yes... Oh," I say, getting back to the topic of Story Hour, "and don't worry, I encouraged everyone to read. I directed them to the 398s and a bunch of people checked out books." I add that last part as if that's the measure of a successful Story Hour—meeting a quota of checked-out books.

"Perfect! Thanks." She checks the time. "Zod, I need to fill out some grant applications in the office. Just let me know when your friend gets here and I'll take over the circulation desk and give you a break for lunch."

I figure I should probably tell her about the research Jack is doing in case she notices that the box is missing from the office closet, so I gesture toward him. "By the way, my friend is looking through those historical records for me. He helped Cole last night too. He wrapped his wet jacket around Cole's burned arm. His name is Tyler." I almost slip up and tell her that his name is Jack.

"Oh, that was him? I was wondering about that jacket. I'll be sure to get it back to him."

She goes over and thanks Jack and then retreats into the office until Cadence and Aiden show up about ten minutes later. I let Ms.

Mason know that I'm going to take my lunch break and she sets up shop at the circulation desk. My friends and I head outside and find seats on the soft grass in front of the Bigfoot mural to eat our jerk turkey, lettuce, and tomato subs and Cajun-seasoned curly fries.

And it is not a bad lunch.

Not bad at all.

———

As we eat, Cadence explains that her dad couldn't get Alfie started, so he'd had him towed to a shop in town and the mechanic friend of his was going to take a look at him and get an estimate for me.

"I really owe you guys," I say.

"It's *y'all*," she corrects me good-naturedly. "You're talking like you're from Wisconsin again."

"Ah, yes. Right. Oh, and by the way,"—I look at her and Aiden— "what do I owe, um... *y'all* for lunch?"

"I'll tell you what," Cadence says, "once you're a famous storyteller and you're making millions, you can buy me lunch. Until then, it's on me."

I know that Cadence's dad probably makes ten times what my dad used to make, but he's never acted like he's better than anyone else, and neither does she. I like that they aren't owned by the things that they own, like so many people seem to be.

As I flip some of my hair out of my face, I catch Aiden looking my direction for a fraction of a second longer than he needs to, and without wanting to read too much into it, I wonder what the lingering eye contact means, if anything.

Jack might have noticed too, because he's looking at me with a tiny smirk.

"You know what I wish?" Cadence says, and then goes on without waiting for anyone to answer. "I wish I was a supermodel."

"Wow," I say. "That came out of nowhere."

"I mean *think* about it," she says earnestly. "It's like the only job that you can stick the word 'super' in front of it and no one thinks you're bragging; they just admire you all the more. You say, 'I'm a supermodel,' everyone's impressed. But how weird would it be if someone said, 'I'm a superdoctor,' or 'I'm a superlawyer,' or 'Oh, hi there. I'm the superplumber here to unclog your toilet'."

Aiden chimes in, "He doesn't just know how to fix a toilet, but boy, does he know how to work the runway."

"Right," she acknowledges graciously. "Anyway, guidance counselors don't usually cover this at career day at high schools. 'Well, Joey, you can be an accountant one day or you can be a superaccountant.' 'I choose superaccountant!' And what's the difference between being a model and a supermodel?" She promptly answers her question before any of us can: "Nothing! There's no difference except the supermodel makes way more money. That's what's so amazing about it. So, I propose that we let people stick the word 'super' in front of their title. Can't hurt." Then she turns to me. "So you, my dear, are a superteller."

"Thanks."

She nods to Aiden. "Superswimmer."

"I appreciate that."

Next, she eyes Jack somewhat curiously. "What are you super at?"

"Riddles," I say on his behalf.

"You, Jack, are a superriddler."

"Thank you, Miss Supernamer... and future supermodel," he says.

We eat for a few minutes and I ask Jack if he found anything about the coffin room in the old documents, but he shakes his head. "I found accounts about how the library is supposedly haunted: ghostly figures appearing, doors opening and closing on their own, books falling off the shelves for no reason, and the smell of cigar smoke lingering in the air even though no one is there smoking—that sort of thing. But I didn't see anything about that room or a murder or suicide in the basement. I'm only about halfway through, though. There are a lot of papers in that box, so there still might be something there."

Since he doesn't know about what happened last night with Lily, I take some time to fill him in. I find out that Cadence hasn't told

Aiden about it either yet, so the two guys pepper us with a bunch of questions and that leads to me telling them what happened to me in the coffin room yesterday. When I'm done, Jack says, "So that's what you meant by 'odd.'"

"Odd is the official, scientific term for it."

"I see."

"About that," Cadence says, "like I told you earlier, I really want to see this [air quotes]—*haunted*—[air quotes] room."

"Hey." I smile. "I'm proud of you, Cade. You used your air quotes properly!"

"[air quotes]—*Whatever*—[air quotes]."

Well, that was short-lived.

"Anyway,' she says, "can you ask Ms. Mason if you can show us the basement after work?"

Though I'm not exactly thrilled about the idea, I do want to see the room again, and having the three of them with me sounds more appealing than peering into it all alone, so I agree.

We finish up our lunches, snap and then post a couple of Bigfoot selfies, and agree to meet up again at three.

Then, Jack and I return to the library while she and Aiden amble off to a coffee shop down the block that just happens to sell the best homemade M&M brownies in town. By far.

———

The rest of the afternoon goes relatively quickly. Ms. Mason and I take turns working the circulation desk, directing people to the books they're looking for, helping them get logged into the computers, and basically filling the time doing library staffish stuff. It's not bad, actually, and after a while I start to feel like I could get used to it. Not the worst part-time job in the world, not by a long shot.

When I return to the front desk one last time, Lore leaps onto the counter, stretches out in front of me and purrs needily, asking me in cat language to scratch his arched back, which I resist doing at first— not being a cat person and all—but I finally oblige him and give in, just because I'm a *compassionate* person, *not* because I'm a cat one.

I'm sure he'll wise up and tire of me soon enough.

Finally, after shelving three books about King Arthur's court that a man who introduces himself as the retired librarian has returned, I glance at the clock I see that it's already somehow five minutes to three.

When I ask her, Ms. Mason tells me that it's fine if we go downstairs to look around but to be careful on the steps with that overhead light not working. "I really do need to get that replaced," she adds concernedly.

"We'll be careful," I promise her.

"Just be back up here by three fifteen so I can close up shop and go see Cole."

"Yes, ma'am."

I'm supposed to call my mom at three-thirty, which should give me plenty of time to show my three friends around the basement, but it doesn't give me something to look forward to after we're done. It's been two months since I've spoken with her and I'm not thrilled about the prospect of hearing her complain to me about me, or berate me just for being alive.

Well, deal with that when the time comes.

For now, the basement awaits.

36

CADENCE AND AIDEN RETURN,

and when the four of us have gathered at the top of the stairs, Jack explains in a hushed and urgent tone that he found something in the box of old papers. "It was scrawled along the edge of one of the railroad ledgers, and if we're going to look in the coffin room, you should all know what happened in that room first."

"What is it?" I ask. "A murder? A suicide?"

"Not quite, but just as bad."

We all look at him quizzically as we try to figure out what that could possibly be.

"So," Jack says, "like Zod told me earlier, this building was originally a railroad station before it became a library and when the trains would stop here, if they were delivering any coffins, they used to unload them and store them overnight in this certain room in the basement because it was the coldest room in the building, to preserve the bodies, right? So, then, when they left in the morning, they'd load the coffins back onto the train once again."

"Okay," Cadence says softly. "But what was just as bad as a murder or suicide?"

"Well, one time... they forgot one."

"What?" Her jaw drops. "They left a coffin in the room?"

"Yeah. Maybe there was a shift change or something and people just never loaded it back on the train. The note doesn't say why." He produces a photocopy of the railroad ledger page from the library's copier, which surprises me: so old school. Why not just take a picture on your phone?

Whatever.

He goes on, "For whatever reason, the train left without a coffin and it stayed down there for another week before the next train that was carrying any coffins came by. And when the railroad workers carried one of those new ones down there, they found that previous coffin that was already there. So, they decided to open it up to see who was in it and—"

"Don't tell me," I whisper. "It was empty."

"Worse."

"What's worse than that?"

"There were scratch marks on the inside of the lid. And the man's fingers were bloody and torn open and full of wood splinters from trying to claw his way out. He was dead when they found him, but... he was still warm."

"Oh, no." Cadence whispers. "So, the guy was still alive when they left him down there the week before?"

"Yes."

"And now his body was warm?"

A nod. "He couldn't have been dead for long."

"Okay," she mutters. "That's troubling."

None of us say anything. We're all trying to let that sink in. A week without food or water, trapped and helpless and dying a coffin. She's right—that is troubling. Enough air must have seeped in through the cracks or slats in the wood to keep him alive.

Alive and suffering. And dying.

Slowly dying.

The thought brings me a chill.

Jack is eyeing me a little bit uneasily and finally, I ask him the question that has risen to the top of the many questions I have at the moment. "You said they wanted to check who was in it. Does it say whose coffin it was?"

"Yes." He hands me the photocopied sheet. "And this is where things get interesting."

"*This* is where they get interesting?" Aiden exclaims.

"Yeah." Jack places a gentle hand on my arm. "The guy's name, the man who died... His name was Conor O'Shaughnessy."

"What?" I can hardly believe that he's telling us. "That's my great-grandfather's name."

"I wondered about that when I saw the ledger."

"But it couldn't be the same person," I mumble, "the same Conor O'Shaughnessy—could it?"

Jack doesn't reply and I wonder if there's more he's not telling me.

I know my great granddad lived in the area, but no one ever told me this story before. If Grams knew about it, she would've certainly mentioned it when she told me about the coffin room.

It can't be the same man.

Still, I find myself gulping as I ask Jack what year this happened in.

He points at the year on the page, and I realize that I can't remember the exact date my great grandpa, whom I never actually met, died, but the year looks close. It might really be him. I'll need to check with Grams to find out what year her father-in-law died.

"Are you still good to go down there?" he asks.

The possible personal connection motivates me to view the room again. To see where he died.

"Yes." I steel myself. "Let's go have a look at that room."

37

THERE AREN'T NEARLY AS MANY
spiderwebs in the stairwell this time, although the spiders must have
been somewhat busy since yesterday because there are already a
number of stringy web threads that we manage to duck beneath on
our way down the dim staircase.

In the basement, as we walk through the stacks, all I can think
of is my great grandfather—if it actually *was* the same Conor
O'Shaughnessy—lying in that coffin, trying frantically and futilely
to scratch his way out, no doubt screaming for help, but being trapped
so far beneath the train station there underground that no one could
hear him. All the while, gulping in just enough air to survive and
probably dying of dehydration or slipping back into whatever type of
coma he must have been in when they first placed him in that coffin
and nailed down the lid.

That was terrifying enough.

But then dying in there all alone, in terror and despair... right
before being found. That troubled me even more.

If that room really is a thin place to another realm, I wonder if
his horrific and tragic death might be part of the reason why. And
maybe, if I'm related to him, that could be why a rift opened up when
I walked in there—because of the connection between us.

We corner the row of bookshelves and discover that the shelf
that's supposed to be blocking the corridor to the three rooms
has been knocked over and all of its books lie scattered across the
concrete floor of the basement.

The shelf's base is so wide that I can't believe it would've just fallen over on its own.

No. Something knocked it down.

An elemental? A changeling?

Or someone, maybe?

A thought: *Lily?*

Huh.

She had substance to her, not like some ethereal ghost. She climbed into the car and wore my scarf. I touched her skin—it wasn't air; it was real.

I guess it's possible that it was her, but I try to hold back from assuming too much in any direction.

Jack is staring at the tipped-over bookshelf. "It shouldn't be like this, should it?"

"No," I say. "Someone has been down here."

For a long moment, we all stare into the rock-walled corridor stretching before us until Aiden looks my way. "And you're saying that last time you felt trapped in a coffin in one of those rooms back there?"

"Yes. With spiders crawling all over me and vying with each other to be the first to squeeze down my throat before I managed to spit most of them out."

"Most of them?" Cadence grimaces uneasily.

"Yes, but not all. They tasted like chicken. Squiggly, juicy, wiggly little chickens."

"Lovely." She scrunches up her face in disgust. "Thanks for that little detail."

"Anytime."

"Well, let's go see the room," Aiden announces. "After all, we've come this far."

"The more I think about it, that might be a bad idea," Jack says.

"The world was built on bad ideas," Aiden replies cavalierly. I'm not sure if he's trying to be funny or brave. "Let's at least take a look."

"Whoever knocked that bookshelf down might still be here," Jack points out to him.

They go back and forth for a minute, until finally Jack gives in and says, "Listen, if we go in that corridor, we need to be careful. And I'm going first."

Aiden has no argument with that. He turns on his phone's flashlight app and Cadence follows suit. After Jack and I glance at each other, we do as well.

I have mixed feelings. On the one hand, I've been here before, I know what to expect, so, theoretically at least, I'm better prepared for what we might see than I was yesterday. So there's that.

But on the other hand, I've been here before... so I know what to expect: terror.

So there's that too.

But now, the decision has been made and one by one, we maneuver past the toppled-over shelf and enter the corridor.

Almost immediately, Aiden notes that the air is cooler.

"Yeah," I say. "And it's going to get even colder than this."

As cold as death, I think.

Cadence turns on her phone's video app and when Jack asks her about it, she says "You know how on those ghost hunter shows they always have cameras and recorders everywhere? If there's anything paranormal in here, I'm going to record it."

She's told me numerous times that she doesn't believe in ghosts, but I don't point that out at the moment. Maybe she's beginning to.

We move slowly through the corridor, passing the first room on the left—the small one—then the first room on the right—the one with the hammer and nails and coffin lid leaning against the wall—and finally, we come to the third room, the final one.

The place where Conor O'Shaughnessy died.

It's vacant. We're the only ones here.

I direct my phone's light into it, through the doorway.

Nothing looks unusual in there, just like it didn't when I first visited here yesterday.

Cadence stands beside me with her phone's camera aimed at the room. "Is something supposed to happen?"

"Not if we just stay here," I tell her. "But if we were to enter it, things would get..."

"Off," Jack says, finishing my sentence for me.

"Yes."

Everyone is quiet and I start to suspect that they maybe don't believe what I told them earlier about all the things that I experienced when I was in this oh-so-innocent-looking room yesterday.

"We should go back now," Jack declares with conviction. "We've seen what we came here to see."

"I want to find out what it's like in there," Aiden says.

"No," I tell him firmly. "And I don't care if the world *was* built on bad ideas, this is one bad idea you definitely do not want to be a part of yourself. Believe me."

"I'm not scared."

You should be, I think, but I don't want to sound scoldy, so I say instead, "We've come far enough. I'm telling you, when I went in there yesterday I almost didn't make it out again."

"But you were alone," he counters. "If we go in together we should be alright. There's strength in numbers right?"

I'm about to reply to that when Jack says to Aiden, "If you're going in there, you're not going alone. I'll go with you."

I stare at him in disbelief. "Jack—"

"I'm going too," Cadence informs us.

"What has gotten into y'all?" I say. "We shouldn't go in there. None of us should."

"It can't be that bad, can it?" Aiden says.

"Oh, it can be. Trust me. It is."

"But what could go wrong with all of us in there?"

I can't believe this. "Talk about famous last words."

"Let's hope not," he replies, to my annoyance.

I'm ready to argue more, but by the look on his face, I can see that there's no convincing him and he does have a point that it *might* make a difference if we are all in there since we should be able to help each other out if one person gets scared or gets in trouble of some sort.

Finally, I rub my head. "Alright, listen: If we go in, you need to promise me that we stick together. We look around and get out quickly. Do not go off on your own. Do we all agree? No more than a minute in there. I'm serious here."

They all nod in agreement.

"One minute, I'm not kidding. I'm setting a timer." I pull up the app.

"Alright." Aiden sounds way too excited about this and I can't help but wonder what's gotten into him. He doesn't seem to be acting like himself.

"Hang on," Cadence says. "Let me leave my phone out here to record if anything weird happens in the hallway while we're in there."

"Good idea," he tells her. "And I'll record whatever happens in there."

He messes with his phone's settings while she props her cell up on one of the rocks jutting out of the wall, positioning it carefully to capture footage of the entire corridor. Then we all face the room together.

"Strength in numbers," Cadence says encouragingly, looking at each of us in turn.

"I'll go first," Aiden announces.

And then, holding his phone in front of him to record whatever we might face in there, he takes a step into the room.

38

I SET MY TIMER FOR SIXTY
seconds, then I take Jack's hand and follow him into the room.
Cadence brings up the rear.

And nothing happens.

It's not like it was the first time I came in here yesterday when I
felt like I was passing into another realm and the air itself seemed to
be pressing actively against me, trying to keep me out.

This time, everything is dusty and cool, there's a touch of mildew
in the chilly air, and we're surrounded by a thick, muffling silence,
but I don't have any terrifying visions or living nightmares. No
ghostly apparitions appear.

No coffins. No spiders. No voices inviting me to stay.

"What now?" Aiden says to me.

"I don't know. The last time I came in here all these weird things
started happening to me."

"Do you think it's because you were alone?" Jack asks me.

He's still holding my hand.

Which I don't mind.

Just like I didn't mind last night when we shook hands.

Lots of not minding going on lately.

"I don't know," I tell him. "That's possible."

We walk to the center of the room.

Still nothing.

Time ticks away.

Forty-five seconds left.

Jack still has a gentle grip on my hand.

I look around, carefully studying the rocky walls. I don't see any lurking shadows fleeing from—or fighting against—the light. Just a plain room. I begin to wonder if my mind might have been playing tricks on me yesterday after all, if my imagination was simply running away with the moment.

No. You saw what you saw. You heard what you heard.

"My shoulder is still sore from when something grabbed me last time," I tell them as my way of reminding myself. "What happened to me is real."

Thirty seconds.

Jack lets go of my hand and takes two steps toward the corner.

And that's when things begin to go wrong.

A cold breath of air shivers past me and I feel goosebumps rise on my arms. I take a faltering step backward as the walls and ceiling begin to dematerialize before my eyes, and a moment later we're standing on a hillside overlooking a tangled forest beside a sweeping valley with a regal palace rising in the mists in the distance. The castle is situated on a cliff rising dramatically above a dark, expansive sea that stretches toward the far horizon.

The sun has just set and the stars are beginning to peek through the darkening sky above us.

One at a time, our phones blink off, leaving us without light just when we need it most, as night begins to shade in around us.

Perfect.

"Are you seeing what I'm seeing?" I say, my words half-gasped, my voice weak.

"I see it," Jack says. "The room is gone. Way gone."

Cadence and Aiden stand beside us saying nothing. In the faltering light, they look as bewildered and overwhelmed as I was the first time I entered this room.

I gaze up at the sprinkling of stars already visible high above us, and that's when I notice that they're off.

They shouldn't look like this.

The constellations that I'm so familiar with and the asterisms that Jack and I made up aren't there. Instead, the star formations that are appearing are all foreign to me. At first, I think of the fact that constellations would be far different on the other side of the world, in a different hemisphere, for instance. Admittedly, I'm not as familiar with those constellations, but of the traditionally recognized eighty-eight, none of the ones that I know of are visible above us.

But I don't think we're on the other side of the world.

Maybe a different world entirely, but not just another hemisphere of ours.

I'm filled with both a sense of curiosity and a growing sense of disquieting alarm. Usually, looking up at the night sky makes me feel like I belong somewhere—yes, that I'm small and insignificant, but also that I am *here*, on this planet at this time, and I can always look up there and find that I have a place in the universe.

But not now.

Not here.

On this hill, the night sky is not my friend and I feel lost in the universe.

I have no idea how much time has passed by now. But it's way beyond one minute.

"We need to get back," I tell the three of them.

"Agreed," Jack says. "But how?"

When we turn around to look for the doorway, there's no door here on the hillside, just a faint trail leaning toward a rugged, snow-capped mountain rising majestically in the night and scratching at the bottom of the sky.

"I've seen enough," Aiden says. "Seriously, how do we get out of here?"

"I have no idea," I say, but then I have a thought. "Maybe it's a hallucination. Maybe we're still in the room. The walls should be about ten or fifteen feet away from us, right?"

"Right." Jack nods. He walks off, maybe twenty feet or so, then goes twenty more. "No walls. No room."

As he returns to my side, Cadence says to me, "Is there something we're supposed to do or say to get back? What did you do yesterday?"

"I gagged on a bunch spiders, spit them out, screamed."

"Let's hope that's not what it takes." Jack is studying the valley.

Yeah. Let's hope.

"Everyone just stay calm." He pats the air softly but urgently in front of him. "Let's figure this out. What do we know? I mean for sure?"

"Somehow, we're on the other side of the rift," I tell them. "Grams would call this the Fairy World. I don't know how to leave it. I'm not even sure how we entered it."

"Well, do we know *anything* for sure?" he asks.

Cadence points toward a trail of six torches fighting off the night breeze as a cluster of people carrying them emerge from the grove of trees about a quarter mile away below us down the hill. "I know for sure we better hurry up and decide what to do." The torchbearers might not see us, but they are definitely moving in our direction. "Those people are coming this way."

Something howls in the not-so-distant distance. Growing up in northern Wisconsin, I've heard plenty of wolves howl, and this sounds *slightly* like that, but deeper and more menacing. If it is the howl of a wolf, it's not like any wolf I've ever heard.

Which makes me think of fairy tales, and how they're usually not tame little stories. They're not typically about dainty fairies flitting around the forest and rainbows gracing the sky and unicorns frolicking with carefree butterflies in tranquil mountain meadows. More often than not, they're about being abandoned in the dark woods and about hungry wolves lurking in the shadows and wicked witches fattening you up in their cages.

Not exactly the type of stories parents ought to be telling their little kids.

And not the type of stories you want to find yourself landing in the middle of.

However, that's how I feel: like we've been dropped into the center of a tale that is not going to have a happy ending.

"Do you have anything enchanted we can use?" Cadence asks me, and I'm not sure if she's being serious or not. "A mirror? A slipper? A key? A forest? It is a fairy world after all."

"Why would I have something that's enchanted?" I say, slightly exasperated. "And a forest? Really? How could I be carrying an enchanted forest around with me?"

"Well, if it's enchanted, it could fit in your pocket."

"Fair," I acknowledge. "But, no. I don't have any enchanted anythings with me, not at the moment."

Jack turns to me. "From what you've told me, everything that's been happening to you has been based on stories that you know or ones that you tell, right?"

"Yes. So far, at least. But it's always a little different, never quite what I expect."

"What story are we in now? If you know this one, it might help us figure out how it ends, what's going to happen next, or how to get out of here."

The howling gets closer and all I can think of is different tales of wolves and changelings and shapeshifters... And Lily's warning that "he"—whoever she was referring to—is after skin... That he's always after...

"Werewolves," I whisper.

"Oh. Let's not even go there," Cadence says as if declaring those words firmly will help anything.

One of the torch carriers shouts something that I can't quite hear and everyone in his group begins to hurry faster toward us, their flames trailing behind them in the air as they run through the night.

They're maybe a hundred yards away.

I search my pockets for a key. A mirror?... A forest?

But I've got nothing—nothing except my phone, that is, but that's not going to get us out of here.

I recall a fairy tale Grams told me once where a young heroine drops a hair pin and it turns into an impenetrable hedge to protect her and her friends from a regiment of soldiers trying to capture them, but I have no hair pin with me, nothing magical or blessed or enchanted.

I call to Cadence, "Do you have a hair pin? Or a hair tie or a claw clip?"

She produces a hair scrunchie. "Just this."

"Perfect. Can I use that?" I accept it from her and say, "Everyone, step back!"

They edge back a couple of steps, watching me curiously as I lift the scrunchie high above my head and then, as hard as I can, throw it to the ground where it lands softly and silently and undramatically on the grass.

Nothing enchanted appears.

Definitely no impenetrable hedge.

Not even a pricker bush.

Well, so much for that idea.

The howling is nearer than ever, but it doesn't seem to be directed at us. Rather, whatever creature that is, it's heading toward the group of people carrying the torches.

All at once, one of them screams, and then another, and another as the torches scatter crazily and chaotically in the night. Some drop. Some go out. The howling doesn't stop, but it changes, becoming wetter, juicier. And so do the sounds of the desperate garbled, burbling screams cutting through the night.

It's not real. None of this is real. It's just a story world.

"Zod, we need to go." Jack is eyeing the bedlam below us. "Not to rush you, but..."

I think of Lily's scream and the scarf and my dad's book.

And I think of poems I've written and stories I've told...

Of heroes and villains.

And of tales I've heard from Grams, searching for clues, a way out, a path forward.

How do the best stories always end? How did Ms. Mason put it? Always with "a valiant choice" or "a selfless act."

But what choice? What act?

The choice has to cost you something... You have to sacrifice something. The more it means to you, the more it costs you, and that's what you need...

I have nothing else with me, nothing except.

My ring.

The ring Dad gave me when I turned sixteen. The ring with my birthstone in it. It's sapphire. It's not enchanted, but it was given to me by someone who loved me. *Truly* loved me. It's precious to me, priceless.

I can't help but gulp as I take it off my finger.

"What are you doing?" Jack says.

"Whatever I have to."

Stepping away from the group to give it some space in case it actually does work—and praying that it does—I throw it onto the ground hoping a magic hedge will appear.

Nothing happens.

"He's coming!" Aiden shouts.

I look up to see one of the torchbearers, with a bow slung over his shoulder and a quiver of arrows, sprinting our way. When he's maybe a hundred feet away, a dark form appears, darting at him from behind, gaining on him. I can't make out what it is, but it's larger than he is and it's faster and he's never going to make it to us before it overtakes him.

"It's right behind you!" Cadence yells to him.

Sahara, you have to do something! You have to help him!

Without my ring, I have nothing left to sacrifice, nothing left to give.

Except.

Myself.

A valiant choice. A selfless act.

I wave my hands in the air and run away from the group over near where the ring landed. "Hey! Over here!" I take another three steps. "I'm here! You want to get someone, come get me!"

39

THE FORM, WHICH IS BEARING

down on the man with the torch, stops chasing him and pivots to face me.

I can't quite make out what it is: if it's a werewolf, an elemental, or something else entirely, but whatever it is, it races toward me, bounding through the darkness, not more than fifty feet away now.

Then thirty.

Twenty.

Ten.

It howls again, and launches itself into the air with vicious teeth flashing in the starlight, and as it passes over the ring, it begins one final howl but never finishes it as it wisps into a cloud of misty smoke that flows all around me, surrounding me.

And all at once, the night and the stars and the castle and the sea begin to recede. The coffin room starts to reappear and, when I turn around, I see the doorway leading back into the corridor. "There!" I yell to my friends.

But the ground beneath our feet is no longer hard-packed earth. Instead, it has become sand, shifting and loose, and we're all beginning to sink into it.

"Hurry!" Jack points urgently toward the door. "Let's go!"

As we fight our way forward through the sand, I keep an eye on the doorway, but just like last night, it seems to be getting farther away every second. However, this time it doesn't just seem to be receding, it almost seems like something's happening to the room itself.

"We're getting bigger," Cadence says uneasily.

"No," I say, "it's the room. We need to get out of here. Now!" There isn't time for a long explanation, so as I struggle forward through the deepening sand, I rush to summarize the climax of the story that has come to mind, all breathless and urgent: "There's an old Celtic story about a shrinking room in the fairy world. It gets so small that no one can get out. And then it gets even smaller, until the only thing that makes it back through to the other side is a gush of blood filled with splintered bones."

As the walls close in and the room shrinks, the sand crowds in deeper around us and Cadence trips and tumbles forward. As she's trying to scramble to her feet again, it must give Jack an idea because he shouts, "Everyone, get down. On your belly. Crawl like a soldier. You won't sink as much!"

It strikes me that he's right: *The more surface area you have on the sand, the less likely you'll be to sink.*

We all flop onto our stomachs and soldier-crawl, arm over arm, toward the doorway, which seems to get farther and farther away the closer we get to it.

You're not going to make it. You're not going to make it out, Sahara.

But I have to.

We all do.

We do.

We will.

All four of us race as quickly as we can as the ceiling descends, getting closer and closer to our backs.

Cadence is in the lead and is the first to make it through the doorway.

Aiden is right behind her.

From here, it looks like Jack and I are maybe fifteen feet away, but I doubt that there'll be time for both of us to make it through, based on how quickly the room is shrinking, I can't imagine there is.

Then, rather than crowd in next to me or edge in front of me, Jack rolls out of the way to make room for me to get through. "Go, Zod! Get out!"

I hesitate for a second before he shouts at me again to get moving, which I finally do, and I emerge into the hallway where Aiden and Cadence promptly help me to my feet.

The corridor is dim, lit only by the light from the basement that's managing to make it this far back under the earth.

As the room shrinks, so does the doorway's opening and now it's only two feet high.

Jack rolls back toward us, throws his hands through the shrinking opening, and Aiden grabs one of his wrists while I grab the other. It's clear that if we don't get Jack through, the rocky enclosure is going to hack both of those arms off and swallow his body and crush him or bury him alive in the sand.

Aiden and I tug with all our might, leaning back and yanking Jack into the hallway just as the doorway behind him closes up like a giant hungry mouth, chomping shut.

Where the opening had been only a moment earlier, now there's only a solid, rock-hewn wall facing us, with the sand and the werewolf and the foreign starlit sky and my sapphire ring sealed far, far, away.

40

"ARE YOU ALRIGHT?" I ASK JACK
breathlessly as he climbs to his feet, brushing off the sand covering his clothes.

"Yes." Then he looks from me to Aiden to Cadence. "Are y'all okay? Everyone okay?"

We all tell him that we're fine. He pats Aiden and me each on the shoulder, being careful to only touch my good shoulder. "Thank you for getting me out of there," he says to us.

"I'm the one who should thank *you*," I say. "For rolling to the side, for letting me go first."

He dismisses that as if it's no big deal. "All good."

A valiant choice.

A selfless act.

Maybe happily ever after was a possibility for us after all.

It's strange how Jack and I seem to both be saving each other lately, while also being saved ourselves, not just here, right now, but also last night at Devil's Falls.

Not a bad deal.

As we talk, the grains of sand that are covering us begin to drop away, disintegrating soundlessly in the air as they do. The doorway that is now a wall begins to open again until it's fully formed there before us once more.

Drops of darkness seem to fall from the ceiling in the room, like giant, slowly congealing drops of blood—but darkness does not drip. And it does not bleed.

Or at least it's not supposed to.

Jack positions himself in front of the doorway as if he's preparing to fight off anything that might come through from the other side.

But nothing does. The dripping stops and a moment later, the room looks as innocent and harmless as before.

Cadence is staring at it. "That was too [air quotes]—*close*—[air quotes] for comfort."

"Yeah," I say. "I'm with you there."

For a moment, I'm tempted to point out that I'd warned them about going in there, but it wouldn't serve any purpose. Anytime someone says, "I told you so," it's always for their own benefit, so they feel better, not for the benefit of others, so I hold back. Besides, I went in there too and frankly, I'm just glad we're all okay.

Our phones click on, and we're finally able to get some comforting light in the hallway.

I check my timer.

It's paused at fourteen seconds left.

It must have stalled out when the phones went dark when we entered into the fairy world.

Cadence retrieves her phone and I think of my mom and how I'm supposed to speak with her in a few minutes. I'm even less excited about it now that all of this has just happened to us since I know I'll be distracted during the call. Right now, I need time to process things, I don't need more stress piled onto me.

"What's on your video?" Jack asks Cadence. "Did your phone record anything?"

She taps her screen and we all watch as the video plays, but there's only about five seconds of footage between when we enter the room and when we rush back into the corridor.

Nothing weird appears in the hallway.

"Did it just stop recording?" I ask.

"I don't know." She checks the settings again, but nothing strange seems to be going on with her phone. She plays the video again. Same result. "But we were in there way more than a couple of seconds," she says, stating the obvious. "At least, what? Five or ten minutes?"

I think of the stars and how they were different than they should have been. "Check the time on your phone," I tell her.

She turns her screen to show us the time: 3:10

I compare my phone to hers and see that my phone shows the time as 3:16.

She looks at me curiously. "What's going on?"

Jack and Aiden show us their phones as well, and they match mine. I imagine they'll recalibrate eventually, but we must be too far underground for them to pick up a signal from any satellites or cell towers.

"It's like time was passing at a different rate in there," Aiden says. "So, what's the real time?"

"Cadence's," I say. "Hers is the only phone that never turned off. Listen, we need to be back upstairs by three fifteen so Ms. Mason can leave to go see Cole. Let's get the bookshelf back in front of the hallway. I'll explain what I'm thinking as we do."

We pass through the corridor and as Aiden and Jack tilt the shelf upright and muscle it into place in front of the passageway, I say, "So, if that is a different realm, whatever world it is, it would make sense that time passes at a different rate there."

"Why's that?" Aiden asks.

"The space-time continuum," Jack says. Then he turns to me. "Is that what you're thinking?"

"Yes."

Cadence is busy gathering and reshelving books. "Space-time? What are you talking about?" she says.

"I'm no expert." I join her in collecting books. "But I know a little about it from studying astronomy. Basically, time and space aren't actually different things, but part of the same fabric of reality. They're entwined together, so that when you travel through time, you also travel through space, and when you travel through space, you also travel through time. Anyway, it has to do with the way that gravity and speed affect time."

"Time isn't a constant," Jack adds. "That's the thing. It's relative. Einstein's theories."

"Right," I say. "The point is: if you go to another realm, another world, it would make sense that time would pass at a different rate for you there."

"Did you say gravity affects time?" Aiden sounds confused.

"Yes. The closer to the earth you are, the faster time passes for you."

"So your brain is actually younger than your pinky toes?" Cadence asks inquisitively.

"Um... Yes." I'd never thought of it quite way before, but she isn't wrong. "That is true."

"That's bizarre," Aiden exclaims.

Reality often is, I think.

We finish up with the bookshelf and check the video on Aiden's phone but find nothing there: As we passed into the fairy world, the screen just flickered off and then went dark.

I think of the howling and the screams we heard in that world and a chill shivers uncomfortably down my spine. I wonder if, in some way, real people really did die in that distant land. It takes me a moment to regroup from that unsettling thought.

I take one more look at the bookshelf hiding all of that away and say, "We need to get back upstairs before Ms. Mason starts to worry about us."

———

By the time we reach the top of the steps, the extra six minutes have disappeared from our phones and the clocks are back to normal, this-world, time. Apparently, they've received their cell signals and recalibrated.

Ms. Mason is just finishing up putting things away when we return. She welcomes us back upstairs. "Perfect timing," she says. Then she asks us how we liked the basement. "What'd you think? It's little creepy down there in places, isn't it?"

"Yes," Cadence says. "That's a good way to put it."

"Some people say it's haunted," Ms. Mason informs us helpfully.

"Do they now?" Cadence replies.

"Huh," Jack adds.

We all share a look.

A moment later, we're telling her that we hope all goes well with taking Cole home from the hospital. We ask her to wish him well. She says she will, and then she ushers us out of the library and locks up behind us.

Once we're outside, I tell my friends to hang on. "I need to take care of something. I won't be long."

I find a place behind the library near the railroad tracks where I can have some privacy, then open the Krazle app on my phone.

Time to talk to my mom.

41

I STARE AT KRAZLE'S FLASHING

icon notifying me that she's already in the video chat room, waiting for me.

All I have to do is tap "accept" to enter.

But I don't.

Instead, I pause, trying to figure out if I'm up to the task of talking to her after all.

You told her you would. You promised.

That might be true, but was I ready to do it now, after what just happened to us in the coffin room and beyond the rift?

Do it. Get it over with, then get back to your friends.

I take a deep breath and peer at the screen, doing my best to put on a believable smile, but I sense that it's only passably convincing.

I remind myself that I can keep this short.

I tap the icon.

And enter the room.

Mom's face comes up.

She looks surprisingly perky and put together. She's let her hair grow out and it's dyed red. Shoulder-length. The bags I remember under her eyes are gone. She's got a sensible amount of makeup on, just enough to accentuate her almond eyes.

"Hello?" I say, as if I don't recognize the person on the screen.

"I still don't understand why you won't just talk to me on the phone like any normal person would." Her words are rushed and impatient.

"Oh, so sorry to trouble you. And by the way, it's good to see you too, Mother."

A sigh. "I'm just saying, do we really need to do this video thing?"

"I don't talk to anyone on the phone anymore," I tell her bluntly. "If you want to conversate with me, I guess you're going to have to look at me." She doesn't know about Dad's voice message to me on the night he died—I've never told her about it and I don't have any plans to. "I have a lot going on," I say. I'm still troubled by the events in the coffin room—or, maybe I should say, the coffin world. "What is it you want?"

She peers at me as if she's trying to see what's behind me. "Where are you?"

"I'm outside the library. I have a new job here."

"Whatever happened to the food truck job?"

"Mom, what is it you want? Why are we talking here, today?"

"I just wanted to see how you're doing."

"I'm fine." I wait. "Is that it?"

"How's your grandmother?"

"Good," I say. "She's good. Everything's go—" I pause. I don't want to say 'good' again because that would sound just plain stupid. Three times in three sentences? Wow. What a vocabulary. "Everything's going really well," I say at last, which isn't much of an improvement.

A tiny sigh. "I know things weren't the best between us when you moved down there, that... Some things were said..."

"Really?" My voice is prickly, but I don't try to soften it at all. "That's what you're gonna go with: 'Some things were said'? Are you even being serious right now? You basically told me that you never wanted me in your life when I was a baby and that you still didn't."

I wonder if she's going to apologize or try to walk back what she said to me right before the arrangements were made for me to move here to Tennessee, but she doesn't.

"Can we put the past behind us for a minute?" she says.

"Just let bygones be bygones?"

"Yes."

"Oh. Okay. Sure..." I wave my hand with a magical flourish over my phone's screen. "There. All done. They're all gone! Wow, that was easy. Is there anything else you wanted to tell me, Dearest Mother? Anything else you'd like to chat about?"

"You don't have to be sarcastic. I'm doing my best here to build bridges."

I feel myself tense up even more. "How's grad school going for you? I imagine it's helpful not having a bunch of distractions like, for instance, your teenage daughter, around?"

She ignores that. "It's going well. I think this is a good break for both of us. A little time apart."

"Uh-huh."

"We can both use some space and then figure out next steps."

I wait, half-expecting her to list those steps, but when she doesn't elaborate, I say, "I have a question."

"Yes?"

"Do you know what year Dad's grandpa died? Grams' father-in-law?"

"What?" The confusion is evident on her face. "No. Not off the top of my head. Why are you asking me that?"

This is not the time to tell her about the coffin being left behind or about Conor O'Shaughnessy's distressing death.

"Just checking on something. I've been thinking about him lately," I tell her honestly. And then, I have nothing else to say to her, nothing more that I'm ready to discuss or bring up.

"Listen," I say. "I need to go." I tell her pointedly to enjoy her space and her break from being near me, then I say goodbye and after a brief silence, she says goodbye to me as well.

Neither of us say "I love you," maybe because we don't love each other, maybe because we just don't know how to say those words to each other anymore.

I hang up.

And I cry.

BEFORE

—

MARCH 27
FOUR DAYS AFTER DAD'S DEATH

The night of the funeral, after we got back to the house, I decided to do what Dad had told me to do in the voicemail he left me when he was dying.

He'd said to check the workbench.

I didn't know why he directed me to go there, and I'm not even sure why I didn't go down right away after we learned about his death, but I needed a few days to at least process things a little bit. However, after the funeral, I knew it was time.

The question had just become bigger and bigger: Why, in his last message to me would he have asked me to go to his workbench? What was he hoping for me to find there?

I didn't go into his woodworking shop very often. It was his space, kind of like my room was for me. When things would blow up between him and Mom, he would disappear downstairs and go at it with his hammer and nails and table saw.

Things hadn't been great between us for a few months.

I don't know if it was just a phase, or a stage, or what. I don't know if it was because Mom was drinking more and he was working more, but the stress was there. It was like this load of emotion pressing down on us all, all the time, and you basically know there are going to be fractures appearing, but you just keep pretending that things are okay. Dad was sleeping on the couch. I didn't ask them why.

Mom was spending more time in her bedroom alone, and more and more empty wine bottles started showing up in the kitchen recycling bin. I noticed them there in the afternoons when I got home from school.

I spent a lot of time at my friends' houses, but when I was at home, I pretty much stayed holed up in my room with my headphones on, doing my best to disappear into my own little world.

I would sketch in my journal and think of stories and write poems. I let homework slack and my grades began to slump. I mean, really badly. And none of my parents' encouragement or orders to start doing better and stop being distracted by my music and private story world was helping. Maybe it *was* making things worse. But it was a way to cope, I guess. And we all need those sometimes.

Dad was retreating more and more to his woodworking shop in the basement.

I'd hear the hammering and sawing and wonder what was going through his mind. Was he cooling off or heating up? Was it helping him escape or was it a way to let his anger out?

Whatever it was, eventually he would emerge with a birdhouse or a bookcase or, in one case, a stand-up desk that he ended up giving away to someone at his office when Mom said she didn't want it.

Some dads have a Man Cave; he had a workshop. Through it all, though, I hardly ever entered it. After all, it was his safe harbor, his place to regroup.

So, when we got home after burying him, I changed out of my church clothes, went downstairs, eased the workshop door open, and clicked on the light.

An overhead fluorescent bulb that needed to be replaced gave the room a slightly blueish, uncertain, jitter-flickery light.

As I walked in, I happened to kick up some of the sawdust on the floor, sending a miasma of it floating up around me, polluting the air and getting in my mouth, dusty and bone-dry on my tongue.

Dad was pretty particular about cleaning up and putting things in their place, and he would have certainly noticed the sawdust and the twitchy, quivering light, so he must've simply not gotten around to sweeping the floor or putting in a new bulb, and now he never would, not anymore. Maybe he'd been planning to replace it on the night he died. No way to know.

The air smelled of freshly cut pine—probably from one of the final projects he'd been working on in here.

An imposing table saw crouched in the middle of the workshop. A sturdy stack of two-by-fours waited in the corner for his next project. Half a dozen shelves on the right side of the room contained dozens of boxes of nails and bolts and screws and some sort of metal fasteners and joists that I didn't even have a name for.

I made my way around the table saw to the workbench, which was situated against the far wall, spanning the width of the room. The pegboard hanging above it held dozens of different-sized tools: a variety of screwdrivers, sockets, hammers, and pliers—but that wasn't really what caught my attention.

Instead, it was what lay next to the portable drill that was still plugged in charging: A leather journal. *My* journal. The reason behind everything.

My idea journal.

My hand trembled as I picked it up and flipped it open. Everything was still there, all of my sketches of dragons and sea monsters and elves and fairies and my snippets of poetry and my story ideas—as silly or outrageous or ridiculous as they might've been. No pages ripped out. Nothing damaged or torn or missing.

The realization of what I'd done overwhelmed me and I collapsed, actually crumpled down to the sawdust-covered floor. I leaned my back against the workbench and wrapped my arms around my knees and drew them in close to my chest and wept for the first time since he'd died.

I couldn't help it. I stopped holding back the tears because, before then, I'd still been trying to deal with my grief and my loss by burying my sadness beneath layers and layers of razory anger. But when I saw the journal, I realized what'd actually happened, how much he really did love me, and why it was all my fault that he was dead.

It was because of what I said to him before he left the house on the night he died four nights ago. The eight words that should never,

ever be said. I thought he had destroyed my journal and I yelled at him, "I hate you. I wish you were dead!"

Those were the last words I ever said to my dad before stomping out of the house, climbing into my car, and taking off into the night.

And I couldn't have been more wrong. I didn't hate him, and I didn't wish he was dead.

I didn't, I didn't, I didn't.

———

I think of that now, here behind the library.

I think of the workbench and the journal and the fact that I never told Mom about any of it, and how she'd hate me even worse if she knew what I'd told him.

Because there's no taking those words back. As much as you might want to—and you're going to want to. As much as you'll beg the universe to let you, you can't. They've burrowed their way into someone in a way that might very well never heal.

But I did say them—*yell* them—at my dad that night.

Is it even possible that Mom could ever love me, ever forgive me if she knew?

I hear my heart shrieking inside of me, *I'm sorry, Dad! I'm so sorry!*

I wish there was someone to tell that to, but he's gone and so is Mom, but in a different way.

And I can't tell Grams. It would devastate her.

The more I dwell on his death and my role in it, the more worked up I get.

I try to calm myself, but I can feel a tremor of regret slicing through me so deeply that I wonder if it'll ever go away.

How do you move on from losing one parent and finding out the other one never loved you at all?

It's like there's a hole in my heart and it's widening, ripping apart more and more, getting deeper every day.

A gash, I think. *It isn't just a hole in my heart. It's a gash.*

PART IV

PETALS AND THORNS

42

I GET RID OF MY TEARS AND

then look at myself in my phone's camera and try on a smile.

My makeup is a disaster.

I clean what I can of it off and try to gather myself so I can face my friends again.

As I'm closing up the Krazle app, a notification comes through for a new text.

From an unknown number.

Oh, no.

I hesitate for a moment as I debate what to do, but go ahead and tap the screen to read it.

And see the words, "Be bold, be bold, but not too bold."

Whoever is sending these is getting closer and closer to the final warning from the story of Mr. Fox about your blood running cold.

My blood running cold.

Not what I need to be thinking about right now.

I'm tempted to block the number, but then realize that the only way we'll ever find out who's behind this is to leave things as they are and hope we figure out a way to track down the sender.

———

I make my way around the library to where everyone is waiting for me on the grass near the Bigfoot mural where we had lunch earlier.

Jack looks at me closely and almost immediately notices that something is wrong. "You okay?"

I don't tell him anything about my talk with Mom or my thoughts about Dad or my recent tears, but just show him my phone's screen.

When he sees it, he tightens up and holds out his hand. "May I?"

Though I'm not sure what he's going to do, I hand him the phone. He types in a message and then gives it back to me.

He has left a warning to whoever sent the text, saying that my friend's dad is a cop and that if any more messages come through he'll be notified.

"Is that true?" I ask him. "Is your dad a cop?"

A nod. "A sheriff's deputy. And this person is harassing you. Those words could be considered a threat. If I need to, I'll have Dad look into it."

Honestly, I'm not sure what his dad would be able to do, but I appreciate his offer and I tell him so.

Everyone is looking at me then, as if they expect me to know what to do next.

Which I most definitely do not.

Cadence breaks the silence. "You mentioned that Grams told you about the coffin room," she says. "Would she know any more about it being a thin place? Should we ask her?"

As I consider what we do know and what we don't, I have an idea for our next step in our quest to get some answers and it doesn't have anything to do with Grams. "Not yet," I tell Cadence. "There's someone else we need to talk to first."

"Who's that?"

"The former librarian, Mr. Indigo."

They look at me curiously.

"Do you know him?" Jack asks.

"No," I admit, "but I do know he lives over on Academy Street, likes to read fantasy novels about King Arthur, and drives a forest green VW sedan."

He follows up with the obvious question. "How do you know all that if you don't know him?"

"He introduced himself to me when he returned three books this afternoon," I say. "When I checked them back in, I saw his address on the computer. And he drove off in a green VW sedan. Plus, yesterday, Ms. Mason said I would need to ask the former librarian about the hallway behind the bookshelf. Mr. Indigo might very likely know about the coffin room. He might even be the one who put the bookshelf in front of that corridor down there in the first place."

"Nice work, Sherlock," Aiden says, and I notice him giving me a warm smile that might be a little too warm.

No one else seems to notice and I start to feel a little uncomfortable, like maybe Aiden might be starting to like me in a way that he should not be liking me, not if he's with Cadence.

I don't want him to be impressed with me.

I want *Jack* to be impressed with me.

And now, as if on cue, Jack is the one who speaks up. "Zod's right. Let's talk to this Indigo guy first. We don't need to tell him anything about what happened to us, but we can at least see if he knows the story of Conor O'Shaughnessy and how he died."

We're all on the same page, so we check our phones to get Mr. Indigo's contact info. Although we can't find his phone number anywhere online, an address for a Mr. Merl Indigo on Academy Street does come up.

"It's only a couple blocks." Cadence taps the geolocation pin that's hovering on her phone's map. "It's a nice day. I say we walk instead of drive. Save the planet."

We agree, pocket our phones, and head along the tracks toward Academy Street. As we do, Aiden seems to linger near me rather than walk beside Cadence, like I would have expected him to do, so I find an excuse to catch up with her and let the two guys bring up the rear.

———

Cadence and I are quiet for a few moments, then she says, "Ever since we left Ms. Mason, I've been thinking about Cole and his burns and about doctors and how the way that they treat you doesn't always make much sense."

"What do you mean? In what way?"

"A couple years ago I went to this doctor with a broken arm—my left one. And he was like, 'I'm afraid it didn't break properly. I'm going to have to break it again to fix it'. And I'm thinking, *What is the proper way to break your arm?* I mean, no one ever teaches you how to do that."

"True enough. And I'm not sure I would want those lessons anyway."

"No kidding," she says. "So, then I just felt worse, like, 'Gosh, I'm sorry, Doc. Next time I'll be sure to reposition myself as I'm falling upside down off the trampoline to make sure I break my bones properly.'"

"Yeah, that's not something you're typically going to be thinking of on the way down."

"I know, right?" I can hear her really gearing up into rant mode now. "Plus, what kind of a treatment strategy is that? Think about it: You walk in with a slash in your arm and he says, 'I'm gonna have to re-slash that for you. You didn't cut very straight the first time.' 'Oh, sorry, Doc.' Or, 'That gunshot wound of yours—not very accurate at all. Let me go get my Glock. And I'll need to you stand over there in the corner near that bullseye target,' Or maybe you get burned, like Cole did, and the doctor is like, 'I'm afraid you didn't burn yourself very evenly there. I'm gonna have to re-burn you. Wait here while I get some kindling and lighter fluid.'"

Despite the humor in her riff on doctors, I hear worry layered in beneath her words. "You really have been concerned about Cole, haven't you?" I say.

"I feel bad for him, even though he was doing something stupid."

Honestly, I do too. I let her know that Ms. Mason told me earlier that it didn't look like Cole would have any permanent scars.

"I'm glad to hear that," Cadence tells me. "I dated him for a minute last year."

"Oh. I didn't know that," I say.

"It wasn't for long, but you know, we were close for a while."

"Sure."

We cross an intersection and when we reach the other side, we find ourselves pausing under the shade of a massive oak afflicted with knobby burls. Cadence looks at me curiously. "Do you think all of this is happening to you because of your great grandpa?"

"Maybe."

I take the opportunity to tell her about being grabbed by the shoulder in the coffin room and then tug the neckline of my shirt to the side to show her the branded hand mark that's still there.

She mutters something incomprehensible under her breath and then says, "Does it hurt?"

"That would be a yes."

I shimmy my shirt back into place and we start walking again. "The connection with my great grandpa does make some sense," I say. "If it really was him in that coffin."

"Maybe the rift opened up for you because you're so in love with stories. I mean, with your imagination and everything, you're sort of living in both realms already. It seems like you, of all people, would be the most likely to find a thin place to a fairy world—especially if that's a place that your family has a dark or, you know, tragic connection to."

Her observations are in line with what I was thinking earlier. "You might be on to something," I tell her.

"I wonder if some people are like beacons calling to other realms?" She turns to me, a bright slightly mischievous gleam in her eyes. "You, Zod, might very well be a superbeacon and you haven't even realized it yet."

"For a second there, I thought you said I might be a 'superbacon,'" I say.

"Now you're making me hungry."

I smile and, after all that's been happening, it feels good to share a light moment with her.

I'm quiet then, and we stroll for a few moments up Academy Street. My phone says it's a five-minute walk to Mr. Indigo's place from here.

We pause and wait for the guys. After they reach us, I slip over to Jack's side and I tell Cadence and Aiden, "We'll catch up with you two down the block."

Aiden looks like he might be about to reply to that when Cadence takes his hand. "C'mon, babe. There's something I wanna talk to you about."

Okay, maybe she *has* noticed how he's been looking at me.

Once I'm alone with Jack, he asks me if something's up.

"Actually, yes," I say. "There's something I wanted to talk to you about too."

43

"HANG ON A SEC," HE SAYS, AS WE
start on our way. "I have something I need to tell you, first."

"What's that?"

"Back there at the library, on the other side of the rift, when you called out to the werewolf—or whatever that was—to get it to chase you instead of the guy with the torch, I'd say that was either extremely stupid or incredibly brave. And I'm mostly in the bravery camp."

"It was all I could think to do," I say.

"And now your ring—it's gone."

"I'll get another one," I tell him, but even as I say the words, I find myself doubting that that'll happen. Even if I did get another ring, it wouldn't mean nearly as much since it wouldn't be from my dad. Honestly, that birthstone ring isn't something that could ever be replaced, no matter how much I might want it to be.

But at least we made it out of there safely, so it was worth losing the ring over that.

"So," Jack says, "I've been wondering: What were you thinking would happen when you threw that ring and the hair scrunchie onto the ground?"

"I was hoping something magical would appear, like an impenetrable hedge or an enchanted thicket that might have surrounded us and protected us."

"Because of a story you tell?"

"Because of one I've heard, one from Grams. Lots of times in fairy tales there are magical thickets and thistles and roses." Then, I add, "Incidentally—different subject entirely—but sorta sort of related: I've always liked that roses are all contradictions and mystery, whether they're in fairy tales or not."

"How's that?"

I consider how to explain it, then say, "They have thorns that try to stab you and a flower that wants to inspire you. Both pain and pleasure. A rose is a constellation of promises, of curses and blessings, both ready to pierce your skin and to heal your heart. It wouldn't be a rose if it weren't both."

"I never thought of a rose as a constellation of promises," he says, "or made up of contradictions and mystery. But I like that you have." Then, after a pause, he adds, "From now on, whenever I see a rose, I'm going to think of you."

"Why's that? Am I all contradictions and mystery too?"

"Yes, as a matter of fact, you are. I can't quite pin you down. You have thorns about you, there are wilds within you, but also, it's like you're a flower that's about to bloom. You're both dangerous and beautiful."

I can hardly believe that he said that I was beautiful. Even if he didn't mean it, I liked hearing it. "Which do you like more," I ask, being unabashedly flirty now, "the danger or the beauty?"

"I haven't decided yet." I wait, but he doesn't elaborate. Instead, he just shakes his head lightly—though I can't read exactly why— and finishes by saying, "You really are like no other girl I've ever met."

I feel a wash of acceptance and affirmation, and I have no idea what to say to him. At last, after abandoning a dozen idiotic replies that would've all fallen short of what I wanted him to know about how much his words mean to me, I decide to tell him what I'd been planning to say a few moments earlier when I asked Cadence and Aiden to go on ahead. "Jack, remember how last night you were telling me that sometimes it seems like billions of miles are separating us even though we might be physically close to other people?"

"Yes."

"And you know how I like astronomy?"

"Sure."

Okay, here we go...

"Well, did you know that in a black hole there's so much gravity that even light can't escape from it, and it just stays there, cycling around and around, maybe for forever?"

"Huh."

"Yep. So you have light, traveling the speed of light, torquing time—because time can't escape a black hole either, and the closer you get to the speed of light, the more time slows down. Right?"

"Relativity again?"

"Exactly. Time either slows, or maybe pauses, or even moves backward in a black hole. I don't think anyone knows what happens when you fold time in on itself, if it would cease to move forward or what. But on the outside of the black hole, for everything else around it, time is going on like it always does."

He's tracking with me, but also obviously curious because he says, "Okay... So, where are you going with all this?"

In truth, I'm not sure I want to tell him how I feel, or what's been going on inside me, but I want to tell someone, especially after the strained talk with my mom that sent me back down again into my own black hole: the gravity of my past, my regrets, cycling around and around, dragging me deeper and deeper into nothingness.

Yes, I want to tell someone.

But not just someone.

Him.

"Sometimes..." I think of Mom and of Dad and of being alone in a vast universe where I can't find my place, where I don't quite belong anywhere. "I feel like I'm trapped inside one and there's no way out."

There. I said it. Now, just to find out what he was going to say.

"You feel like you're trapped in a black hole?" Jack says.

And a flood of thoughts overwhelms me: *Yes, where all my dreams and all my most precious memories—all the stuff I want to hold onto the most—all of that has been ripped away and left behind. Yes, where all of my hopes are sucked down into darkness and I'm stalled out in time, trapped in an endless, meaningless loop. Yes, where I'm held back by a force so strong that I won't ever be able to pull free.*

So many thoughts.

So much confusion.

"Yes," I say simply. "And I can't escape it. I feel like time is going on without me, that everyone else is moving on, moving forward, but they're all leaving me behind. Life is leaving me behind."

After a long pause, he says, "That must be terrible, to feel that way."

It is, I think, but I remain quiet, trying to figure out the best way to respond.

Part of me wishes that someone was in the black hole with me, but that would just be devastating for them as well, and that realization only makes me feel selfish and guilty all over again.

You need someone strong enough to pull you out of the past, out of the gravitational tug on your heart.

And then, I don't know exactly why, but the admission comes out. Maybe it was my conversation with Mom or the momentum now that I've told Jack how I'm feeling, or the fact that he said I was beautiful and unique and like a flower that's about to bloom, but whatever it is, I blurt out *why* I'm feeling this way, and I tell him what sent me plummeting into the black hole in the first place: "I feel like it's my fault that my dad is dead."

Immediately, I regret letting that slip out.

It was too much to tell him, too soon to say it.

"Why would you feel that way?" Jack says concernedly. "What happened?"

"I'm sorry," I backpedal. "I shouldn't have said that."

"No, it's—"

"No," I fumble. "I'm sorry."

Cadence and Aiden have stopped a few houses ahead of us beside a mailbox, and I can tell from the number on it that it's the address we're looking for.

"I'll be okay," I say to Jack. "Forget I said that."

"Hey." He touches my arm gently, and we both stop on the

sidewalk. "Zod, you're not alone, okay? No one's leaving you behind. If you want to talk about it, we can. But we don't have to. I'll still be here for you either way. Alright?"

I feel a tear coming, but I hold it back and stuff it back in where it won't bother anyone, won't sneak to the surface, won't be visible.

Back in the black hole.

"Thank you." My words are soft and delicate and I hear my voice crack. "I appreciate that."

Telling him all of that about my loneliness and my guilt about Dad's death and having him still accept me doesn't make everything better, but it makes the moment better, which, for now, is enough.

I'm not sure if I'll eventually tell him what happened the night Dad died, but I might.

And he would be the first one, the only one besides me, to know.

It's all I can do to keep myself from leaning into Jack's strong arms, but I manage to hold back, and we join Aiden and Cadence beside Mr. Indigo's driveway.

The green VW sedan sits parked in front of his house. I don't know if he lives alone or not, but I take the car's presence here to be a strong indication that he's home.

"How do you want to do this?" Cadence asks us. "Will it be too much if all four of us walk up to his door and ask him to tell us about a terrifying room at the library where you enter a world of coffins and shrinking rooms and torches and castles and werewolves in the night?"

"That might be a bit much," I say. "I think we just ask him about the corridor in the basement, see what he says." Then I add, "And I can do it by myself. It's fine. We don't all need to go."

"What if he wants to know why you're asking him?" she says.

Before I can answer her question, Aiden offers to tell Mr. Indigo that he's doing a research project for school and needs to know about the library's history.

However, I'm not a fan of us lying to Mr. Indigo like that, so I say, "How about I just remind him that I work at the library and tell him that the bookshelf got knocked over in the basement and that we saw the hallway back there with the three rooms in it. I can also mention that Ms. Mason said she didn't know anything about the corridor and that I should ask him about it. That's all true."

They agree, and we decide to go to the door together rather than leave three people lurking at the edge of his driveway while one of us knocks on his door.

"Okay." Aiden gestures gallantly toward Mr. Indigo's porch. "Ladies first."

———

With my friends beside me, I knock on the front door and wait somewhat anxiously as I hear movement inside the house, the sound of footsteps from someone approaching the door.

Finally, it opens and a short wisp of a man who looks like he's in his late sixties appears. He studies the four of us for a moment, then repositions the wired reading glasses perched on his nose and says, "Can I help you?"

"My name is Sahara," I tell him. "I work at the library. We met briefly, earlier today. You like historical stories about King Arthur."

"Ah, yes... And you must be here about the overdue book that I forgot to return?"

"Actually—"

"No, I'm just kidding." He offers us a smile, but it's short-lived. "You're here because of the basement, I'm guessing? The three rooms?"

"Um... Yes."

"Come on in." He opens the door wider. "I've been expecting you."

44

EXPECTING US? WHY WOULD HE

be expecting us?

Mr. Indigo welcomes us into a brightly lit living room with a skylight dappled with variegated autumn leaves that must have fallen onto it from some of the trees in his yard.

"I don't have much to offer you," he says, "but would y'all like something to drink? I have some sweet tea, or there's water or Cheerwine soda—or, do you kids these days drink coffee? Never could get into that stuff myself, but I can make some. My wife left some after the divorce. But that was eight years ago, so it might not be all too fresh."

"No." I answer for all of us. "We're good. We don't need anything. But thanks."

"Okay." He looks at me and my friends curiously. "So, you're Sahara... And y'all are?" After some quick introductions, he says, "Well, then, let's get down to it: You've seen something, haven't you? Down in the third room?"

"How did you know?" I ask.

He waves off the question. "That doesn't matter. What matters is what happens next. Before I worked at the library I was a school bus driver. I drove the bus for nearly twelve years before landing the library job, and I was there for another thirty until I retired last spring. It's on one of those buses that you'll find the answers you're looking for."

"On a school bus?" Aiden has a puzzled look on his face. "One that you drove thirty years ago?"

A nod. "Bus 916."

"Where is it?" I ask.

"Just outside of town, at Terence's Auto Salvage Yard, out past Limestone Cove on the way to Buladeen."

"The school bus graveyard," Cadence says solemnly.

"Huh. Is that what they're calling it these days?" He chuckles softly. "Well, I suppose it is. You find bus 916 and you'll find your answers." Then he adds, "It's our family's property. My brother takes care of it, but if he's not out there, you have my permission to look around. I'd go with you myself, but I'm expecting a delivery this afternoon. Water heater. I need to be here when it arrives."

I'm left speechless.

I came here with a pile of questions about the library and the rift and thin places, and now there's an even bigger pile forming on top of them: Why search an old school bus? What are we supposed to even be looking for? How will this give us answers? And most of all, why was this former bus driver and librarian expecting us to show up at his house?

I decide that I need to at least get an answer to that last one, but before I can ask him about it, Cadence speaks up: "Mr. Indigo, you worked in the library for thirty years—did you ever get the impression that it's haunted?"

"I'm not sure 'haunted' is the right word for it, but I've seen things that I can't explain."

Jack, who's been listening intently, says, "I found an old railroad ledger with a story, handwritten along the margin, about something that happened to a man named Conor O'Shaughnessy, down in the room where I guess they stored coffins sometimes. Does that name mean anything to you?"

Mr. Indigo takes a deep breath, glances toward the kitchen as if he's expecting someone to appear, and then, when no one does, he says, "I think it might be best for y'all to stay away from that room and keep anything you've seen in there to yourselves."

"Did you put that bookshelf in front of the corridor?" Aiden asks him.

"I knew it wouldn't be enough." He sighs. "But I was hoping it would at least... Well... You went into the third room." He states that as a conclusion, not as a question. "What did you see?" He looks at me when he asks that.

"It's hard to explain what we saw," I begin, "but it was—"

"Out of this world," Aiden offers, perhaps trying to be funny, but he's not wrong.

I go ahead and ask Mr. Indigo what he knows about the coffin room, as we'd agreed to do out front before I knocked on the door, and he says, "I know there's a darkness there. When I went in there, I felt a sense of dread, like I was trespassing—that's the best way to put it. I got out of there as quickly as I could. That's why I put the bookcase in front of that hallway. That's not a place that should be visited, or disturbed, or trespassed in."

"Earlier, when we were outside," I say, "you mentioned that you were expecting us. Why is that?"

"I'll tell you what—go out there to the school bus graveyard, look for bus 916, and then come back here and I'll tell you all everything I know about the strange things that have happened in that library over the years."

I study his face to see if I can discern any clues as to why he would say that. His ebony eyes are striking, dark and deep, but give nothing away.

"But what are we looking for there, exactly, on that bus?" I ask him.

"You'll know when you find it," he says unhelpfully.

I see his cell phone on the end table beside the couch and I think of how everything is related. "Mr. Indigo, this may seem like a strange question, but have you been texting me lines from an old English folktale?"

"Me? No. Not at all." And then, "What folktale are we talking about?"

"Mr. Fox. Do you know it?"

"I do. You kids be careful." Then, somewhat cryptically, he adds, "Some doors were never meant to be opened. Some tales were never meant to be told."

"Mr. Indigo," I say, "By any chance, are you familiar with the book *Haints in the Hollers: Southern Appalachian Ghost Lore*?"

"No, no, I'm not."

––––––––

Back outside, we regroup on the sidewalk again and Jack asks the rest of us, "What did you make of that?"

"It was bizarre," Cadence says. "It was as if he was hiding something, but also like he was doing his best to help us—both."

That was a good way to put it.

Her phone vibrates as a text comes through. After checking it, she informs us that she has to get going. "It's my mom. I need to head home to watch Brin while Mom runs some errands, but I should be able to get away later tonight again if I need to."

When she mentions her baby sister, it makes me think of the conversation I had with Grams earlier about changelings, and how fairies will sometimes target babies. "Keep a good eye on her," I tell Cadence.

A curious look. "Why do you say that?"

I'm not thrilled to bring up how fairies try to steal babies or how changelings exchange places with your loved ones, so I just say, "With all the things from the fairy world happening, I just think it's probably best to be careful, especially with those who are the most helpless."

She says nothing but I can tell by the look on her face that my explanation wasn't entirely satisfactory.

Aiden explains that he needs to go too, to help his dad get ready for a Haunted Hayride that his dad's tractor company is putting on tonight.

"I'd invite y'all but I think it's going to be pretty lame. Just riding along on a trailer on a hay bale while every once in a while someone in a cheesy Halloween costume jumps out from behind a tree and waves a knife or chainsaw at you."

Yeah, that doesn't sound amazing.

Aiden scoffs. "If I were an insane psycho killer, I can tell you one thing: I would definitely not use a chainsaw."

"Why's that?" Jack asks.

"A bunch of reasons. Too unwieldy, first of all. Too hard to maneuver, too easy to end up accidentally swinging it into your own leg, for instance, which would seriously suck. Second: too messy. Do you really want to be wearing pieces of someone else all over your clothes? Moist, little bits of skin gristle everywhere? I can't think of too many ways to kill someone that are messier than that. And it's not just you, it's the whole chainsaw. It'd be gooped up with people juice and would spray everywhere around the room—not just blood, but also—"

"Okay, okay," Cadence flags a hand up to halt him in mid-sentence. "You can stop. We get it. And did you just say, 'bits of skin gristle' and 'people juice?'"

"I might have. Anyway, the whole sociopathic chainsaw killer bit was obviously dreamed up by someone in Hollywood to be dramatic, but it's just not very practical. That's all I'm saying."

"I'm still stuck on people juice," Cadence notes.

"Me too," I say.

Jack holds a finger in the air. "Unanimous."

"Sorry," Aiden says, apologetically. "I didn't mean to gross y'all out."

Cadence says to him, "I mean, seriously, 'wearing pieces of someone'? Who even thinks about things like that?"

An insane psycho killer, I think. *A sociopath.*

"I've seen a few scary movies," Aiden tells us.

"Maybe a few [air quotes]—*too*—[air quotes] many," Cadence notes.

"Maybe," he admits.

"Zod and I will go to look for bus 916," Jack says, pivoting away from the people juice conversation and volunteering me to spend more time alone with him all in one fell swoop, which I have no argument with. "Sound good?" he asks me.

"Sounds good to me," I tell him. "Let's go find that bus."

45

THE WALK BACK TO THE LIBRARY

seems to go faster than the trek to Mr. Indigo's house did.

Once we're there, Cadence and Aiden take off, and since my car is still in the shop, I climb into Jack's car with him and we leave for the school bus graveyard, which looks like it's going to be about a twenty-minute drive.

I'm mostly thinking of Jack and how he said I was both dangerous and beautiful, like a rose.

I feel myself flush and I'm just glad he's got his eyes on the road and not on me.

We don't say much on the ride. I'm admittedly still distracted with Aiden's offhanded comment regarding "wearing pieces of someone." I recall what Lily said about someone being after skin.

Of course that had to come to mind.

As we turn onto the property's gravel road, Jack says, "So what was all that with Aiden about the chainsaws and skin gristle? Did that weird you out?"

"Um. Yes. I was just thinking about that, actually."

"Do you know him really well?"

"Only through Cadence, really," I say. "You?"

"Not that well. No."

"He seems to be acting a little weird today," I tell Jack. "Almost like he *wanted* to go through the rift to the other world."

"Maybe he's just curious."

"Maybe."

We park in front of the salvage yard and walk together to the slightly-falling-apart and desperately-in-need-of-a-paint-job office building's front door.

Jack knocks.

No one answers.

I was wondering if Mr. Indigo would have called his brother to make sure he would let us onto the property, but he obviously didn't do that yet, or if he had, his brother decided not to show up.

"Mr. Indigo did say we had permission to look around," Jack reminds me. The sprawling, fenced-in salvage yard lies back a few hundred feet behind the office. "Maybe his brother is out in the yard, or somewhere else on the property? I vote we head back there and see if we can find him."

"I second that."

We walk back to the yard and find the gate padlocked shut, but a trail leads through a small grove of trees paralleling the fence and we figure that it might lead us to another, unlocked, opening.

"Well, if we can't get in there"—Jack points to the yard—"at least it wasn't a wasted trip."

"It *wasn't* wasted?"

"Exactly."

I look at him curiously. "How's it not wasted if we *don't* find what we're looking for? You lost me somewhere. Is this backwards day?"

He doesn't answer right away. "I think, Zod, that no time I spend with you is wasted."

Oh.

For real?

"And see?" I say. "That was *definitely* the right thing to say."

As we wander back along the trail, colorful autumn leaves caught in the breeze drift down slowly around us. It's ridiculously romantic, really, the forest tossing leaves down just for us as if they might be confetti at a fairy tale festival or special celebration.

Especially in light of what he just told me.

It's crazy how quickly things can shift and change. It wasn't much more than twenty-four hours ago that I was reading my essay in class and noticing Jack looking my way with those striking, green hazel eyes, which now appear slightly brown, perhaps because of the tint of late afternoon sunlight, but what matters is that those eyes have been looking at me. In class, I was wishing that he might possibly just talk to me, and since then, we've already made up asterisms together, visited another realm, and saved each other from certain death multiple times.

Not bad.

We don't see anyone on the other side of the six-foot-tall metal mesh fence surrounding the property and when we call out, no one answers.

There are warning signs to stay out, that it's private property, with imposing "Beware of Dog" signs attached to the fence at regular intervals, but I don't hear any barking.

Jack points up ahead to where two sections of the fence meet, about fifty feet away. "It looks like there might be an opening up there."

"You think it's okay to go in the yard?" I'm standing beside another Beware of Dog sign that shows a ferocious dog barking.

"You can buy signs like that at any hardware store and it's a lot less money and effort to just post them on your property than to actually buy and train and care for a guard dog. But if you want to stay here, I can go in by myself and look for the bus. No worries."

"I'm good. I just don't really like dogs."

As we start toward the opening, I'm thinking of an old Appalachian story about Wiley and the Hairy Man, where a boy outwits the dangerous Hairy Man by tricking him into making all the rope in the county disappear, freeing the dogs that are tied up or on leashes, and they all come after the Hairy Man.

The Hairy Man doesn't like dogs either.

A clever boy, that Wiley.

Beyond the fence, at least fifty or sixty school buses languish in various states of crumpled-up-ness. Based on the different models and designs, some were obviously left here decades ago to rust away in the yard.

When we see no sign of an actual dog, we decide to go and look for bus 916.

We find a small opening where those two parts of the metal fencing overlap. Somewhere along the line, one of them got peeled away from the other and, even though there isn't much room to spare, when I exhale my air and press the flexible fencing to the side, I'm able to squeeze through, just like I did yesterday when I snuck between the bookcase and the wall in the library's basement.

Jack is bigger than I am, but he's also stronger, so he's able to press the loose fencing further away from himself as he maneuvers through to join me on the other side.

However, one of the snaggily-sharp metal burrs on the fence catches his left arm as he passes through. The torn fabric on his long-sleeve T-shirt reveals a wicked slash, maybe six inches long on his forearm.

It makes me think of Cadence's riff earlier about doctors offering to re-break a bone or re-slash an arm.

But I don't offer to re-slash Jack's arm for him.

"You okay?" I ask him.

"Yes." He stares at the cut for a moment, then plays it off as no big deal. "All good."

"You sure? That looks kinda deep." The blood is already soaking through the edges of the ripped fabric and staining his shirt.

"I'm sure." He covers the wound with his free hand to put some pressure on it. "I'm fine."

I wish I had something to wrap around his arm to keep that nasty gash from bleeding, but I don't have anything with me.

"Let's just get going," Jack says. "We can worry about my arm later."

———

All throughout the salvage yard, bus windows are broken out. In some cases, the bus hoods are popped open. Crude graffiti is rampant on the sides of many of the buses. Sometimes, tires are missing or the engines are gone entirely. Some buses have grass or bushes sprouting out of the empty engine blocks. There's even one that has a small tree growing out of its open hood.

The buses are parked—or abandoned might be a better word for it—in six slanted rows spaced about twenty feet apart. Most of the property is overgrown with thickets and vetch that would be tough to hack through with a machete, let alone walk through without one, so we stay on the vague path that meanders through the rows of buses that someone must have created to allow access to the vehicles.

Thorns everywhere.

No roses.

It reminds me of the impenetrable hedge surrounding the tower where Sleeping Beauty awaited her awakening. In Grams' version of the story, the princess remains fast asleep, as the years and then decades passed by and the deadly thorns surrounding the tower skewered and killed valiant prince after valiant prince, leaving their vanquished corpses exposed in the thicket to turn to bleached skeletons beneath the blazing, indifferent sun.

With that on my mind, I edge forward with Jack toward the first bus in this row of eight.

"So what exactly are we looking for on bus 916?" he asks.

"I have no idea."

"Do you know any stories that might fit in with this?" he says. "Any clues from tales you've heard?"

"About school bus graveyards?"

"Well... Yes."

I shake my head. "Nothing in particular." Just Wiley and the Hairy Man and Sleeping Beauty, but neither one seems worth mentioning. "Nothing with school buses," I tell him.

We discover that the buses have their numbers emblazoned on their sides near the doors and, as long as the underbrush isn't so high as to obscure them, we're able to make them out from a distance.

The buses are in no particular order, so bus by bus, we begin making our way through the salvage yard, searching for 916.

———

It takes about ten minutes to eliminate the first half of the buses. We've just started on the next row when Jack points. "There."

Sure enough, the bus he's indicating, maybe eighty feet away, looks like it has the number 916 on the side, but I can't make it out for certain from here.

We approach it cautiously and attentively, trying to discern what Mr. Indigo might have been referring to when he told us this bus would give us the answers we were in search of.

Yes, it's 916.

An old shovel leans propped up against the side of a nearby bus. Jack grabs it and holds it in front of him like a weapon as we walk toward 916's front door.

Most of the windows are shattered but aren't completely clear of glass, and the persistent jagged shards remaining embedded in the frames remind me of deadly teeth. For some reason, I find myself thinking of the horrid injuries that would result if anyone tried to climb out of one of those windows and slipped or wasn't careful. I can't help it. That imagination of mine again.

And what I picture is not pretty.

At all.

Something right out of one of Aiden's scary movies.

The hood is propped up and the rusted and ruptured engine inside of it tells me that this bus has been here for a long time. Also, the design of the bus looks decades-old, matching what Mr. Indigo told us about the timing of when he was still driving school buses.

Because of a missing front tire on the passenger's side, the bus lilts toward us, canted at an awkward angle and leaning inelegantly against the dirt.

"I'll go first," Jack offers.

After a slight hesitation, I nod.

The door is jammed shut and Jack wrestles with it for a moment, trying to pop it open, but it fights against him the whole time, resisting obstinately, until he really throws his weight into it and finally, with an angry metallic screech, it gives way and grinds open just wide enough for us to get through.

"You ready for this?" he says.

"I'm ready."

He angles the shovel in front of him.

In the distance, I hear the rough, guttural barking of a dog, but it doesn't sound like it's on this property. Too far away. Still, it makes me cautious and a little uneasy.

I think of the howling earlier this afternoon, on the other side of the rift. And I think of werewolves.

Which isn't exactly what I need to be thinking of at the moment.

What if that's what knocked over the bookshelf in the basement?

Admittedly, that's a stretch, but my imagination is right at home considering things that are a stretch. It's sort of my imagination's specialty. And, after all that has been happening to me since yesterday evening, I'm not really sure anymore what's a stretch and what's not.

We enter the bus and begin to search for... What?

Who knows.

That's the thing.

As I think about it, I realize that Mr. Indigo was never quite clear about what answers we'd find, just that we'd find them—but to which question? Why the rift opened up for me in the first place? A definitive reason for why it's even there in the library's basement? How to seal it back up again? Why he was even expecting us in the first place?

I don't know.

And that makes it tougher to pinpoint what to look for.

He said we'd know when we found it.

Well, let's see if he was right.

Figuring that since he was the driver, the clue might be in the front of the bus, Jack and I spend a few minutes looking through that area in-depth.

However, nothing appears to be out of the ordinary around the driver's seat, near the console, or on dashboard. No notes. No messages. No enchanted mirror or slipper or key or forest. No clues.

Finally, we begin to make our way toward the back of the bus, studying the seats and the floor as we go. I take the right side; Jack takes the left.

The sound of the barking outside is getting closer and it makes me think that the dog might actually be on this property after all.

"You hear that, right?" I say.

"I do. Let's finish this up and get out of here."

Both of us dial up the urgency of our search.

Many of the grimy seats are split open and spewing out their insides like soft, fluffy intestines. A scattering of leaves that've blown in here from the grove of trees nearby dots the floor and seats, bringing a touch of color to the otherwise drab interior.

I find a few empty cans of spray paint, a pink hair barrette, and an empty bottle of whiskey, but can't imagine that any of those are the things we're looking for.

I'm getting less and less confident that we're going to find something helpful in this old bus and more and more anxious by the sound of barking coming this way.

We're two-thirds of the way through the bus when Jack says, "I think I found it."

He bends over the seat, retrieves something from the floor, and then, with a look of confusion on his face, turns to face me.

He's holding my sapphire birthstone ring, the one from my dad, the one that we left behind on the other side of the rift.

And that's when the dog arrives.

46

I'M REELING FROM WHAT JACK just found, but also distracted by that little rather necessary thing called survival.

He hands me the ring and I confirm that it's mine. How could it have gotten here? It's supposed to be in the fairy world where we left it. Plus, why would it be in a bus that's thirty years old?

But I slide those questions aside for the moment as I pocket the ring and glance out the window.

It's time to get out of here without getting mauled by the hulking, raven-black dog that's bolting through the salvage yard toward the front door of the bus.

I try to calculate if we'll be able to get back to the fence's opening in time, before the dog can get to us, but I'm not confident we can make it.

"We need to get gone," Jack says.

"Yes, we do."

But that requires getting off the bus, and with the dog arriving at the door, that's not going to happen.

This dog looks like it's pushing a hundred and twenty pounds. It tries to squeeze through the door's narrow opening at the front of the bus, but he's so big I'm not sure he'll be able to make it in.

But he's so aggressive that I'm also not sure he's *not* going to make it.

I'm no expert on dogs, but I did an assignment on guard dogs when I was in middle school and, based on the way this one looks, with its size, short black coat, and focused intensity, it's maybe a

Cane Corso—but I hope not. They're seriously ferocious and are supposedly unaffected by pain—even electric fences won't stop them. So there's no way either Jack or I will be able to, even with that shovel.

Escape through the windows?

Not gonna happen.

There's no easy roof access either.

Which only leaves us the emergency door at the back of the bus.

The dog's hoarse barking and low growls are becoming more menacing, and I hope that he'll get stuck or not be able to make it through, but he throws himself at the opening repeatedly until he's able to squeeze through onto the bus.

He starts up the steps.

Rather than sprint toward us, he takes it slow and snarls in the back of his throat in the way that only dogs can do, and only do when they mean you no good.

I run to the back of the bus while Jack stays in front of me, slowly backing up toward me as the dog stalks toward him. Jack waves the shovel's blade threateningly at the dog, but it doesn't seem to be intimidated by it at all.

I yank at the emergency release bar on the bus's rear door, but it's jammed or maybe rusted in place because it doesn't want to move, which makes sense if it hasn't been opened in three decades.

"Now would be good," Jack tells me unnecessarily.

"It's stuck." I try again, but it's no use. "Either you're going to have to do it," I tell him, "or I'm going to need the shovel."

After a slight hesitation, he grabs a shard of glass that I can't imagine will be much use against the dog. He angles it in front of him like a knife blade and hands the shovel back to me.

I hurriedly cram the shovel's blade into the gap to lever the release bar open, press down, and at last it gives way all at once, surprising me. The door bangs open abruptly and, since I'm leaning forward and already off-balance, I tumble out heavily and awkwardly, into the underbrush, ensnaring myself in a tangle of thorny branches and thistly vines.

As I land, all I can think of is Cadence's words about broken bones and falling in such way that they break properly—which I definitely have not done.

I free myself from the branches entwined around me, assess all my limbs and find that, although I'm scratched up a bit from the thorns, there doesn't appear to be any major damage, nothing broken, and nothing poking into or out of my skin that's not supposed to be.

"Come on," I yell to Jack. "It's open!"

I reach up to help him down if he needs it, but he leaps athletically from the back of the bus, launching himself past the bush that I landed in.

Before slamming the door shut, I snag the shovel from where it dropped inside, hoping that my idea will work to keep the dog from following us.

It's bounding forward now, directly toward me.

Hastily, I close the door and lean back against it and feel the dog wham into it, jarring it behind me.

I'm guessing that this door wasn't designed to be locked from the outside—why would it be? Then someone could trap children inside during an emergency.

So, once it's closed, though I try to latch it, I'm not surprised when it doesn't want to stay shut.

Thus, the shovel.

Jack anticipates what I have in mind. "I'll get it."

I pass the shovel to him and he wedges the blade against the ground and jams the handle up against a groove on the door's exterior, down near its base.

The propped-up shovel looks less secure than it did in my imagination and I'm not sure how long it's going to last.

We both back up.

The Cane Corso doesn't take the hint that we prefer to be left alone, or left alive with our throats intact, and it lunges violently against the door, trying its hardest to knock it open.

The shovel holds, but the force of the dog's weight slamming against the door buries the blade a little further into the dirt. I'm anticipating that enough force on the door could jar it loose. We probably should have wedged it against the door upside down.

But there isn't time to switch it now.

Jack indicates the fence. "Let's go!"

Together, we sprint along the path through the thicket, staying on the trail as much as possible, angling our trajectory toward the gap in the fence that we came through earlier.

When we're a few seconds away, I glance back. The shovel is still in place, but I can hear the dog continuing to bark and bang against the bus's rear exit door.

Probably burying the blade in further.

Probably getting closer to freeing itself.

Probably—

We dash forward, get to the gap in the fence, and wrestle our way between the metal fencing until we're safely through on the other side.

I look over Jack's shoulder and see the shovel suddenly torque to the side and drop to the ground. The door bursts open and the dog leaps fearlessly from the bus. All I can think of is that if we were able to get through the opening in the fence, the dog will likely be able to as well.

"How are we going to stop it?" I gasp.

"I'll tie the fence shut."

"With what?"

He whips off his shirt. "With this."

Okay, that'll work.

The dog is darting toward us, much more confident on the trails than we were, and running much faster than we were able to do.

We need to make this quick.

"Hold the fence pieces shut," Jack says.

Very quick.

While I press the two flaps of the fencing into place, he threads the arms of his shirt through the two sides of the metal mesh, cinches the gap closed, and then quickly ties the shirt into a secure knot.

Breathing heavily, we both back up.

As the dog leaps viciously toward us.

Crashing heavily into the fence.

The makeshift shirt lock holds.

For the moment.

We back up a couple more steps as the dog mounts up again, brutally throwing itself against the fence, barking and snarling.

Shapeshifters come to mind.

And changelings.

I'm half-expecting the dog to morph before my eyes into a viper or a deadly basilisk and writhe through the fence to get to us, or into a facinorous vulture and swoop over the fence to attack us, or into a mountain troll who can rip apart the metal fence, and then do the same with us, limb by limb, with its bare hands.

But none of that happens.

Thankfully.

The dog remains a dog.

And the fence remains closed, secured with Jack's shirt.

"You okay?" he asks me.

"Yeah. You?"

He nods. "I'm good."

I can't help but notice that he indeed does look good without that shirt on—except for that six-inch-long gash in his left arm, which does not look good at all. It's bleeding again. Or maybe it never stopped.

"We need to clean out that cut," I say. "When was the last time you had a tetanus shot?"

"Maybe a year or two ago, I think. I don't remember exactly."

"Still, we should get you to a doctor," I say. "You probably need stitches and antibiotics."

"I'll be alright. I just need to clean it out, smear some first aid cream on there, and throw on a bandage. All good. I've gotten hurt way worse than this skateboarding."

Leaving Jack's shirt in place and the guard dog snarling behind us, we head through the copse of trees toward Jack's car.

"My house isn't too far," he says. "We can swing by there, clean this arm up, I'll grab another shirt, and then we can figure out from there what to do next."

Which makes me think again of the ring that my dad gave me.

I check.

Still in my pocket.

Unbelievable. How could this happen?

"How did my ring get on that bus?" I ask Jack, speaking my thoughts aloud.

He shakes his head. "I don't know, but someone put it there. And it had to be someone from the fairy world because that's where it was left."

That gets me thinking.

"Mr. Indigo sent us here," I say. "Is it possible he put it on the bus?"

"But why?" Jack says. "And when? We headed to his house pretty much right after leaving the basement ourselves, and if he had been in there somehow, we would have seen him leaving the library."

"Yeah." I nod. "You're right. It couldn't have been him... Unless... Huh."

"What is it? What are you thinking?"

"Remember how we were talking earlier about time," I say, as we traverse the trail. "And how it passes differently in the fairy world?"

"Yes."

"I'm wondering if that might explain how the ring got in the bus. I mean..."

"What are you saying? Time travel?"

"Retrocausality."

"Okay, and that is...?"

We pass through the trees and I notice the wind kicking up, bringing more leaves down around us now than on our way in.

"Basically," I say, "there's something called quantum entanglement. It has to do with changing the spin of a subatomic particle and when it's entangled with another one, it'll instantaneously affect the other particle—even if it's on the other side of the universe. Anyway, since most physicists believe that the fastest thing in the universe is the speed of light—"

"Aha." Jack anticipates where I'm going with this. "Something must be off, because whatever travels between the particles telling the other one to be affected would be moving faster than the speed of light."

"Very good." I'm impressed. "So, to get around that, some scientists have suggested that since time is relative, the information goes into the future and then travels back to cause what preceded it."

He takes a moment to process that as we pass the office building and approach his car. "So what comes first," he says, as he clicks the unlock button on his key fob, "the cause or the effect?"

"Nothing can happen that isn't caused," I say, "but does that cause come from the future or the past? That's the question."

"Huh. Can you cause the past?"

"Yes... Well..." Suddenly, I'm not sure my explanation holds up. "I mean, I'm just throwing it out there. I have no idea if it's true—even scientists have no idea if retrocausality is real. It's all really just speculation at this point."

"But the ring isn't speculation," he says. "That's real."

"Yes. It is."

And it got there somehow.

We arrive at his car and I take one last look at the salvage yard. Mr. Indigo told us we'd get answers here, but it seems like all I ended up with is more questions, just like when we visited him in person.

"Okay." I open the door and climb into the passenger seat. "So what's the plan?"

Jack scrounges in the trunk and comes up with a roll of duct tape. He folds up a leftover McDonald's napkin, places it over the cut to

protect it, and then uses the duct tape to wrap around his injured arm
for now, as a rudimentary bandage.

"Let's head to my house and get this arm patched up. Mr. Indigo
said we should return to him. Maybe there's still time to do that
today. Either way, we can see if Cadence and Aiden can join us at
my house—as long as Aiden's done helping his dad get ready for the
Haunted Hayride."

Skin gristle.

People juice.

Ew. Double ew.

As Jack fires up the car and as we take off for his house, I study
the ring to make sure it really is the same one that my dad gave me.

As far as I can tell, it is.

I wonder once again how it got onto that bus.

And who might have put it there.

And why.

47

AFTER INFORMING ME THAT
it's about fifteen minutes to his house, Jack is quiet during the drive,
which gives me a chance to put a video call through to Grams.

Since she doesn't always keep her ringer on, I'm not sure if she'll
pick up, but after six rings she does.

"Sahara," she says in her careful, sensitive way. She looks tired.
"How was work?"

"Hey, Grams. It was good. You doing alright?"

"Yes. And how did the call with your mother go?"

Oh, that's right. She knows about that.

Of course she does. She's the one who told you to set it up.

So, how to do this...

I contemplate how much to tell her, but finally opt to keep the
summary of my terse conversation with Mom as short as possible.
"We tried to let bygones be bygones," I say vaguely. "Grams, I have a
question. We came across an old railroad ledger at the library that...
um... mentioned a Conor O'Shaughnessy. I was wondering if it was
referring to your father-in-law. Do you by any chance know the year
he passed away?"

When it comes to some things, Grams' memory is as sharp as
a tack, but in other things, time has been eating away at some of
her memories, so I'm not sure if she'll know the year off the top of
her head.

But she does, telling it to me almost immediately, and it matches
the date in the ledger, which makes me think it has to be the same
Conor O'Shaughnessy.

"A ledger?" Grams looks at me questioningly. "What did it say?"

"Um... It referred to him being taken to that coffin room you were telling me about." I hesitate, but then say, "How did he die?"

A small pause. "What is this about?"

"I'm just trying to sort out what we found at the library."

"It was his heart." She sighs softly and sadly at the memory. "He passed away in Ohio and they brought him back here to be buried on the family farm, but I think there was some confusion about which train his body was on and his coffin didn't arrive at the funeral home 'til a week later than it was s'pposed to. That's about all I know."

So, she doesn't know anything about him being left for dead and trying to escape from his casket in the coffin room.

But how could she not know?

Sahara, if you were one of the railroad workers who was responsible for forgetting him down there, would you have told the family?

Good point.

I decide that informing her about the details regarding Conor's death is probably best done in person and not over the phone, so instead, I say, "Grams, let's say there's a thin place. Could tragedy cause it to tear open?"

"Has something happened?" Both her voice and her face are filled with concern.

"Yes," I admit. "But I can't get into everything right now. I will, though. I promise."

"Are you alright? Are you safe?"

I assure her that I'm fine, then explain that I'm planning to hang out with my friends for a while tonight.

She offers to make a late dinner for us, but I tell her not to bother, that I'll just get some leftovers later when I get home.

"I'll text you when I know a specific time," I tell her. "And I promise not to be late this time and I'll fill you in more when I see you."

"You be careful now," she cautions me, "and make good choices."

"I will," I promise. "I mean, I'll do my best. Don't worry. I'll talk to you soon."

We end the call, and after I check in with Jack to make sure he's doing alright, I connect with Cadence on another video call to tell her what we found at the salvage yard.

When she picks up, I hear her baby sister crying in the background, which makes me concerned. "How's Brin?" I ask.

"A little fussy," Cadence says, "but she's alright. Did y'all find anything at the school bus graveyard?"

"You're not going to believe this: We found my ring—the one from my dad. The one that got left behind in the fairy world."

"What? That makes no sense." She squinches up her eyes slightly in confusion. "How did it get there? And why?"

"Your guess is as good as mine," I tell her. "When do you think you'll be done watching Brin?"

"Mom should be home any minute."

"Do you know where Jack lives? We're heading over to his house now. We were thinking we could all meet up there."

"Text me the address. I'll leave as soon as I can. Also, I'll see if Aiden can make it too. As long as he doesn't bring along a chainsaw."

"Good thought."

After she hangs up, Jack tells me his address and I send it along to Cadence.

"We'll be there minutarily," he says. "Six, maybe. Seven tops."

I take the opportunity to flip open the ghost lore book that I brought with me from the library, studying the dogeared pages—stories about a ghost hitchhiker, a girl with a yellow ribbon around her neck, a shrinking room—all stories that have come true to some extent in the last twenty-four hours.

An unsettling chill grips me.

Who marked those pages?

Dad?

The last dogeared page is a story about an elemental at Leap

Castle in Ireland and how some people who'd traveled there claimed
to have seen it in the Appalachian Mountains as well.

That's what's coming.

The next few minutes pass quickly, probably because I'm deep
in thought about the book's stories and time travel and rifts and
retrocausality and if it would be possible that cause and effect really
could be reversed at certain times or in certain places in the universe.

Since I'm so used to time passing in the same direction as
cause and effect, it's hard to think about it all happening the other
way around.

What really did come first—the chicken or the egg? Or both?
Or neither?

Could a future event really cause one in the past?

Jack pulls into his driveway and parks in front of a modern two-
story house painted in a contemporary gray and white design that's
tucked up against a thick forest that extends up a steep mountainside.
We're about two miles from town. No neighbors close by.

It's nearly dusk.

On the right side of the house there's a large oak tree that contains
an impressive treehouse. The tree's stout branches reach close enough
to the second-story window that it looks like someone could climb
out onto them.

Jack seems like the kind of guy who might have done that, if that
was his bedroom window, and I wonder how many times he might've
snuck out over the years. Maybe to see a girl. Maybe to go to a party
or hang out with friends.

"Nice treehouse," I say.

"Yeah," he says offhandedly. "I always liked it growing up."

As we exit the car, I leave the ghost lore book open on the
passenger side seat and ask him, "Did you ever form any of those 'No
girls allowed!' clubs?"

"If I did, I can tell you for certain that I'm over that stage."

"I'm glad to hear that."

Through the garage door window, I catch sight of a sheriff's department squad car parked inside.

As Jack leads me onto the porch and opens the front door, I'm reminded of the Mr. Fox story again and I'm thankful there's no sign above this door inviting me to be bold.

———

Inside the house, Jack asks me to wait for a second in the living room, then he disappears into the bathroom to grab some first aid cream and bandages for his arm.

While he's gone, I take in the room—the pristine, unblemished white leather couch facing the television, the recliner in the corner, the fireplace mantle holding a clutch of family pictures. Very stylish. Pretty immaculate. The place hardly looks lived in.

A hallway extends past the dining room toward a partially propped open bathroom door and a stacked washer and dryer, with another door, possibly to the basement, on the right.

I find my way over to the fireplace.

The photos show Jack and his parents on the shore of a lake, fishing, then at a campsite with snow-capped mountains in the background, and then standing together at Times Square in New York City. In all of the photos, the three of them look genuinely happy.

Jack's school portrait shows him with a sly grin, his eyes, sharp and hazel-colored. They look greener in the picture than they have recently, but maybe it's just the lighting. Beside the portrait, there are two plaques containing sheriff's department awards that his dad has won.

Kinda the perfect family. It looks like Jack has a good relationship with his mom and dad and that they actually enjoy spending time together.

Imagine that.

It makes me wonder what that would be like—to do stuff like

that with your mom and have her enjoy it, instead of her simply having to put up with spending time with you.

One of the photos off to the side shows Jack and another guy at a skateboard park. It takes me a second to recognize him, but then I realize it's Ryan, the shirtless guy from the bonfire who was the first one to jump over the fire.

Huh. I wasn't aware that the two of them knew each other.

———

Jack returns, carrying some bandages, a couple of washcloths, a glass of water, and a tube of triple antibiotic ointment. He leads me to the dining room. "There's more room here than in the bathroom," he explains. "I figured it might be a little easier to get it cleaned up out here."

We take a seat at the table.

"Here. I'll do it," I offer.

He doesn't argue with that, so I moisten one of the washcloths, warn him that it might hurt, and then carefully remove the duct tape that he'd wrapped around his arm earlier, and begin to clean off the dried blood and dirt surrounding the ragged gash.

The photos of Jack smiling beside his father make me miss Dad all over again.

"Is your dad here?" I ask him.

"What? No. Not today."

"Oh. I saw his squad car in the garage."

"He has another car he drives when he's not on duty."

"Right. Gotcha."

I'm as tender as possible, but getting the cut cleaned out requires a bit of scrubbing. However, through it all, Jack barely flinches. Some of the blood has dried and it takes me dampening the washcloth several times to get the wound clean.

"I saw the pictures by the fireplace," I say. "Looks like you and your parents are pretty close."

"It's not perfect or anything, but I'm thankful they're still together. They went through a rough spot when I was in grade school. Since then, they've gotten along as well as you could hope for anyone."

A pause. "Remember earlier," I say, "when I told you I felt responsible for my dad's death?"

"Yes."

"I've never told anyone what happened between us the night he died."

"I understand. It's all good. You don't—"

"But I want to tell you."

He looks at me with what appears to be genuine understanding. "Are you sure?"

I nod. "It'd probably be good for me to tell someone about it," I say. "I just haven't found the right someone yet."

Until now, I think, but I keep that to myself.

I take a deep breath. "Alright, here's why I feel so guilty, what happened the night my dad died—and why it's my fault that he's dead."

48

I TELL JACK ABOUT THE

problems at home in the months before Dad died and about my struggles keeping my grades up and how Dad kept telling me I needed to stop being so distracted by sketching and writing poetry in my idea journal all the time and to buckle down and get my homework done if I was ever going to get any sort of scholarship to college.

"It was one of those things we always argued about," I say. "It was a big deal to him that I went to college. It wasn't really a huge goal for me, but it sure was for him. I was happy just daydreaming, escaping into my own world, but he had other things he wanted me to be focused on. He tried everything he could to get me back to feeling like myself again, back to doing my homework, but I wasn't really onboard with that, and something had to give."

I explain how I came home late from a friend's house on a Saturday night in March and how I went to look for my journal in my bedroom but it wasn't there.

"It's where I would write down all my story ideas," I explain. "It was important to me. Not really a diary so much, but a place where I could let my imagination run wild, run free. And it was weird because I couldn't find it anywhere, and I was getting really confused because I remembered leaving it on my desk."

"Where was it?" Jack says.

I finish cleaning out the cut and smear some triple antibiotic cream liberally across it.

"While I was looking," I say, "Dad comes and knocks on my bedroom door and he says he needs to talk to me about something.

And I'm like, 'Not now. I need to find my journal.' And he says, 'It's about your journal.'"

And then, as I carefully cover his wound with a bandage and wrap soft gauze around his arm to keep the cut covered, I lose myself in the story, in the memory of it, in the telling of it:

So I stare at Dad. "What do you mean? What are you talking about?"

"I took it. It's time to move on."

And I feel this giant stone sinking inside of me. "You what?"

"You're spending way too much time writing there and daydreaming instead of actually studying in school. You need to—"

"Then you talk to me! You don't invade my privacy and take my stuff."

"I have talked to you, Sahara. You know I have. Time and time again, and—"

"Don't you know what that journal means to me? Do you have any idea what you've done? You took it—what does that mean? Where is it?"

"It's not here anymore, Sahara. It's been too much of a distraction."

"You can't throw out the stuff that's the most important to me!"

"You're smart. You could get a scholarship to college and your mom and I can't afford to send you there without—"

"What if I don't want to go to college? Did you ever think about what I want instead of just what you want for me?"

"I don't want to argue. I just—"

I can feel a hot tear leaking out of the edge of my eye. "You went too far. That's ME in that journal!"

"It's not as bad as—"

"I hate you."

"You don't mean that, Sahara."

I snatch up my car keys and look him in the eye and say The Five Words You Can Never Unsay: "I wish you were dead."

And then I push past him and storm out of the house, climb into my car, and take off onto the icy road, into the fog-enshrouded night.

And that was the last time I ever saw him alive.

I look at Jack's arm and realize I'm clinging to it, like it's a lifeline and I'm drowning, afraid to let go.

"I'm so sorry," I mutter and release my grip abruptly.

"It's okay." He rotates his arm, then makes a fist, testing out how his arm feels. He unclenches the fist and then pats the gauze wrap affectionately. "Good as new."

I'm still caught up in the emotion of the memories and find it tough to regroup and be present here, with him.

Jack twists slightly in his chair so he can face me. "You were saying that you left, went driving into the fog. But how is it your fault that your dad died?"

"He came looking for me."

He's dead because he loved you.

He took your journal because he loved you and wanted what was best for you.

He went out in search of you because he loved you.

And he called and tried to reach you when he was dying and you wouldn't let him. You wouldn't pick up.

"The thing is," I say, "the roads were icy and he wouldn't have been out there driving on them if it hadn't been for me saying those things and leaving like that. So, I drove around for a while and then saw this call from him come through, but I didn't answer it because I was still pissed at him. When I got home, I turned off my phone and went to bed, and later on, the cops showed up and told Mom and me that his car had been found. He drowned in a lake, trapped under the ice. I was the reason he went out that night. If I hadn't left, or if I'd answered the phone when he called me, he might still be alive."

Jack lets all of that sink in.

"I'm thirsty," I say. "Can I grab a drink of water?"

"Yeah, sure. The glasses are above the sink."

As I pour myself some water my hand is trembling.

"And is that why you don't talk on the phone anymore?" he says. "Because of that night?"

"Yes." I drink some water, trying to calm my shredded nerves, but it doesn't really help.

"Zod, what happened to your journal?"

I set down the glass. "That's the thing, I found it after his funeral. He hadn't thrown it away, just took it away. It was on his workbench downstairs in the basement."

"He lied to you?"

"I mean, I can't remember exactly if he just said he took it or if he said that he'd actually gotten rid of it. But he was trying to motivate me, you know? To get me to get my priorities straight. He did it for my own good. He was going to give it back. He just got carried away and took it."

"I think you might be cutting him too much slack."

I let that pass without comment.

"All I know," Jack says, "is that we can't change the past, but we can let it change us today. My soccer coach used to tell us, 'Let your losses inform you, not define you.' I wish I knew what else to say. You're more than the mistakes you've made. Like I told you earlier, you're a flower about to bloom."

I think of what I told the hikers this morning about Erwin's past and how we can learn from history and change as a result of it, and I can't help but notice the parallel to what Jack is telling me right now.

Learn. Grow. Adapt. Mature.

Or wither away and die.

Grams warned me about letting pain become my home and how anger gets tougher and tougher to remove the deeper you let it grow its roots in your heart.

Yeah, no kidding.

To escape the black hole, you have to let go of your hurt, not let it control you more and more.

Let the past inform you, not define you.

Let it equip you, not limit you.

"Jack," I say, "thanks for listening, for not judging me. You're very wise for your age."

"Don't let the word get out, it might ruin my reputation."

I feel a smile cross my face. "Your secret is safe with me."

The sun has dipped down below the mountain behind the house and the room is draped in a cascading reddish glow.

It's almost exactly twenty-four hours since I first ventured into the coffin room.

I'm overwhelmed by thoughts of the past and by the possibilities of what leaving it there behind me might mean, the chance to actually, finally, escape the black hole, what it would look like to stop letting the past claw into me so deeply, to stop letting it define me. I'm processing that when I see a text from Cadence that she and Aiden just drove up.

"They're here," I say.

"Let me throw a shirt on," Jack says. "I'll be back down in a minute."

He grabs the bloody washcloths to tidy up the dining room and then heads upstairs to his bedroom to change while I go to open the front door for Cadence and Aiden.

But I don't make it.

Because as I'm walking past the hallway, I hear the muffled cries coming from behind the door beside the washer and dryer.

49

I PAUSE, WONDERING IF MAYBE

I'm hearing things, but I don't think that's the case.

I walk over to the door and edge it open. "Hello?"

It's the door to the basement stairwell.

And there are definitely sounds coming from down there. Muffled cries.

Something's wrong.

I hurry to the front door and let Cadence and Aiden in. "I think someone might be hurt," I tell them before they can say anything.

"What is it?" Cadence asks, a flash of concern in her eyes. "Who?"

I lead them to the top of the basement stairs. "Listen."

We can all hear the urgent, distressed cries, but they're not clear, as if someone—or maybe more than one person—is gagged or has something in their mouth.

"Who's down there?" Aiden asks me.

"I don't know. I'll go get Jack. Wait here."

I run to the stairs leading up to the second floor and call out, "Jack, someone's in your basement! I think they're hurt!"

The reply comes: "What? The basement?" Then I hear the sound of his footsteps pounding toward the stairs. "I'm coming!"

He appears with a gray T-shirt on and a moment later he's flying down the steps to my side.

We hustle over to join Aiden and Cadence, who are waiting for us at the top of the basement stairs.

Aiden flicks out a knife I didn't know he had and Cadence pulls out a canister of pepper spray from her purse, which might have been helpful against the werewolf in the fairy world—if she even had it with her—but who knows how susceptible werewolves are to pepper spray.

But that's all past and gone.

Right now, tonight, we need to help whoever's down here.

Jack, weaponless, takes the lead, followed by Aiden carrying that knife of his. I follow after him, with Cadence bringing up the rear.

It sounds like chains scraping across the floor. There's also a muffled sound that might be someone calling out from somewhere further back in the basement.

"Jack, who is that?" I ask.

"I have no idea."

The stairs are wooden and creaky and, honestly, I'm a little nervous that with all four of us on them, they might just collapse under the weight.

But that doesn't keep us from tromping down them.

And they hold up.

The further down we go, the louder the sounds become.

At the base of the stairs, I see that the basement is still unfinished, with drywall needing to be put up, ceiling panels waiting to be fitted into place, and a concrete floor in need of being carpeted. A toolbox sits beside a pair of sawhorses in the corner.

However, despite the renovations going on, a door to a room across the basement has been hung in place, and now, a heavy clasp bolted to the doorframe holds a padlock that secures the door shut.

We run toward it and Jack pounds on the door, trying unsuccessfully to muscle it open.

"Mom?" he yells. "Dad?"

I hadn't thought of that.

The cries become more urgent, but still impossible to decipher.

Jack tries the door one last time. "There are some bolt cutters in the garage," he says to us. "I'll be right back. Don't go anywhere, and stick together." He turns toward the stairs and darts up them, taking them two at a time.

The bottom of the locked door doesn't quite reach the floor and it looks like, if I get close enough to the ground, I might be able to see to the other side.

I kneel and press the side of my head to the floor. I can't see much, but I can make out several lengths of thick chain on the concrete as well as four shoes: two that might be from a guy and two that look like they're women's shoes.

"What do you see back there?" Aiden asks.

"There are two people," I tell him. "A woman and a man, I think."

I call out beneath the door, "We're here! We're going to help you!"

More muffled sounds. Maybe the people are relieved? Maybe scared, warning us to get away? I can't tell.

I push myself to my feet as Cadence looks around the basement and comes up with a hammer from the toolbox.

"Use this." She hands it to Aiden, then checks her phone and shakes her head. "No bars. Must be because we're in the basement or behind that mountain."

"I'll go upstairs and call 911," I offer. "There's gotta be reception up there."

"Jack said to stick together," Aiden counters.

"I won't go far. I'll be alright."

I whip out my phone and head to the stairs as Aiden approaches the bolted door with that hammer.

I run up the stairs to the kitchen. I haven't used my phone as a phone in nearly seven months, so I'm a little weirded out tapping in 911, but I do it anyway.

"Emergency services," a woman says, her voice calm and measured. "What is the nature of your—"

"There are two people chained up in a basement," I tell her urgently, trying to catch my breath.

"Is anyone hurt?" she asks.

"They're chained up! I don't know. Maybe. Probably."

"Are you in any immediate danger?"

"I don't think so."

I hear the sounds of the hammer smacking wood to pieces in the basement. So, Aiden must have decided that prying the clasp free with the claw end of the hammer wasn't going to do the trick and he'd resorted to trying to break through the door instead.

Hmm. Good for him.

The dispatcher goes on, "Are you in a safe place?"

"Just send some cops," I say. "And an ambulance. Send them now." I give her the address. "We're at Deputy Beck's house. He might be hurt."

My phone vibrates in my hand. I look at the screen.

The text message is from an unknown number.

Based on what's been happening, I'm expecting it to be the next line from the story of Mr. Fox, the final part of the tripartite warning, but that's not what I see.

"Hang up the phone," it reads instead. "And check upstairs."

50

I'M TORN—GO UP THERE LIKE
the text says, head back down to get Aiden and Cadence to join me,
or find Jack, who went to the garage.

Find Jack.

Yes.

I emphasize to the 911 dispatcher to hurry up and send those cops
and the ambulance right away. Before she can reply, I hang up the call
as the text commanded me to do.

As I run through the kitchen toward the garage door, I think
of the old urban legend about the babysitter who gets the call from
someone who says, "Go upstairs and check the children." And when
she has the call traced by the police, they find that it was coming
from that address. The caller, the killer, was already there in the
house, upstairs, waiting for her.

I get to the garage and throw open the door. The patrol car is still
there, parked in front of me, but there's no sign of Jack or the bolt
cutters he came up here to find.

"Jack? Are you here?"

No reply.

I check the car and find it unlocked.

He's not in the front or back seats.

The trunk?

I hit the trunk release.

Empty.

Under the car?

I look.

No one there.

With the babysitter story on my mind and Jack missing, I hurry back to the living room and grab a fireplace poker from beneath the mantle.

I glance at the framed photos and plaques once again: sheriff's department awards, Jack and Ryan at the skatepark, Jack and his family together.

He and his parents all look so happy. So glad to be together, and I pray that if those two people in the basement really are his parents, everyone will end up being alright at the end of the night.

When I spoke with Grams last, she said, "Make good choices."

Yeah. Keep that in mind.

Light is fading. Night has fallen.

The gloaming.

That's what people used to call it, the term they used to use.

In fairy tales.

And in real life too.

Jack must be upstairs.

I think of that urban legend: *Check the children.*

And the text: *Hang up the phone and check upstairs.*

Who would send such a text to me? Who would want me to hang up the phone with the dispatcher?

With my heart hammering out of control, I slowly ascend the stairs. I can't help but think about all that's been happening to me over the last twenty-four hours.

Visiting the coffin room.

Meeting Lily.

Finding out about Conor O'Shaughnessy's death.

Traveling through the rift and entering the fairy world.

When I reach the landing above the steps, I call out, "Jack?"

Nothing.

But I think of Mr. Fox and of Mary and what she found upstairs in the story—the bones and teeth and hair and blood inside the closet in Mr. Fox's bedroom.

As I'm starting down the hallway, I receive another text: "Be bold, be bold, but not too bold, lest your heart's blood run cold."

Who is sending these?!

Who knows the story?

Mr. Indigo?

Cole? Could he be here?

Someone else from the party?

Wait.

Aiden has been acting weird. You've never been near him when you've gotten one of these text messages.

But what? Really?

No. I discard that possibility. It couldn't be him. How would he have known to text my phone?

Then a thought: What about Ryan? There's a connection to him through Jack's interest in skateboarding. Is it possible...?

I think of Lily and the graveyard and how things ended up playing out differently than I expected last night, but also in a way that made sense based on the stories I know.

In the babysitter story, the caller, the killer, was already in the house.

Already upstairs.

Let it play out differently, now. Please, let it play out differently.

There are two doors on the way down the hall, with a third, the bathroom door, open at the end of the hallway.

Taking a deep breath, I start down the hall and nervously lean over and peer into the first room.

...Be bold, be bold...

There's a cell phone on the bed and it's lit up, as if someone has just sent a message.

I make sure the room is empty, then check the phone and see that, yes, a text has just been sent—the one I received, the warning about my heart's blood running cold.

I don't recognize the phone or its case. As far as I can tell, it's not the phone of anyone I know.

...But not too bold...

It's unlocked. The home screen has a photo of Jack's parents. I tap it, go to settings, and check to see whose phone it is.

His dad's name comes up. I recognize it from the sheriff's department awards downstairs: Anthony Beck.

What? Why would he be sending me these texts?

I have no answers.

One more room.

I leave Mr. Beck's phone there, return to the hallway, and walk to the final bedroom.

...Lest your heart's blood run cold...

I hold the poker securely, lean the unlocked door open, and then edge around the corner.

And see someone lying motionless on his back, on the bed.

Jack.

51

I RUSH TO HIS SIDE. AT FIRST I can't tell if he's breathing or not, but then I finally notice his chest rise.

And fall.

He's alive.

I squeeze his hand. "Jack, wake up."

No response.

Just his steady breathing.

His chest rising and falling.

He has the same T-shirt shirt on and his arm is bandaged, but something's off. It doesn't look like the gauze wrap is in quite the right place. Maybe I didn't secure it as tightly as I'd thought.

I shake him gently to awaken him, but he remains unconscious.

I study the room. Based on the posters on the walls, the clothes tossed around the floor, the soccer trophies, and computer gaming setup, I decide this has to be Jack's room.

As I process everything, I realize that there's one more option. One more possibility that hadn't occurred to me earlier.

I gulp.

And reach for the bandage.

But even before I edge it to the side, I suspect what I'm going to find.

I peer beneath it.

There's no cut.

Yes, just as I thought.

Across the room, near the window that overlooks the treehouse tree, a closet door waits ominously for me.

Oh, no.

...Lest your heart's blood run cold...

Steadying myself and gripping the fireplace poker tighter, I cross the room. If it has been Mr. Beck reenacting what happens in the Mr. Fox story, as the text messages from his phone might indicate, then I know what I'm going to find in that closet: blood and skin and teeth and hair.

But whose? Jack's mom's?

Then who are those two people chained up in the basement?

Everything is tied together.

Yes, so far it has been.

From what I could tell when I looked beneath the door in the basement, it's a man and a woman: Could it be Cole and his mom down there? That Ryan guy and a girl from the party? Lily and her dad? Was that even a possibility?

Maybe, but how? And why?

However, I don't suspect that Mr. Beck is the one behind all of this. Not anymore. I think someone else has been using his phone.

Still, I need to see for myself what's behind this closet door in front of me. I have to know for sure.

In the fading light of day, I place my hand on the doorknob, turn it slowly, and open the door.

52

AND DON'T SEE ANYTHING

strange or out of place inside the closet—but then I realize someone might be hiding behind the hanging clothes.

There's no light in the closet and, with the darkening day outside, it's tough to make out what's in here.

Apprehensively, I study the shoes on the floor, looking for legs rising from them, checking the right side of the closet first.

Clear.

Then the left side, which is tougher to see because of Jack's pants and button-down shirts hanging down...

I use the poker to prod into the dark corners of the closet and press the clothes aside.

No legs.

No intruder.

Nothing on the floor except for a skateboard and a bunch of sneakers and soccer cleats.

Okay.

Quickly, I return to Jack's side.

There's no cut on his arm, and it couldn't have healed already.

Unless...

This isn't Jack.

Because it's Tyler instead.

Footsteps in the hallway.

Deputy Beck? Mr. Indigo? Ryan? Cole? Aiden?

No. I don't think so. I don't think it's any of them. I remember

Jack's eyes. How they look in the photos downstairs, how they've always looked: green hazel.

Not brown.

I've never known him to wear contacts, so that's not it.

But is what I'm thinking even possible?

Nothing that happens is impossible. And nothing that's impossible ever occurs.

The footsteps pause just on the other side of the hallway wall as whoever it is stops, just out of sight.

"I know who you are and what you've done," I call out. "You made one mistake."

"Oh? And what mistake is that?" a familiar voice says.

"The eyes." He still hasn't come into view, but it's him. I know it is. "You have the wrong color. You were close, but you didn't get them quite right."

"I'll keep that in mind for next time." Jack appears in the doorway wearing a short-sleeved button-down shirt, the jagged cut visible on his arm. "Hello, Sahara."

Yes, just as I'd suspected. It's him. Not the hero of the story. The villain.

"Jack."

I glance from him to the person on the bed, the real Tyler Beck, the guy from my class, the person Jack stuck the bandage on to try and fool me.

They look identical.

Just like a changeling would.

"You knew right where to place your hand, didn't you?" I say to Jack.

"My hand?"

"When we were talking out at Jameson's Gap last night. You knew where I was sore on my shoulder because you were the one who grabbed me in the coffin room and tried to keep me from leaving. That's where you touched me. That's why."

"A moment ago you said it was my eyes," he replies.

"Yeah," I say. "You added too much brown. Lily was trying to warn us about you. She said someone wanted skin. All the while it was you."

Jack watches me quietly, his gaze shifting momentarily to the fire poker, and then back to my face. And somehow, he changes the color of his eyes, makes them match the color from the photos. I'm not sure anyone would be able to tell him apart from the real Tyler Beck, not anymore.

Crap. You shouldn't have told him about the eyes.

"Are you the shadow that I saw the first time I went into the corridor?" I say. "Is that how it works?"

He remains silent.

There's a faint smell of smoke and for a moment I wonder if it's from a nearby wood stove or a brushfire, but then I remember that there aren't any neighbors close by.

I'm nervous, but I know what I need to do: The cops are on their way. If I stall long enough, they'll get here, and they'll be able to overpower Jack and save my friends as well as the two people chained up downstairs.

Just keep him talking.

"And you didn't fall backward on accident, did you?" I say. "Up on Devil's Falls? You fell on purpose. But why? To get me to come out there with you? Oh... Were you going to throw me off? But then Cadence and Aiden arrived and you couldn't chance it."

"At the time I thought it would have been easier," he tells me. "But, hey, part of finding your way through a story is adapting when necessary. Pivoting toward new possibilities, right?"

I'm not thrilled to know he was planning to throw me off the waterfall. "And when I heard the whispering up there at the falls, it wasn't the devil, was it? No... Somehow it was you. The whispering only started when I touched your hand."

"I wondered when you might realize that."

He enters the room and I level the poker in front of me, ready to use it however I need to, but he doesn't come toward me. Instead, he walks directly to the window and latches it shut, taking away any chance of escaping onto the tree branches outside or through the treehouse.

Then, he rounds the bed and stands between me and the door, sealing me in.

Not good.

Yeah, there's smoke. There sure is. But, with the window is closed, latched—where's it coming from?

From inside the house. It has to be coming from inside.

No. Not good at all.

"So, you came through the rift," I say, "knocked down the bookcase, and then what, replaced Tyler? And you know his memories?"

"Enough of them. I've been making up what I need to along the way to get by."

"And down in the basement?" I'm examining the bedroom, trying to figure out if there's some way out of here—but also realizing that if I run, Tyler would be left behind and who knows what Jack would do to him. No, I can't run. I need to somehow overpower Jack. "Who's chained up down there?"

"Tyler's parents," he says.

Wisps of smoke are starting to curl in through the doorway and up through a nearby air vent on the floor.

I gulp and look at the bed. At my classmate. At the guy I've had a crush on all year.

Unconscious. Helpless.

Chest, rising.

Falling.

"What did you do to him?" I ask Jack.

"He's asleep."

"He's more than asleep."

"Yes," he admits. "More than asleep."

I let that sink in. "How do I wake him up, Jack?"

"That depends."

"On what?"

"On you. On what you choose to do."

"What does that mean?"

He doesn't reply, just takes a couple of steps toward me until he's about eight feet away.

I angle the poker at him and he stops.

"The police are coming." I try to make it sound like a threat, but he just shrugs it off.

"They're not going to make it in time," he says.

"Before what?" I say, but I think I already know.

The fire. He started a fire.

He intends to kill us all.

And I didn't tell the dispatcher to send a firetruck.

Jack's only response to my question is to approach me. I grip the poker in both hands, holding it like a baseball bat. I aim it high, but he's not intimidated and is able to back me into the corner near the closet door until I'm literally standing up against the wall.

"Give me the poker, Zod."

"You don't get to call me Zod."

He stays just out of reach of the poker, if I were to swing it at him.

Keep him talking! As long as he's talking, you're not dying, and neither are your friends.

"So, you used Tyler's dad's phone to send me the texts. I get that. But why?" I shake my head. "Why are you doing this—any of this? Why did you come to our world? What do you want?"

He smiles and raises an eyebrow at me, and, with a chill, I realize that maybe it's not me who's stalling.

Maybe it's him.

"How about a little riddle?" He doesn't wait for me to respond, but immediately goes on, "You answer this and I'll answer you: 'The life you have isn't yours to give. You yearn to suffer, to die, to live. You cannot take a final breath. So what is a fate that is worse than death?' Solve the riddle and I'll tell you why I'm here and how you can save Tyler. I'll give you one minute."

He consults a timer on his phone. "Starting now."

53

"TELL IT TO ME AGAIN."

As he does, I process every word, trying to figure out what they have in common with each other, tracing their logic toward an answer: "The life you have isn't yours to give," he says.

And I think, *How is it possible to have a life that you can't give away? Does that mean you're not alive at all? Can you give away someone else's life? Is that what he's saying?*

He goes on: "You yearn to suffer, to die, to live."

Who would yearn to suffer and also to die and to live? That makes no sense! Or does he mean that you have to suffer in order to die, and die in order to live?

"You cannot take a final breath."

What can't take a final breath? Something that can't die? That's never been alive? But if something's not alive, how can it yearn to suffer and die?

Finally, he says, "So what is a fate that is worse than death?" finishing the riddle for a second time.

How's it possible to suffer more than dying? I think. *What fate could he possibly be talking about?*

"Forty seconds," Jack says.

Okay, okay, okay. Think, Sahara...

I consider everything that's happened since last night, and when I think of death, my mind races back to my discussion with Grams this morning—about the coffin room and changelings and elementals, and the sermon she was listening to on the radio comes to mind, those words from Revelation about seeking death and watching it flee from you. Desiring it, but not being able to experience it.

Well aware that the seconds are ticking away, as quickly as I can, I process Jack's riddle, the paradoxes within, the implications extending out of it.

I have the sense that the ghost lore book might give me some answers, but I didn't get the chance to get all the way through it. I—wait.

That last dogeared page.

I think I might know the answer.

"Ten seconds." Jack grins at me. "You don't know the answer, do you?"

"I do, but before I tell it to you—"

"You're stalling. What is it?"

"*The life you have isn't yours to give*—someone can't give away what they do not have, so you're not alive yet. *You yearn to suffer, to die, to live*—but what could it be that's not alive and yet yearns for something?"

He looks at me confidently. "I don't think you know."

I go on with my explanation. "And what cannot take a final breath? Only something that's not alive or that cannot die. And what's a fate worse than death? Wanting to die but you can't: You seek it, but it flees from you. And so, that's the answer. You're an elemental. And that's your fate—to be unborn, unable to suffer, and unable to die."

A cold shadow slides across his face as he realizes I've solved it. "I prefer saying that I'm *liminal*," he tells me.

"Because you dwell in the in-between." I eye him, trying to be ready in case he makes a move on me. "The realm between worlds."

"But not anymore."

Is it true that he can't die? Then how can you stop him? What about now? Now that he's in our world?

The smoke in the room is growing thicker by the second. I have no idea how I'll be able to get past Jack and get Tyler down the stairs.

There's no way I'm strong enough to carry him, even if I were able to get Jack out of the picture.

Jack cocks his head at me. "If you think it's terrifying to realize that you're going to die, imagine how terrifying it is to be trapped and suffering and alone, yet unable to die—ever."

Trapped. Suffering. Dying. That makes me think of the coffin room again. "And Conor O'Shaughnessy?"

"Oh, it was delicious watching him die. I savored every moment—all that dread, that hopelessness, his desperate, futile, final screams."

Jack's words chill me, but also enrage me, and that gives me added courage. "You said you'd answer my question if I solved your riddle. So, why? Why are you doing any of this?"

He indicates Tyler. "Because I want something he has that I don't."

And then it hits me. "Skin," I say.

"Yes. And bones and life—and pain. Without a body, you can't feel it. I can't feel the warmth of the sun on my skin, or the chill of the night air and the goosebumps it brings. Imagine never being born, never growing old, never being able to die. This world of yours, though, it's so startlingly, vibrantly *tangible*. So much like the rose you were telling me about—all contradictions and mystery, all danger and beauty, all loss and love and disappointment and hope. I'm doing this because I want to able to *feel*, and then one day to die."

I grip the poker securely. "Come a little closer and I can help you with that last part."

He shakes his head slowly. "I'm afraid I don't intend to do that for a very long time."

Where are those cops?!

"You said the cops wouldn't get here in time," I say, my throat dry from nerves and the smoky, chalky air. "Is that it? You're going to kill us all here in the house?"

"I don't want you dead, Sahara. That's the answer to the other part of your question. I could have killed you at the falls, but I changed my mind. It's much better this way, for all of us."

I can hardly believe how easily I fell for him. "And all those things you said to me," I mutter, "that I was beautiful, that you liked spending time with me, that I wasn't like any other girl you'd ever met, all that—those were all lies?"

"All true, actually. That's what makes this a little more... complicated."

I let that sink in. "You said earlier that I could make a choice that would awaken Tyler. What is it?—Wait... Like a fairy tale... You've been trying to get me to fall in love with you. Is that the only way you can stay here? Oh... and let me guess, just like in a fairy tale, you had one day to do it? By sunset? And now that night has fallen..."

"It's not quite that specific, but you're not wrong. You opened the rift, Sahara. You're the key. A good ending always requires a sacrifice. If the choice costs nothing, it means nothing—am I right?"

"What does that mean? What are you saying?"

"What are you willing to give up to awaken him? I'm afraid there needs to be an exchange. Someone will need to return to the fairy world."

"Me."

"A kiss is all it takes." He taps his cheek gently.

"But why would I do that?"

"To save Tyler."

"And then you get to live—but what about him? He won't survive the fire."

"He might. He'll have a shot. It's your decision."

Sleeping Beauty. A kiss to break the curse.

Or, in this case, to transfer it to me.

There's gotta be another way.

"But you were going to push me off the falls," I say. "Do you want me dead or not?"

"Not dead. No. Not anymore. That was just my instinct to kill—it was tough to hold back. But when I realized I was starting to like having you around, I decided I wanted you to live."

For a happy ending, you need a valiant choice or a selfless act.

No. Helping Jack would be a betrayal.

"I'm not alone, Sahara," he tells me. "There will be more. And the queen we all serve—she knows about the rift. And she's not content to stay where she is. The rift is open. This is just the beginning."

"No," I say, "it's the end."

A valiant choice.

Raising the poker, I rush toward him and swing it violently at his temple. But he's too quick and backs out of the way, then grabs the end of it, draws me close to him, and then shoves me brutally against the wall, knocking the breath out of me.

He wrenches my arm backward and as I struggle to get free, he manages to twist the poker from my hand.

He tosses it aside, then manhandles me into the closet, slams the door shut, and locks it.

"Goodbye, Sahara."

54

"NO!"

I hear his footsteps recede as he leaves.

"Hey! Open the door!"

I try the doorknob, but that's useless.

I'm going to need another option.

I know that Cadence has no cell reception bars in the basement, but I wonder if a text might go through so I send her one: "Tyler and I are trapped upstairs in a bedroom. Get out of the house, but help us if there's time!"

Certainly, she must know about the fire. She and Aiden might've already fled and made it outside.

I kick the closet door, pound it, slam my shoulder against it, but it remains solid and immovable in front of me, imprisoning me.

Grabbing the skateboard, I smash it against the locked doorknob again and again, but that does nothing.

I study the doorknob and see one of those holes that allow for emergency release—if you have a nail or something to slide in there.

Which I don't.

But I have something else.

I grab a wire hanger, straighten out the end, and try fitting it into the hole, hoping to jimmy the lock mechanism enough to get the door open.

It doesn't cooperate.

With the smoke thickening, I'm forced to grab a shirt and wrap it around my mouth and nose to block the smoke.

Trapped.

Dying.

Alone.

You're not going to make it out of here.

I think of my dad, trapped and dying last March. Under the water. Under the ice.

He reached out to me, but not just to me. He told me to tell Mom that he loved her.

And I never did. I never have.

Grams warned me not to let pain become my home, not to let anger grow deep roots because it'd be tougher to weed out when the time comes.

Yeah, and now it has.

I tap in Mom's number.

It only takes two rings before she picks up. "Sahara?"

"Mom! I need to tell you something."

"I thought you didn't talk on the phone anymore?" she says, her voice biting.

I ignore her question. "The night dad died, he called me. He left me a message."

"What? What was it?"

"He left a voicemail. He told me... He told me to tell you that he loves you. He wanted you to know that before he died."

A long pause. "Why didn't you tell me this earlier? Why did you wait?"

"I don't know. I was angry. I was sad. Look, it doesn't matter, okay? But he loved you—all the way to the end. And I do too. I love you—or I want to. We both need to. We don't need for everything to be right between us, but we need that to be."

All the while I'm talking to her, I'm trying to get the lock free.

And now, it clicks. The doorknob turns.

"I'll talk to you soon," I tell her, even though I don't if that's true. Then, I hang up, pocket the phone, grab a shirt for Tyler's mouth and nose, and throw open the door.

Smoke is everywhere now.

What do I do? I'm not strong enough to carry him to safety.

Sleeping Beauty.

There must me a choice.

There must be a sacrifice.

Grams' story: a century of sleep.

You have to do whatever it takes. You have to help him.

It might be his only chance.

A kiss to break the curse...

I lean over and close my eyes and kiss Tyler, a gentle kiss, a fairy tale kiss, and then, my heart slam-hammering in my chest, I step back.

I'm hoping he'll magically awaken.

But he doesn't.

I shake him like I did earlier. "Come on!"

His chest, rising and falling.

"Tyler, wake up! Tyler—"

And then he does.

He shudders, then slowly opens his eyes, blinks them closed again, and then coughs in the choking smoke.

I tie the extra shirt around his nose and mouth to keep out the smoke, to help him breathe.

"Can you stand?" I ask him urgently.

"What?" He's staring at me, confused. "Sahara? Is that you?"

"There's no time to explain. We need to get out of here. Now."

He sits up, groggily, and I help him swing his feet to the floor.

I put one arm around him to support him, and we make our way out of the bedroom to the hallway, which is nearly filled with smoke.

Ideally, we would crawl beneath the smoke, but he's still weak and that's not going to happen.

"What's going on?" he says.

"Long story. Let's go. Hurry."

Hobbling through the hallway, we get to the stairs and begin making our way down them.

Heat is radiating up the staircase and pulsing toward us.

The crackling hiss of the fire gets louder.

Halfway down the stairs, the flames become visible, eating their way through the living room furniture and climbing up the walls, trying to overtake us.

I decide that the best thing is to get him to safety and then come back in for Cadence, Aiden, and Tyler's parents, if they're still here in the basement.

However, by the time I get to the first floor, I see Cadence and Aiden emerging from the basement stairwell, coughing, sputtering for breath, and helping two people who still have chains shackled to their ankles. I recognize them from the photos: Tyler's parents.

So, Aiden must have been able to get the door down there open, to free them.

Excellent.

Well done.

We all hurry out the front door, onto the driveway, and past Cadence's car.

Tyler leans up against the side of it.

I would've thought that his parents might be hesitant to be near him since they would think he was the one who chained them up in the basement, but Jack might not have taken on Tyler's form yet when he imprisoned them down there.

They go to him and hug him and Cadence and Aiden and I turn to look at the fire.

Cadence says, "Everyone always says that you shouldn't panic, that 'This isn't the time to panic.' Actually, there are some moments that are made precisely to panic. They have panic written all over them—and that, being in the basement, was one of them."

"I'm with you," Aiden says.

I hear them, but I'm a little fuzzy. I wonder if it's because of a lack of oxygen from being in the smoke. But that's not what it feels like.

It's different. Deeper. Queasy and faint.

"Something's wrong," I tell them.

And then, with a gulp of horror, I realize what it might be.

Police car sirens sound as a sheriff's department cruiser comes flaring down the road and into the driveway.

"What?" Cadence asks me. "What is it?"

"Do you have your pepper spray?" My words sound like they're coming from someone else.

The house is going up in flames quickly, as if it's in a hurry to turn into ash.

She looks at me curiously. "Sure, why? What's up?"

"I might need it."

"For what?"

"Werewolves."

I hold out my hand and she digs it out of her pocket and hands it to me. I hand her my phone and the sapphire ring, just in case what I'm thinking of, what I'm afraid of, happens.

"What are you doing?" she asks me.

"It's going to be okay," I mutter as believably as I can.

I'm uncertain on my feet, but I make my way over to the three family members comforting each other just a few feet away, beside Jack's car.

I see the ghost lore book still on the passenger seat waiting, right where I left it.

Deputy Beck says to me, "Thank you for getting Tyler out of there. We owe you everything."

"It's not Tyler," I whisper.

He looks at me curiously. "What?"

Holding the pepper spray steady, I study the gauze wrap. With a trembling hand, I reach over and yank it all the way down.

The cut is still there.

This isn't Tyler.

It's Jack.

"It's you!" I yell.

He switched places while you were in the closet. He wasn't trying to get away, he was trying to get you to kiss him.

I aim the pepper spray at his face and Tyler's mom steps back, gasping. His dad tells me in no uncertain terms to drop the pepper spray.

"Where is he?" I ask Jack urgently. "Where's Tyler?" But my words are even fainter now and I'm not even sure anyone else can hear them.

I look past Jack to the house. It's too far gone, the fire has devoured too much of it, spread too quickly. There's no way any of us could get back in there, get upstairs and search for Tyler.

And then, I'm collapsing, dropping heavily to the ground.

I have the pepper spray in my hand, but I can't aim it anymore, can't move.

Just like Mr. Fox in the story. Helpless at the end.

No, no, no. Tyler was in the house.

I whisper his name, or I try to.

But I'm sure I only end up mouthing the word.

I turn my head toward the burning house and see that the window beside the tree branches that Jack had latched shut is open. Maybe Tyler was able to get out, maybe he was able to get to the tree...

"Sahara, are you okay?" It's Jack, leaning over me, his face just inches from mine. His eyes, the perfect shade. No one will be able to tell he's not Tyler.

In the version of Sleeping Beauty that Grams told me, the prince sacrificed himself for the princess. With his kiss, he took her place and accepted the curse to sleep for a hundred years.

Now that's all I can think of, that's all that I know.

And Jack grins at me as I fade away and he whispers, "Goodbye, Sahara. Welcome to your new home. Say, 'Hello,' to the queen for me."

55

I'M CAUGHT IN A DREAM THAT'S

curling around me. It's like I'm sinking and floating at the same time. I'm nowhere and yet also here, lying on the ground, on the grass.

I can feel it with my hands by my sides.

Yes, I'm on grass, not on a driveway.

I feel someone shaking me softly.

"Dazia, are you okay? Wake up."

I must still be dreaming. Dazia was the girl from the story I told to the kids at Story Hour. The one with Princess Alamore and the dragon and the riddle and the troll.

"Dazia?" the person repeats.

I finally manage to open my eyes, blinking against a bolt of bright sunlight overhead. But it should be dark, after dusk. I should be able to see Tyler's house.

But, no. It's day.

And there's no house.

I look at the person who has been shaking me, a guy about my age that I don't recognize. "There you are, Dazia. Are you alright?"

A steel-gray horse whinnies beside him.

"My name is Sahara," I say softly. "Not Dazia."

A small look of confusion. "You must have hit your head. Just rest for a moment."

But I have to see, I have to know.

So, I sit up and catch sight of the grove of trees and the valley and the castle rising in the distance, and the vast and open sea, and, when I turn to look back, the snow-capped mountains behind me.

The rift.

I'm on the other side.

The young man reaches out his hand for me, to help me to my feet. "If you're feeling better, if you're alright, we should go. The queen wants to see you."

The guy has a bow slung across his shoulder and a quiver of arrows strapped across his back, just like the person who was being chased by the werewolf.

Is it possible he's...?

As I look around, only a few feet away from me in the grass I see my sapphire ring glistening in the light of the midday sun, in the place where it was left the last time I was here.

How much time has gone by?

I pocket the pepper spray and then pick up the ring and carefully slide it onto my finger. Then, I stand up and join the young man, climbing behind him onto the back of the gray steed.

"Yes," I say. "Let's go see the queen."

Sahara will return in

PORTAL

RIFT TRILOGY, BOOK TWO

Coming in April 2025

DISCUSSION QUESTIONS

1. Sahara was impacted by the stories Grams told her. Who has been a storyteller to you? A relative? A teacher? A friend? What is one of the stories that you remember? Why is that one so memorable to you?

2. The book begins with this line: "Some words have the power to impale your heart." Do you agree with that? How powerful are words? Why do you think that is?

3. What are some of the moments of courage in the book? What do the choices of the characters tell you about what matters most to them?

4. What are the different types of rifts that happen in the book? Are all of them in a thin place, or are any of them inside of the characters? Explain what you mean.

5. Do you think that struggles change us or reveal us for who we really are? Does Sahara change in this story, or is her true self revealed? Why do you say that?

6. If you could be any of the characters in the book, who would you choose? Why? What is it that draws you toward that character?

7. Sahara feels like there's a gash in her heart from the loss and rejection she has experienced. Have you ever felt that way? What did you do about it? How did you find help?

8. If you could journey to another realm, one that has bits and pieces of stories you know in it, what are some of the things you'd like to see there? What are some things you hope would never appear?

9. Grams likes to celebrate told stories instead of written ones—even to the point that she doesn't want them written down. As she says, "They'll keep flowering as long as they're told and retold and allowed to grow in the wild. You write a

story down and it's stuck there forever, encaged in a bunch of little squiggles on a page. Let it live. Don't write it down." Do you agree with her? Does she have a good point?

10. Jack mentions that sometimes he feels billions of miles apart from the people close to him. Have you ever felt that way? What did you do about it? What are some ways to bridge the gaps between us?

11. If you were to make up an asterism from a story that's important to you, what would it be? Why not go ahead and find one?

12. What was your favorite twist or surprise in the story?

13. What would you say is Sahara's biggest fear? What does she desire most?

14. Sahara deeply regretted the words that she spoke to her dad on the night he died. Have you ever sought forgiveness for things you've said to someone? How can we find healthy ways to move on after we've said or done things we regret?

These questions are intended to be used for discussions and reflection about Rift *and are provided by the publisher for classroom, library, and reading club use. Photocopy permission is granted for these purposes.*

SPECIAL THANKS

Thanks to Linda for her encouragement, to Ms. Hardin's class for their stories, to our Carter County tour guides, to Hannah for her feedback, to Liesl for her patience, to Rebecca and Steve for their vision, to John for his professionalism, to Josh for taking me back into the hills, to Trinity and Scott for their perspective, to Betty for her insights, and to Suzy for introducing me to the coffin room.

Also, thanks to Elisabeth, Katherine, and Mei Li for helping me see the world through the eyes of a girl.

Thanks also to the staff at the Unicoi County Public Library for your cooperation. As you'll notice, I changed some of the geography of the basement. This was simply for narrative purposes, but still, the basement is creepy. I'm just saying.

And, finally, thanks to Elliot for appearing as Lore in this book. Purr.

ABOUT THE AUTHOR

Steven James is the critically acclaimed author of twenty novels and many nonfiction books for teens and adults. He is also an award-winning storyteller and once won the South Carolina Liar's Contest, making him the official liar for the state of South Carolina that year. (Yes, that's actually a thing.)

When he was young, his uncle told him stories and instilled in him a love for storytelling. When he's not writing or telling stories—or lost in his imagination daydreaming—you'll find him hiking, playing basketball, or sneaking out to see a matinee.

To find out more about Steven's books, visit him at *www.stevenjames.net* or listen to his weekly podcast The Story Blender, on which he interviews some of the leading writers and storytellers in the world on the secrets to telling great stories. Check it out at *www.thestoryblender.com*.

For the inside scoop on Sahara and her friends and their upcoming adventures, check out *www.riftbooks.com*.